HARD FALL

OTHER TITLES BY J. B. TURNER

J. B. TURNER
HARD FALL

THOMAS & MERCER

This is a work of fiction. Names, characters, organizations, places, events, and incidents are either products of the author's imagination or are used fictitiously. Any resemblance to actual persons, living or dead, or actual events is purely coincidental.

Published by Thomas & Mercer, Seattle

www.apub.com

Amazon, the Amazon logo, and Thomas & Mercer are trademarks of Amazon.com, Inc., or its affiliates.

ISBN-13: 9781542049993
ISBN-10: 1542049997

Cover design by @blacksheep-uk.com

Printed in the United States of America

To my late father

One

It started on a lonely coastal highway.

Jon Reznick glanced in his rearview mirror. The black SUV was edging closer. It had been six long miles. And the crazy fuck was still shadowing him.

Reznick decided to make a move. He hit the gas pedal and sped down the near-deserted road toward home. Swirls of red leaves whipped up as he drove hard to lose the trailing vehicle.

Suddenly, the SUV accelerated and pulled up to within inches of his truck's bumper, flashing its headlights.

"What the . . . ?" Reznick said.

He accelerated hard to avoid being rammed. He took a sharp left turn, sped off the highway, and got on Camden Road, hoping to lose the crazy driver.

He checked his mirror again.

The SUV was still following. The road forked. Reznick's mind began to churn through options and possibilities. Was the guy armed? Drunk? Just a backwoods crazy? Or maybe the guy was fucking with him. But then again, maybe it was a sign of something far more serious.

His mind flashed back to an attack on an American convoy near Baghdad Airport when a Saddam loyalist had rammed the rear car before opening fire, killing two US soldiers.

Reznick glanced in the mirror again. The guy was still there.

He'd had enough. The road was deserted apart from his car and the vehicle following him. He put a few hundred yards between them, then spun the steering wheel to the left, pulled on the handbrake, and came to a grinding halt. His truck now faced the oncoming SUV.

He jumped out and crouched down on the grass verge at the side of the road. He pulled out his 9mm Beretta, aimed, and shot out the right front tire of the SUV.

Screeching brakes. The smell of burning rubber. The vehicle swerved and flipped over. Time seemed to slow. Frame by frame like in a film. Metal crunched as the car slammed into the asphalt. The SUV shuddered to a stop. Smoke billowed out of the engine as its alarm emitted a high-pitched beeping.

Reznick ran across the road and kicked in the front-left window. The driver was wedged between the inflated airbag and the seat. Reznick leaned in and dragged him out, blood seeping out of a nasty gash in the man's forehead and from a burst lip.

He pressed his gun to the man's bleeding forehead. "You wanna play fucking games, is that it?"

The guy stared up at him blankly, blinking away tears.

"Answer!"

Slowly, the expressionless look on the man's face began to change. The guy started to smile through the blood dripping onto the road.

"What the fuck is so funny?"

"Jon . . . Easy, man. It's me." The man held out his open palm.

Reznick stared at the skeletal figure's wide, staring eyes.

"It's me, Jon. It's Jerry. Jerry White. You remember now?"

The name crashed through Reznick's brain like an oncoming truck.

"Way back, Jon."

Reznick was struggling to take it in. "Jerry? Are you fucking kidding me? I thought your car was trying to run me off the road or something."

"It's not my car. I stole it."

Reznick stared long and hard at the emaciated figure in front of him. "You stole it? Jerry, what the hell is going on? You could've gotten us killed."

"I'm sorry, man, but I'm desperate. I needed to see you."

Reznick was shocked at the puny frame of a guy he remembered as a phenomenally fit and perfectly honed warrior. "See me about what?"

Jerry pointed at the gun. "Jon, you wanna ease up?"

Reznick put his Beretta back in his waistband and helped the ex-Delta operator to his feet. "What's going on, bro?"

"I'm in trouble."

"What kind of trouble?"

"I'm scared. I want you to help me. That's why I came up here. I saw you purely by chance about ten miles back. I've been driving throughout the night and all of today. I'm on the run. Been up to your house. I drove around a bit. Then I saw you. Started to tail you. I wanted to get your attention."

"Slow down . . . My attention?"

Jerry White seemed like a broken man, not the guy he'd once known. Reznick was standing beside a former Delta hard man who'd helped him through the loss of his wife after 9/11. A fearsome Special Forces soldier. "Shit, Jerry, is this really you?"

He blinked away the tears. "I knew you'd still live here. Remember when me and some of the Delta crew came up here?"

Reznick clasped his old friend's shoulder. "How could I forget?"

"We drank ourselves shit crazy."

"That we did." Reznick shook his head as he stared at Jerry's haunted face. "You look terrible. What the hell's the matter with you?"

Jerry stared at him. "I'm so scared."

"Scared? Of what? You've nothing to be scared of."

"That's where you're wrong, Jon. There are people who'll come for me. They *will* come for me. But you can't let them."

"Remember who came and got you out of Sadr City? It was me. You remember? Trust me, I got this."

Jerry stared at him blankly, blood dripping from his forehead.

"I won't let anyone touch you. Ever."

"I don't know who I am anymore," he whispered. "There's something happening to me."

"Like what?"

"You have to protect me. Hide me. For the love of God, don't let them get me. They're gonna kill me."

Two

The lowering autumn sun cast long shadows. Gold and rust-colored hues dotted the trees as they drove back to Reznick's oceanfront home on the outskirts of Rockland, in midcoast Maine. He knew the villages and towns around Penobscot Bay like the back of his hand. The quiet, pine-lined roads. The peaceful harbors and unspoiled beaches just off US 1. The tourists were long gone by mid-October. But encountering an old friend on his trip back from Camden, after some deep-sea fishing on a charter boat, wasn't how he had envisaged his day ending.

He wondered what to do about the stolen—now damaged—BMW. He made a mental note to call Bernie to retrieve the vehicle. He'd get it fixed and returned to the owner. Reznick would pick up the tab.

In the passenger seat, Jerry began clawing at his arms, digging his nails into his skin. Blood oozed through his shirt.

"What the hell are you doing, Jerry?"

Jerry stared straight ahead as they turned down the dirt road to Reznick's home. "Just look after me, Jon. Promise?"

"I promise. You have my word."

"What about the car I stole?"

"I know a guy who'll get it sorted. We need to get you cleaned up. You hungry?"

Jerry nodded, occasionally touching the wound on his forehead. Blood had dried across his face. "They don't feed me too much."

Reznick could see that from Jerry's bony frame. "Who's they?"

Jerry closed his eyes and began rocking back and forth, as if for comfort.

"I said who's they, Jerry?"

"Don't let them take me back."

Reznick wondered what the hell had happened, whether this was some post-trauma thing. "OK, relax, man. Nearly there."

The salt-blasted wooden house his late father had built with his own hands appeared in the distance. He drove down the dirt road for a mile before pulling up. He got out and headed inside, Jerry close behind.

"Make sure you lock the door and all the windows, man," Jerry said.

Reznick could see Jerry was in the middle of some sort of mental breakdown. "Will you relax?"

Once Reznick had gotten him inside and reassured the bug-eyed ex-Delta that things were fine, he handed him a fresh set of clothes, two sizes too big, and ushered him into the shower. Afterward, he sprayed antiseptic wash on the gaping wound on Jerry's forehead.

Jerry grimaced at the pain.

"Gonna have to stich this motherfucker up, Jerry, OK?"

Jerry nodded.

Reznick got a needle and thread out of a first aid kit, dabbed the needle with alcohol, then began to stitch up his old friend.

"Fuck!"

"I'll be quick."

Once the wound had been stitched, Reznick swabbed antiseptic cream over it and bandaged it up. Then he cleaned the minor wounds on Jerry's busted lip and the scratches and abrasions on his arms.

"There, good as new, right?"

Jerry sat down by the log fire and pushed back the cuticles on his fingernails. "Thanks, man." He looked at a picture of Reznick and Lauren taken in Central Park in New York on her eighteenth birthday. "Is that your little girl, Jon?"

"Yeah, that's Lauren."

"She's beautiful, man. You're a lucky guy."

Reznick nodded.

"Last time I saw her she was about four or something, just a little girl."

"She's all grown up now. At college."

"College? Good for her. Smart girl. I like smart girls."

Reznick looked at his old friend. "So what's going on with you?"

"You've no idea what's going on."

"Look, how about I fix you something to eat? You want some soup?"

"What kind?"

"Tomato. Out of a tin."

"Tomato is good. Yeah, sure."

Reznick heated up the soup and took Jerry a piping bowl on a tray, alongside a plate with buttered white bread.

Jerry slurped the soup greedily and ripped chunks off the bread, chewing ferociously. "That's fucking good, man. Thanks."

Reznick got two cold bottles of beer from the fridge. He went back into the living room, with its views over the darkening waters of Penobscot Bay, and handed one to Jerry.

Jerry held it for a few moments, transfixed. "Not had one of these for months." He took a long gulp and sighed. "Long time. This is nice here." He put down his beer and finished the soup and bread.

"You want any more?"

Jerry shook his head. "That's enough, man. If I have any more, I'll puke."

"Why you not eating?"

"I told you. They don't feed me. Rations almost. I go days without food. I'm ravenous most of the time. I have ringing in my ears. I'm hearing voices."

Reznick took a swig of beer. "Tell me what's really going on with you. And don't give me any bullshit."

"I can't tell you some of the things I've seen."

"Maybe we should take you to a hospital and get you looked over."

"Jon, that's not what I want. That's where I've just been—in a hospital."

"A hospital? Where?"

"I don't know. Near Ithaca, I think. That's what I heard."

"What . . . is it a veterans' hospital?"

"I don't know, man. Just had me down there going crazy. They're trying to drive me out of my mind. When I close my eyes, I see things—myself killing people. That's all I see."

Reznick kept his expression neutral. He'd seen guys like this before. Guys who were hanging by a thread. Jerry needed urgent psychiatric treatment, not cozy chats over bottles of beer. He was gone. "Listen to me. I know a guy . . . a doctor. A friend of mine. He might be able to help you."

Jerry began rocking back and forth. He sobbed hard, tears streaming down his face. "I've got things in my head, man. I see things. I keep on hearing the same words. Over and over again."

"I know."

"I've had my fill of doctors. Sick fuckers . . . what they've been doing to me. Do you hear me?" Jerry glanced out the window. "You mind pulling the blinds? It's getting dark."

"Sure." Reznick made a quick tour of the house, shutting the curtains to obscure the view inside. "So, here's what I'm thinking. You can spend the night here. And tomorrow morning I'll drive you across to the doctor I know. He's a good guy. He'll make sure you're taken care of."

Jerry finished the rest of the beer, hands shaking. "And you know this guy?"

"He's a former Marine. Went to medical school. Smart guy. And I swear he'll look after you."

Three

They talked into the early hours.

Reznick listened while his old friend tried to explain what had happened to him over the years. Jerry talked of being a panhandler down on Ocean Drive in South Beach after he'd returned from Iraq, unable to handle life at home. Begging for cash. Food. Drink. Drugs. Sleeping in doorways. Dumpsters. Under bridges. Abandoned lots. Then he'd been arrested and taken to a hospital in Hollywood, Florida.

A few months back, he'd been flown to a hospital in upstate New York. He talked of hearing whispered voices in the dark. Voices from the shadows. People filming him. And then more voices. Repeated voices. Imploring him to kill.

The more Reznick listened, the more certain he was that his friend was acutely unwell. A psychiatric illness, for sure. And the sooner he was given the help he needed, the better.

Jerry ground his teeth. His eyes darted across the room. "Did you hear that, Jon?"

"Hear what?"

He pointed to the ceiling. "Like someone's on the roof."

"Just the wind. Got a couple of loose roof tiles I keep meaning to fix."

Jerry closed his eyes for a few moments and began to take deep breaths, as if trying to relax.

"You going to be OK tonight? Do you need any medication?"

"Just a sleeping pill. Might calm me down."

Reznick went into the bathroom and rummaged in a cabinet. He found an old bottle of sleeping pills he'd been prescribed years earlier. He handed Jerry a couple, which he washed down with a glass of water.

After fifteen minutes, Jerry's breathing became shallower, his eyes heavy. Half an hour later, he'd drifted off to sleep in the frayed chair opposite—the one Reznick's father had sunk into after work at the sardine-packing plant.

Reznick fetched a blanket from his wardrobe and wrapped it around Jerry. He took the empty bottle of beer and the tray with the plate and bowl to the kitchen. He washed the dishes and then sat down, watching over his old friend.

Hour after hour Jerry tossed and turned, moaning in his sleep. Agitated, as if trying to escape someone's clutches.

Reznick listened to the old grandfather clock in the corner ticking, the crackling logs on the fire. He wondered whether to text the psychiatrist he knew and ask him to see Jerry first thing in the morning. He reflected on that for a few minutes, then decided to wait until daybreak, hoping Jerry would enjoy a good sleep.

He made himself strong black coffee and sat back down in his seat. His old friend twitched, the spasms interspersed with an occasional groan. Perhaps a recurring nightmare.

Reznick was no stranger to searing nightmares. The worst had come after his wife died. He'd picture her over and over each and every night, silently screaming from high up in the Twin Towers, black smoking billowing out into the pristine blue September sky. He'd wake up in a cold sweat, shaking for minutes.

A loud moan from Jerry snapped him back to reality.

Reznick sipped the scalding coffee, enjoying the caffeine buzz. A few more gulps washed down a Dexedrine, his drug of choice to keep him awake and alert.

The night wore on. He wondered if he should do something more worthwhile. Read a book, write an email to his daughter, watch an old movie. But he didn't.

It was plain as day—his blood brother was starting to lose his grip on reality. Jerry needed someone to watch over him. Reznick thought back to the countless times he'd grabbed thirty minutes or maybe an hour in the night as they'd hunkered down in some shithole in Iraq. Jerry had watched over him like he'd watched over Jerry. That was the way it was. The firefights. The search-and-destroy missions in Baghdad. Fallujah. The ensuing mayhem. The deaths. And the seemingly constant suicide bombings. Both al-Qaeda and the Islamic State used that tactic to take strategic villages. The effects were inevitably devastating. But a suicide bomber could also be used as a diversionary tactic, sometimes as part of a secondary attack.

Then there were improvised explosive devices inside dead dogs, waiting to blow up soldiers, Iraqis, anyone. Sometimes armored convoys were attacked by roadside IEDs triggered remotely by cell phone. Sometimes by jihadists in their line of sight a few hundred yards away, filming the whole thing.

Putrid anger boiled over. Delta didn't take prisoners. And neither did the former Baathists. Loyalists. Republican Guard hard core. And then came the infiltration and influence of the Iranians. Quds.

Reznick, Jerry, and other Special Forces soldiers had seen it all. The torture victims found dead. Bound and gagged. Eyes missing, limbs hacked off, gunshot wounds to the back of the head. Bodies thrown off buildings. On and on.

Jerry stirred for a few moments before drifting back into a fitful sleep. The embers of the fire were still burning.

Reznick sat in silence and stared at the flames.

Four

Just before dawn, headlights shone through the blinds of Reznick's house.

As Jerry slept, Reznick drew his 9mm Beretta, pulled back the slide, and headed out the rear of the house. He crept around his home and down the side path. He spotted one SUV and an ambulance. He approached the SUV and yanked open the passenger door.

A middle-aged woman with a black bob haircut wearing bright-red lipstick stared at him, unfazed. Two heavyset men occupied the rear seats.

Reznick pressed the gun to the woman's head. "Who are you?"

She cleared her throat. "My name is Dr. Eileen MacDonald." She handed him a business card. "We've come for Jerry White."

"Why?"

"He is a patient of mine. I have reason to believe he's here with you."

One of the men in the back handed Reznick a piece of paper. "Just ease up. He's a patient at our facility."

Reznick looked over the paperwork, which seemed legitimate, and moved the gun away from her head. "The Wittenden Institute. Ithaca. Never heard of it."

"Jerry is a very sick man," Dr. MacDonald said. "We need to take him back for his own good, Mr. Reznick. You are Mr. Reznick?"

"How do you know my name?"

"This is your house, right?"

Reznick wondered how they knew so much. He was very careful to protect his identity and the details of his life. "You need to explain how you know who I am and where I live."

"It's complicated."

"I don't need to know *it's complicated* bullshit. How the hell do you know who I am and where I live? Answer me!"

"Calm down, Mr. Reznick. We learned that a man who stole a car earlier today matched Jerry's description. The GPS on the car indicated it was near Rockland. Jerry's file shows he has family in the area, and he also indicated in interviews with myself and other doctors that he came to Rockland to visit you many years back. I believe you were both in Delta."

"Yeah, but how did you know where I live?"

"I'm not at liberty to say."

Reznick saw a red flag. "Bullshit. You need to do better than that."

The doctor glanced to the two men in the back, who shrugged. "Our facility treats veterans, Mr. Reznick. Vulnerable veterans. And we have access to the databases of several government agencies."

Reznick wondered what government agencies, apart from the IRS, would have his details. He sensed they weren't telling him the full story.

"I very much hope you'll hand him over without further problems."

"Not so fast. I need some reassurances."

"There are two ways we can do this. You can either hand him over to us, or we can call the local cops to help us. But then it might get messy."

"The local cops? What the hell does this have to do with them?"

"Jerry White needs urgent medical care. He needs to be treated by us."

"I don't doubt that Jerry is very ill. But he's petrified of going back to your hospital. Can't he just be looked after here? What about his family? Doesn't his father live up near Camden?"

"His family want nothing to do with him. Besides, Jerry has, unbeknownst to me, not been taking his medication for nearly a week. And it's made him psychotic."

Reznick folded his arms. "Are you kidding me? So you're telling me you haven't been doing your job right."

The doctor flushed. "I think that's unfair."

"Is it?"

"He had been concealing the medication he should have been taking. So it's now vital that we take him back without any further delay."

Reznick sighed. "I have to tell you, he's in a heightened state of anxiety. How long has he been a patient of yours?"

"Several months. He's suicidal. And in this current state, he's a risk to himself and to others. He has classic signs of PTSD. Recurring nightmares. Jerry has also admitted self-harming. He's talked of hallucinations. Paranoia."

Reznick contemplated the right thing to do. He wanted Jerry to get treatment. But Jerry was terrified of being returned to the hospital.

"Mr. Reznick, is Jerry inside?"

"He's sleeping. But when he finds out you guys are here and want to take him away, he'll freak."

MacDonald turned around and pointed to the two heavyset men in the back seat. "Mr. Laurence Cray is the head of security, and he and his colleague are both well trained in restraint."

Reznick glanced at the men in the back. "I don't doubt that."

He wondered how the heavies would treat Jerry for absconding. Would he be put into restraints back at the hospital? But the reality was, Jerry needed help. That was clear. And despite Jerry's concerns—real or imagined—about the doctors and the hospital, medical care was essential.

"So how are we going to work this, Mr. Reznick?" Dr. MacDonald looked over his shoulder toward the house. "Damn . . ."

Reznick turned around.

Jerry was standing on the front porch, bandages still on his lower arms, knife in hand.

"I trusted you, Jon!" Jerry shouted. "I fucking trusted you! You're a brother to me. How could you do this, man?"

Reznick took a few steps toward him, hands in the air. "These people are here to get you better."

"Like fuck they are!" He pointed the knife in MacDonald's direction. "That bitch is trying to control my thoughts. She messed with my head, Jon. Why don't you believe me, man? How could you do this?"

"Jerry, these people are from the hospital . . ."

"It's not a fucking hospital. It's a nuthouse. A hospital gets people better. Why am I not getting better, you bitch?"

MacDonald stepped out of the SUV. "You haven't been taking your medication, Jerry. That's why you've regressed. And you'll start having seizures if we don't act soon."

"You lying bastard!" He looked at Reznick. "She's lying, Jon. Don't believe her."

Reznick took another step forward and reached out his right hand. "Jerry, gimme the knife."

"I thought you were my friend, Jon."

"I am your friend. But you've got to gimme the knife."

"You called them, didn't you? Are you working with them too, Jon? Is that what it is?"

"Categorically not."

"You know what they're going to do? They're gonna take me back there and start playing all those words over and over again, trying to brainwash me. They're controlling my fucking thoughts."

MacDonald turned and looked at Laurence Cray in the back of the SUV. He stepped out.

"Don't fuck with me, Cray," Jerry shouted.

Cray said to Reznick, "Sir, can you move two steps back? We need to defuse this situation."

"Don't antagonize him any further, you hear me?"

Reznick watched as the second man got out of the SUV and walked over to Cray.

"Well . . . it's the goon squad." Jerry held the knife up higher. "So do I have to take you all on, you miserable fucks? Don't fucking try anything."

Reznick said, "Jerry, put down the knife before someone gets hurt."

Cray took a step forward.

"Not another step, you fat bastard. Torturing me like some fucking lab rat. You get your kicks like that, huh?"

Cray said, "One last time, Jerry—put down the knife. And we'll get you the help you need. I promise."

"The nurse won't stop talking. Talking and talking, trying to tell me what to think." Jerry began violently slashing his left wrist. Blood spurted onto the wooden porch.

Reznick rushed forward and kicked the knife out of Jerry's hand, then got him in a headlock and brought him down to the ground, pinning his body with his own.

Jerry writhed hard, blood streaming off his fingers. "Get the fuck off me!"

Reznick used all his upper-body strength and leaned in hard, restraining his former Delta buddy. "Can't do that, Jerry. Don't struggle, man."

Jerry saw Cray approaching out of the corner of his eye. "Get him away from me!"

Cray pinned down Jerry's right leg while his colleague took the left. He then jabbed a syringe into Jerry's thigh.

"You fucking bastards!" Jerry screamed. He struggled and shrieked like a cornered animal.

Then he went limp.

Five

It was nearly dark when the SUV and the ambulance arrived at Wittenden.

The headlights glinted off the razor-wire fence and penetrated the darkness cloaking the Institute. Watching from his third-floor executive office, Dr. Robert Gittinger stared down through the rain-streaked windows.

Gittinger felt a charge of excitement go through his aging body. He had imagined his twilight years filled with strolls and swimming with his wife in a gated community in Boca Raton. But here he was, in his late seventies, back in the shadowy world he loved and thought he'd left behind. The project that had been shelved in the 1960s was back in business. And he was at the helm.

Who gave a shit about aqua aerobics sessions in a gated community when you could control a man's life?

He had started out all those years ago as a bright-eyed graduate of MIT with big ambitions to be a leader in his field. In the early days, Gittinger, like many of his colleagues, had felt strongly that the program's experiments were essential for the well-being of America. But as the years passed, his idealism had given way to an enjoyment of psychological torture masquerading as science. The crazy music on a loop. Play it backward. Turn up the volume. And intersperse it with people screaming. Throw hallucinogens into the mix. He was transfixed by their impact on men. How they became so afraid. He had that power over them. His work hadn't received any recognition—that wouldn't have been allowed—but he was an expert in his field.

And now, as the director of the Institute, he could indulge his whims as and when he required. It was like a drug to him.

Then there was the money. He didn't know any other employer in North America that was paying psychologists $1.5 million a year. He was in the second year of a three-year contract. And the money would help put his grandchildren through their fancy prep schools and college.

But he had other reasons. Personal reasons.

He watched as the security personnel stepped out of the floodlit guardhouse at the perimeter fence and carefully checked the documentation the occupants of the SUV and the ambulance provided. A few moments later, both vehicles were ushered through.

He shut the blinds, sat down at his desk, and opened his laptop. He watched CCTV footage of an unconscious Jerry White being carried out in a straitjacket from the back of the ambulance and placed on a gurney. Gittinger monitored the progress carefully until White was safely back in his private room—the lights on full brightness, twenty-four separate cameras monitoring his every movement, and six hidden microphones picking up every utterance from the room.

The nurses carefully removed the straitjacket and lifted White onto his bed. Then they secured him with leather ties strapped across his chest, thighs, and ankles.

A nurse injected a drug into his left arm; it would knock him out for at least forty-eight hours. She said, "Play loop one and then repeat." From the speakers came a recorded male voice. *No past, no future, no now.* And again. *No past, no future, no now.*

Dr. Gittinger smiled. All the hard work would have to begin again.

Six

It was late as Reznick reflected on what had happened earlier. He sat wrapped up on his deck, staring out over the dark waters of Penobscot Bay, watching silhouetted lobster boats bobbing in the swell, thinking of Jerry. It was strange that the doctor from the hospital and the two security guys had managed to track down not only Jerry but where Reznick lived. He wondered if he had done the right thing handing Jerry over. The whole thing didn't sit right with him.

He thought Dr. MacDonald had sounded defensive. And Jerry's physical appearance and the look in his eyes worried him greatly. It wasn't the guy he knew.

The more he thought about it, the more uneasy he felt. His friend was clearly on edge, if he hadn't already tipped over into a full-on psychotic breakdown. But why would they just turn up like that in person? Wouldn't they have left it to the cops to find Jerry and take him back?

It just didn't make sense.

Reznick watched TV, killing time. Despite the late hour, he decided to go for a run, thinking of his old Delta buddy. He changed into his sweatshirt and pants, black Nike running shoes. He headed out into the dark. The chill autumn wind was biting through him. He pounded the near-deserted sidewalks of Rockland, leaves blowing and swirling down

Main Street. He headed out of town and onto a beach, illuminated by the full moon. Pounding the sand. Mile after mile.

He returned home feeling better. He headed down to the basement, which he had converted into a boxing gym. He pulled on his old leather gloves and hit the punching bag and speed ball until the sweat was pouring off him.

He did another twenty minutes on the punching bag before calling it quits, showered, and put on some fresh clothes.

He made himself some supper. Tomato and mushroom spaghetti sprinkled with a liberal amount of Parmesan cheese. Then he took a bottle of cold beer out of the fridge.

He switched on the radio and listened to the shipping forecast as he sat down at his kitchen table. It was something that reminded him of his father, listening in for weather conditions at sea. He ate alone and stared out the window at the dark waters.

After he had finished his meal and the bottle of beer, he washed the dishes, wiped down the counters, and emailed his daughter, at Bennington College, in Vermont, asking her how she was. She hadn't emailed him for nearly a week.

A few minutes later, his cell phone rang.

"Dad, I'm so sorry that I haven't been in touch." It was Lauren. It was good to hear her voice.

"Hey, stranger, how goes it?"

"Is it OK to talk, Dad? It's a bit late, I know."

"Not a problem."

"I'm so sorry about not emailing. I'm snowed under with essays and assignments and all sorts of stuff."

"As long as you're working hard, honey."

"What about you? What've you been doing?"

"This and that."

"This and that," she parroted. "What does that even mean?"

"It means not very much. Just enjoying my own company. I like my own space."

"I know you do, Dad." A silence opened up between them. "You OK? You sound a bit distant."

"Just a guy I knew turned up yesterday out of the blue following me in a stolen car and then freaking out a bit. Ex-military like me."

"Are you kidding me?"

"No. I put him up for the night."

"At our house? Dad, is that a good idea?"

"I can't give up on an old friend. He needed help yesterday. Bad."

"Where is he now?"

"This morning first thing he was picked up by people from the hospital. Started slashing at his wrists, he was so psychotic. Said he didn't want to go back."

"Are you OK, Dad?"

"Don't worry about me, I'm fine. He's back where he came from."

"And where is that?"

"Some psychiatric hospital. Escaped, apparently."

"He's a mental patient? And he stayed with you? At our house?"

"I couldn't turn my back on him, could I?"

"I guess not. That's awful. Who was it?"

"Guy called Jerry White. You might remember him."

"I remember the name. You said he visited you after Mom died. At the house."

"That's right. You called him Uncle Jerry when you were younger."

"I did?"

"He was around a lot at the time. He even read you stories."

"I don't remember that."

"He also, if I remember correctly, stopped you from getting scalded after I knocked a pan of hot water off the stove. He put his arm in front of you. He was the one who got burned."

"Oh my God, Dad. Really?"

"He did that. He was around for me a hell of a lot after your mom died. I was a mess. He also taught you to tie your shoelaces. You were only two or three."

"I remember you showed me a photograph of the two of you. Why didn't you tell me all that stuff about him?"

"I'm telling you about it now."

"You're really closed off, Dad, do you know that? Can you find the photographs for me to look through when I come back?"

"I don't even know where they are."

"You've got a big pile of them up in the loft."

Reznick made a mental note to check them out. "Jerry was a one-off."

"Yeah, you said he was a good guy."

"He was. He's really gone now."

"What do you mean?"

"I mean he's gone schizoid or something. It happens."

"But he's getting help now?"

"I think so."

Lauren sighed. "He's not dangerous or anything, is he?"

"Only to himself, I think."

"He read me stories?"

"Fairy tales. That kind of thing."

"I think I've still got the book in my room."

"I know. It's sitting right beside *Anne of Green Gables*. Your mother loved that book."

They said their loves and goodbyes and hung up, but Reznick kept hearing those words: *You said he was a good guy.*

Reznick fixed himself a tumbler of single malt Scotch. He got the box of old photos Lauren had mentioned down from the attic. He rummaged around for a few minutes in the box, glancing at old photos of him with

Elisabeth. Photos of him in his early twenties, Delta operator, pre-9/11. Fort Bragg, North Carolina. A different person. A different world. Then Delta focused on possible missions. They examined advancing tactics, techniques, and procedures. When there was a conflict, it was invariably short and sharp. South America to take out a member of Shining Path. Colombia to kill a FARC guerrilla leader. Then it would be back to the grind of training. And more training.

Eventually, he caught a picture of him and Jerry drinking in a Rockland bar. Post-9/11. It was taken by another ex-Delta—now sadly dead—Harry Leggett. He looked at Jerry's staring eyes. But also his own blank expression.

Reznick's mind flashed back to the time after 9/11. A hardened young Delta operator, still in his twenties, drinking himself crazy for weeks. He'd shipped his baby daughter off to his in-laws in New York for a time. He knew he wasn't coping. He couldn't even look after himself. He was just a shell.

Twelve-hour drinking sessions each and every day. Eventually, weeks later, he was left alone as everyone went their separate ways. Reznick descended into an even more self-destructive pattern of behavior, until somehow, after some serious conversations with an old friend of his father's, he stopped the drinking. Stopped for his daughter but also his country.

He had skills that were prized. He was part of the elite Delta cadre. A few months later, he cleaned up. Then two years after 9/11 he was in Iraq with Delta. Shootings, killings, assassinations, on and on in blazing heat like he'd never experienced before. It was like Dante's *Inferno*. Blood, dust, pain, death, on and on and on.

He was able to disassociate. His personality was like that. The same was true of most of the Delta guys. They just did what had to be done.

Reznick had an abiding memory of Jerry White in Iraq still burned into his mind. His very soul. The hell that was Fallujah. He remembered Jerry had been cut off from the rest of Delta during a fierce gun battle.

He had been kidnapped off the street at gunpoint and taken to a make-shift torture chamber by Sunni jihadists. Baathists. They pulled out his fingernails. Beat him to a pulp looking for names of Iraqi informers and translators. He gave them nothing. He fed them plausible lies. They stabbed him. Tried to drown him.

Reznick and two others managed to locate him in a warren of shitty dusty streets. They killed every goddamn enemy. Reznick carried Jerry out to a Humvee, where his heart briefly stopped while Special Forces medics fought to keep him alive. Eventually, they got him to a US military hospital emergency room. And after three operations, Jerry White was saved.

Jerry thanked Reznick countless times afterward. And after Reznick lost his wife, Jerry was the first who turned up in Rockland, supporting him through his darkest hours. He stayed with him, drank with him, and watched as he attempted to drink himself to death. He was the one who put his arm around Reznick's shoulder and said he needed to find strength to go on for his daughter. *Don't let it destroy you. Because if it destroys you, it will destroy your daughter. And she will have no one.* Those were his words.

Slowly, Reznick had begun to emerge from his haze.

He began to realize he had responsibilities. Lauren needed him. Jerry was the one who hung around; he was the one who didn't leave his side as Reznick howled on the beach, down in the cove by his house.

He flicked through a few more photos and saw himself at Jerry's wedding at a hotel in New Jersey with his wife, Patti, way back in 2008. Smart gray suits. But even then there were signs that Jerry was out of control. Patti was a recovering addict who had her own problems. But she had confided in Reznick that Jerry had threatened to jump to his death if she left him.

He wondered where Patti was now.

Reznick picked up the photo of Jerry, Patti, and himself. He remembered that Logan Township was her hometown. He also remembered

Jerry saying that when he first met her he'd had to head across into Camden and score her some heroin. He eventually got her off it. But Jerry was never convinced she was clean.

Her eyes were always way too glassy, her reactions a fraction too sluggish. She was a sweet girl but pretty damaged. Which probably made them perfect for each other.

Reznick rifled through the rest of the box and saw a picture of Patti with her brother, a burly cop named Jimmy Gonzales, who policed the meanest streets of Camden. Reznick liked him a lot. Didn't say too much; just drank and watched what was happening.

Reznick wondered if he was still in the job. Gonzales might be able to tell him more about what had happened to Jerry. He might even want to pass on the information about Jerry's whereabouts to his sister, if she didn't already know. He pulled up a number for the police HQ and called.

A female voice answered.

"I'm looking to speak to Jimmy Gonzales. Friend of his sister. Was hoping he could help me."

"What's your name, sir?"

"Jon Reznick."

"Hang on."

A silence opened up down the line until the gruff voice of Gonzales said, "You gotta be kidding me. Jon Reznick?"

"You got it."

"Jon, how the hell you doing, man?"

"I'm OK. And you?"

A long sigh. "Got fired a few years back and then rehired at a far lower salary, but hey, what the fuck, right?"

"Indeed. Jimmy, I won't take up much of your time."

"Is it about Jerry by any chance?"

"Yeah, it is."

"He's crazy, you know that."

"Yeah, I know. I was hoping to speak to Patti."

"Patti? She doesn't want anything to do with him. Can't say I blame her."

"I understand that. I just wanted to find out what exactly has happened to him."

"Patti's trying to get her life in order. And she's got a good job, and I don't think it'll do any good to resurrect memories of Jerry, if I'm honest."

"Sorry, I thought you could help. Or maybe explain his situation. The doctor who picked him up mentioned post-traumatic stress."

"Is that right?"

"When was the last time you spoke to Jerry, if you don't mind me asking?"

"About a year ago. Patti had left him months earlier and he was still bugging me, wondering why she wasn't visiting him at the hospital."

"What hospital was that?"

"The Palm Hospital, down in Florida. Burned-out wack-job veterans mostly."

"And he called from there?"

"Yeah."

"And that was the last you heard?"

"That's it. Until you called."

"The doctor at the hospital he's in now said his family didn't want anything to do with him."

"Well, Patti said she doesn't want anything more to do with him, that's true. But I felt sorry for him. I visited him a couple of times down in Florida."

"How did he seem to you?"

"In a pretty bad way. Self-harming, threatened other patients. He called to say he had been picked to undergo new rehabilitation therapy up in New York. He was excited about that. Doctors had told him that the treatment had excellent results with veterans with psychiatric conditions."

"What was this place called?"

"Wittenden or something."

"Did you visit him at this place?"

"I called, but they said that wasn't possible."

"What about the last time you visited him down in Florida? What was he like?"

"Jerry was wired. Babbling about killing people and stuff. Said he needed to get a knife. Talked about the Taliban operating across Florida. Needed to sort them out. Was too much for me, so I didn't go anymore."

"Did anyone else visit him in Florida as far as you know?"

"His father."

"What's his name?" Reznick asked.

"Hank White. Retired to Bar Harbor, just up the coast from you. You want me to let him know?"

"Yeah, give the old man a call. Let him know Jerry's at the Wittenden Institute in Ithaca, New York."

Seven

The following day, Reznick's cell phone rang. He didn't recognize the number.

"Yeah, Reznick speaking."

"Jon, it's Jimmy Gonzales. I thought you should know. You know, after your call?"

"Sure. Did you manage to get in touch with Jerry's dad OK?"

"Yeah, I did. But last night—late last night—I got an irate call from Hank saying he wasn't being allowed to visit Jerry at Wittenden. Really cut up about it. Said he had a right to see his son. Which I absolutely agree with and understand."

"Sure."

"Anyway, he called in the middle of the night, about two in the morning. I've got to be straight with you. When he called, he sounded out of his brains. Really crazy drunk. And he was threatening to go down there."

"Go down where?"

"To the hospital where Jerry is, in New York."

"Wittenden?"

"Right. So he was screaming at me over the phone that he wanted to speak to the doctors, demanding to see his son. Threatening to go to his congressman or senator or some such shit. Said he'd called them up again and said he was going to get the press to highlight this disgrace, as he called it. Eventually, after raving for a few minutes, he just hung up on me."

Reznick sighed. "Shit."

"Anyway, I just got off my shift and I called Hank. No answer. Called twenty, maybe thirty times over the last hour or so. And still no answer."

"Maybe he's sleeping off his hangover."

"Maybe. I was just thinking, well, Jerry is still family. He's not a bad guy. He's crazy, sure. But he's not a bad guy. And his dad is family as far as I'm concerned."

Reznick said nothing.

"So I was wondering if it was possible for you to head on up to see how he is."

Reznick considered what he was saying. "Hasn't he got anyone in Bar Harbor?"

"Not a soul, man. Not a goddamn soul. Burned all his bridges."

Reznick thought of his Delta buddy in a hospital without anyone to visit. He would have wanted someone to at least look in on his dad. "Leave it with me, Jimmy."

The sun had dipped below the horizon, spreading a dark autumnal glow across Bar Harbor, when Reznick pulled up at Hank White's trailer. The door was open and a golden Labrador was barking its head off.

Reznick patted the dog on the head. "OK, boy, how you doing?"

The dog barked some more, increasingly louder.

Reznick knocked on the open door. "Hey, it's Jerry's friend, Reznick. You decent, Hank?"

No answer.

Reznick knocked again and waited for a few moments. "Jimmy Gonzales said to give you a visit. It's about Jerry." He sighed. "Hank,

I'm just coming in." He popped his head inside and looked around. Disheveled mess. Old TV dinners strewn around with empty bottles of vodka, wine, and Scotch, the sickly smell of pot heavy in the air. "Jesus . . ."

He looked around the trailer, then out the back window, which overlooked some woods.

The dog's barking didn't let up.

Reznick checked the collar and saw it said *My name is Max. I belong to Jerry White.* He looked over toward the woods. He felt that Hank White wouldn't be far. Maybe crashed out there after going for a walk.

He stepped out of the trailer and headed down a leaf-strewn dirt path toward the trees.

Reznick took out his gun and pulled back the slide, purely as a precaution. He walked on, pale moonlight showing the way into the woods. The dog was barking, walking beside him, occasionally jumping up on him. "OK, Max, behave."

The dog ran on ahead.

Reznick followed and headed farther into the woods, along a trail. A canopy of dark-brown and black foliage. The prolific aroma of damp and leaves and soil. He walked nearly a mile or so. The light was fading fast. Up ahead the dog was barking furiously.

He went in that direction, the only sound twigs snapping underfoot.

He sensed something was wrong. Maybe a hunch. The open door of the trailer. Had Jerry's dad gone for a walk and had a heart attack? Maybe he'd collapsed in the woods drunk and fallen asleep somewhere among the trees. That was the most likely explanation.

The more Reznick thought about it, the more he wondered what the hell he was doing out in the middle of some goddamn woods outside Bar Harbor, Maine, trying to find out if his ex-Delta buddy's dad had fallen ill or collapsed.

Reznick called out. "Hank, are you out there? It's Reznick, Jerry's friend. Jimmy called me. He's worried something happened to you."

The dog's barking was the only sound that split the chilly air.

Reznick walked on and on. He was determined to make sure he'd given a proper look before he called the cops to report a missing person. "Hank, it's getting dark. You need to get yourself back to the trailer. Your goddamn door's wide open."

Up ahead, shrouded in darkness, was something Reznick couldn't make out.

He ran forward until he stopped dead in his tracks. He peered through the gloom. High up on a mossy oak, he could see Hank White hanging, belt around his neck, eyes open and mouth agape.

A few moments later, he sensed movement behind him.

He spun around. Two cops were approaching, their guns trained on him.

"Not a fucking move, son!"

Eight

Deep in the bowels of the Wittenden Institute, Director Dr. Bob Gittinger and Dr. Eileen MacDonald were standing outside the reinforced one-way mirror. On the other side of the Plexiglas, Jerry White lay on his bed, heavily sedated, leather restraints across his chest, waist, thighs, and ankles.

From the speakers came a recorded male voice. *No past, no future, no now.* And again. *No past, no future, no now.*

Gittinger watched, transfixed. "Do you believe he will allow the words into him?" he said. "What I mean is, when will he no longer resist?"

"Jerry is strong willed. He is very resourceful. And he is highly dangerous. But the cognitive tests we've done with him show he follows orders almost compulsively. So we are confident the trigger words will be followed. We have had three psychological evaluations, and they all say the same thing. He's the best candidate for successful completion."

Gittinger glanced through the glass again. "What do we anticipate the effects on him will be with the more intensive therapy we're planning?"

"No one really knows."

"Best guess?"

"Our best guess is that Jerry might feel overwhelmed for a short period, but we're not expecting any regressive reaction to his course of treatment."

"Very well, I want a first-day update tomorrow at 11 p.m."

MacDonald nodded. "I'll send that to you as soon as we have the vital signs and figures and all the efficacy predictions of the treatment."

Gittinger took one long look at Jerry White lying prostrate, knowing what lay ahead for him. He headed back to his office and shut the door. The more he thought of the experiments they were resurrecting, the more excited he got. His mind turned to his wife, dutifully at home, thinking his work was required for his country. And in a way it was.

As a young man in the early 1960s, when he had first joined the group in Canada conducting the experiments, he had felt that something was not right. That maybe what he was doing was unethical. But as the years had passed, those feelings had dissipated. Now the tests sent a frisson of tension to the very pit of his stomach. He loved nothing more than gazing at a subject as they were put under his spell.

He'd kept copious notes since the earlier days, details of each and every experiment, hundreds of notepads locked away in his basement office. And they knew that. That was part of why they'd approached him shortly after his retirement eight years earlier.

The work was of national importance, they said. Secrecy was paramount. The program was beginning again. But this time he would be in charge. He would run the show how he wanted. There were other reasons. Reasons that were known only to a handful.

Fifty years ago, Gittinger had fallen out with numerous colleagues who had dismissed the efficacy of the tests and the results. They said the tests were barbaric. Inhumane. Unlawful. He didn't care. He claimed that, with modifications to those selected and the medication they were given, the tests would eventually result in stunning breakthroughs for mankind. Deep down even he didn't believe it.

But the escape of Jerry White had unsettled him.

He wondered if it wasn't just a matter of time before the program was fully exposed. That thought weighed heavily on his mind.

Someone somewhere would surely connect the dots, eventually.

His cell phone rang, snapping him out of his morbid thoughts. He recognized the caller ID. His heart sank. It was the boss.

"Dr. Robert Gittinger," he said.

"Thought you'd want a heads-up, Bob."

"Regarding?"

"Jerry White's father."

"What about him?"

"I'm hearing he's no longer with us."

Gittinger took a few moments to let that sink in. "What happened?"

"Think he was depressed. Took his life, apparently."

Gittinger knew that wasn't the case. It was too much of a coincidence. It had to be related to the escape of his son. He understood that those outside the experiment were just collateral damage in his line of work. "Are you sure?"

"He'd threatened to go to his congressman. From what I gather, he didn't call. But he'd looked up the congressman's phone number and email address."

"But it didn't come to anything."

"That's right. Very sad. But Hank White is gone. And he won't be bothering you or anyone at the Institute ever again."

Nine

The sound of a cell phone ringing roused Reznick from a fitful sleep.

He awoke and looked around. He was lying on top of a bed in a cold Bar Harbor police cell, an assistant director of the FBI staring through the bars at him, phone to her ear.

Reznick took a few moments to realize it really was Martha Meyerstein in person. He was well known to her and the Feds. His work as a black-ops specialist had come to the attention of Meyerstein several years earlier. He had been tasked with carrying out a high-level hit. But it was a setup to kill an innocent government scientist. He ended up protecting the man and handing him over to Meyerstein and the FBI, subsequently helping the Feds foil a biological weapons attack on the DC Metro. And since then he had been called in to help Meyerstein and her team when there was a threat to national security. His covert skills had been instrumental in tracking down and killing an Iranian hit squad who wanted to neutralize former Delta Force members. He'd brought down the head of the Russian mob and rescued Meyerstein after she'd been kidnapped and held prisoner by the Bratva. He had also been called in when a senior American security adviser had gone missing. But it had transpired that the kidnapping was part of a much wider conspiracy involving a CIA cabal who wanted to kill the President.

He wondered how she had gotten involved in this. He certainly hadn't contacted her. So who had?

Meyerstein spoke into her phone. "I'll call you back this afternoon, sir," she said, ending the call. "What the hell is going on, Jon?"

"What are you doing here?"

She shrugged. "Trying to figure out what the hell you're doing in a six-by-four cell."

"It's a long story. Listen, this doesn't concern you."

"That's where you're wrong. I was woken up in the middle of the night."

"By who?"

"It doesn't matter. I get to hear things. If the cops search your name in a database, the FBI will get to hear about it. Do you understand?"

"What do you want?"

"I want to get you out of here."

"OK, let's do it."

Meyerstein stared long and hard at him. "Not so fast. I can get you out of here. But remember our little conversation? Well, I'm still waiting to hear your answer."

"I'm still thinking about it."

"Then I can't help you, Jon. I'm sorry."

"Gimme a break."

"Here's the deal. Either you agree to work with us, in effect formalizing the role you've had, and sign a form confirming that, or I'm just going to have to leave you to the good officers here in Bar Harbor."

Reznick shook his head. "You're really going to pull that stunt on me? Seriously?"

"It is what it is, Jon."

"It's blackmail."

"Don't be so dramatic. It's business."

Reznick sighed. He always felt uncomfortable being tied into formal arrangements. His work with the FBI had purely been on an ad hoc basis. And he had been unwilling to commit to a role that might have him focusing on more mundane Fed inquiries. He was happiest doing high-level jobs.

He felt instinctively uncomfortable at the thought of being part of an organization like the FBI, which had particular ways of doing things. He enjoyed the freedom of doing operations as and when required.

But as it stood now, Reznick needed every friend he had.

"I can't believe you're using this as leverage."

"Jon, listen to me. We want to help you. We want to get you out of here. And we can. But we cannot do a thing if you aren't assigned to the FBI. If you come under the auspices of the FBI, you have my word that we will do our utmost to help you. But first you have to help yourself."

"What I'm doing is probably not on the FBI radar. But I need to pursue this thing, even if I sign that bit of paper. I can't turn my back on my friend."

Meyerstein thought long and hard. "Fine." She handed the paper and a pen through the bars.

Reznick scanned the legal jargon pertaining to national security. He scrawled his signature and printed his name, then handed back the paper and pen. "You play hardball, Meyerstein, I'll give you that."

She folded the paper and put it in her pocket, along with the pen. "Let's cut the crap, Jon. If I get any more sleep-deprived, I'll have to be admitted to the hospital."

"Nice of you to come in person."

Meyerstein shook her head. "Let me tell you, the Director is less than delighted that you've ended up in jail for the night."

"It's not so bad. Been in far worse than this, let me tell you. It's not the Plaza, but it's not bad."

Lieutenant Jackson walked into view holding some paperwork and a plastic padded mailer with Reznick's belongings. He unlocked the cell. "Assistant Director Meyerstein is vouching for you, so that's good enough for me. At least for now."

Reznick shook his head. "For now?"

"As of now, the FBI is taking full responsibility for you. But if we require you to answer more questions, then the rules are that you will comply. Alrighty?"

"Whatever." Reznick took the padded mailer with his gun, cell phone, and wallet. "Appreciate the hospitality, Lieutenant."

Jackson shrugged as if he'd heard it all before. "Try and stay away from Bar Harbor, Mr. Reznick."

"I'll see what I can do."

Meyerstein drove Reznick across to a diner overlooking the water. They sat down at a window booth. She ordered a breakfast of freshly squeezed orange juice and coffee; Reznick opted for pancakes and maple syrup with black coffee and the orange juice.

When they were finished, Reznick spoke first. "I appreciate you getting me out."

"You mind telling me what all this is about?"

He recounted the story from when Jerry White began tailing him until he found Hank White hanging in the woods, just before the police arrived. "Something is wrong. Very wrong."

"The police know that. They still consider this a homicide. But they don't think you're telling the full story. I can understand how the cops thought your version sounded less than plausible. Prints all over the trailer, discovering the body, and that following an incident with his psychotic son. I'd be asking questions myself."

Reznick ordered more coffee for them and their cups were refilled. He took a gulp. "I'm guessing this sort of stuff is small-time and outside FBI jurisdiction."

"Unless there are terrorism issues, cybersecurity, or major threats to America, you're right; an old guy hanging himself in the woods in Maine doesn't really register on our radar."

"So why didn't you just ignore the call from the Bar Harbor cops?"

"I was sorely tempted to, let me tell you. But the last thing the FBI needs is for local reporters to be alerted by a desk sergeant tipping them off that an ex-Delta guy—who has close links to the Feds—is being interviewed after a body is found hanging in the woods."

"I'm assuming you didn't have to come all this way. Why didn't you get the guys from the Boston field office who oversee Maine?"

"Not having a field office does make it challenging. But I couldn't risk an FBI asset being compromised. I wanted to be here to oversee this myself. I also don't want the Boston Feds crawling all over this wondering exactly what the extent of your role has been for the FBI."

Reznick nodded.

"Probably just as well I'm here on the ground. The cops have a real thing for you in this investigation, Jon."

"That's nice."

"It's no laughing matter. I needed to smooth things out. I spoke with Maine's attorney general, and I was able to explain that to the lieutenant, who seemed more than eager to off-load you, at least for the present."

"Well, whatever, I appreciate it."

"I think it's important that our organization looks after its assets. Speaking of which, the Director will be pleased you've signed, although he'll be less pleased by the circumstances."

Reznick nodded. "Attracting attention isn't something I enjoy."

"Gunshots on a road on the outskirts of Rockland, crazy friend staying the night, psychiatric hospital having to haul him out of your house. Not exactly low profile."

Reznick sipped some coffee. "I can't turn my back on Jerry. He's not allowed visitors. And now his dad is gone, I just don't want to abandon him."

"You're not abandoning him. He needs help. And hopefully, in a few weeks or months you can see him."

"I've never seen Jerry like that. A guy like that, tough—that's how I remember him—but now he's like a fucking shell. Said he wasn't being fed."

"Crazy people say crazy things."

"I know . . . but something—and I can't place what it was exactly—about the fear in his eyes really troubled me."

"Was he psychotic?"

"That's what they said."

"But you don't think he was."

"I don't know. He'd seem lucid for a few minutes, and then he'd be gripped by a terrible inner terror. He said when he closed his eyes he saw himself killing people."

"Post-traumatic stress?"

"I guess. He thought the doctors were trying to drive him out of his mind. He said he thought they were going to kill him too. It was all a bit out there."

Meyerstein went quiet for a few moments as her gaze wandered around the diner. "Tell me about Jerry when he was well."

"Jerry was the one, above all my other Delta crew, who was with me in the days and weeks following Elisabeth's death."

Meyerstein averted her gaze.

"He was there as I sat on the beach, down in the cove, drinking myself into oblivion. He drank with me in every bar in Rockland. Twice. And still helped me get home. He slept on the sofa. He heard me wailing every night. But he never said a thing. He was just there for me. Eventually, he said, 'OK, enough. You need to move on.'"

"You were close?"

"We were close. You know how it is. People go their separate ways, lose contact. When I left Delta, he was still there. He left a couple of years after me. But he didn't get in touch. And to be fair, neither did I. You get on with things."

"I understand."

"I don't owe Jerry anything. But I feel I do. That's why I came up here to make sure his dad was OK, not knowing that I'd find him like that." Reznick looked out over the water. "Jerry loved the ocean. Loved looking at the water. Listening to it hit the shoreline. Made him calm. Relaxed him even. This all probably doesn't make much sense."

Meyerstein sighed. "It makes plenty of sense. You look out for people. I admire that. We all have our reasons why we look out for people. Or at least certain people."

"I must be a pain in the ass for you."

"Life is never dull with you, I'll give you that." She took out the paper he had signed. "You need to date it." She handed Reznick a pen.

Reznick looked at the papers and marked down the date.

"Do you not like commitment, Jon? Is that it?"

"That's not it. It's just got to be the right time for me. Today is the right time. And I don't mind committing myself to some high-level stuff. But I need some time to help Jerry."

"We won't be waiting around forever. You're now part of the FBI."

"I got it."

"You've got to be careful, Jon. One fuck-up and you'll be back in jail."

"How long can I spend looking into Jerry's situation?"

"You've got a week. Not a day more."

Ten

It had been a couple of years since Reznick had met up with Tom McNulty, an ex-Marine and now Rockland psychologist specializing in post-traumatic stress. It turned out he and McNulty shared a mutual friend, Bill Eastland, former chief of police and a Vietnam vet buddy of Reznick's late father. McNulty was a good listener. And he had offered to work with Reznick if he ever needed help.

Reznick hadn't taken him up on the offer until now. He'd much prefer to deal with his emotions and moods in his own way. Usually by walking along the shore. Forgetting himself, at least for a few hours. Forgetting the memories.

It was late morning when Reznick pulled up outside McNulty's waterfront property in Owls Head, not far from Rockland.

Reznick got out of his car and rang the front-door bell. A few moments later, the mustachioed McNulty opened the door, holding a mug of coffee. He wore a burgundy sweater, dark jeans, and cowboy boots.

"Well, Jon Reznick, long time no see," he said. "Come on in. I've only got a few minutes to spare, so it'll have to be quick."

Reznick headed inside and was shown into a spacious waterfront room filled with books. Two adjacent sofas were positioned near a marble table with old copies of *Newsweek* and *National Geographic* piled on top.

"Sit down. You want a coffee?"

"Don't mind if I do, Tom, thanks. I appreciate you seeing me on such short notice."

"Not a problem." McNulty headed to the kitchen and brought back a piping-hot mug of black coffee. "The way you like it, as I remember."

Reznick smiled and took the mug, placing it on a coaster on the table.

McNulty put down his mug and sat on the opposite sofa. "So what can I do for you? You said when you called it wasn't about you but rather a former friend of yours. Ex-Delta, right?"

"Yeah, pretty much."

"What do you want to know?"

"First, this is not a consultation as such. This is just a chat."

McNulty smiled. "Whatever you want to talk about, I'm listening."

"You know what it's like, Tom. I mean, when you're in battle. It's fucking nasty. Does things to your head."

"No question."

Reznick went over again what happened when Jerry White came back into his life.

"That's a very traumatic series of events by itself," McNulty said. "Together it must've had an impact on you."

"Maybe."

"Is that something you want to talk about? I can book you in."

"Not really. What I'm interested in is trying to visit the hospital Jerry's in. I don't know . . ."

"What don't you know?"

"I'm not really good at this opening-up stuff, Tom, but Jerry looked after me when I was at my lowest and I want to at least be there for him. You know, just to visit him and say, 'It'll be alright, pal'—that kind of thing."

"Perhaps Jerry's doctors feel that in his current condition he's just not ready. Might be worth leaving it to the doctors to get him back on track."

"Maybe you're right."

McNulty looked at Reznick. "You're dying inside, Jon. I can see that. You're really cut up about this, aren't you?"

"I don't want him to languish in a goddamn psychiatric hospital for months. I'm wondering if you, maybe in your capacity as a psychologist who knows about post-traumatic stress disorder, maybe you could contact them, at least try and gain access. Maybe they'd allow you in."

"I don't as a rule interfere in the workings of other hospitals, unless the person is a patient or former patient. But in this case—just this once—I'll put in a call for you."

"Tom, that's much appreciated. That's a real weight off."

"Not a problem. So . . . Jerry White." McNulty leaned over to his desk and picked up a pad of paper and a pen. "What's the name of this hospital Jerry's being cared for in?"

"It's in upstate New York."

"Know that area well."

"Place called the Wittenden Institute."

McNulty scribbled the name down and went quiet for a few moments.

"Jerry said it might be in the Ithaca area or thereabouts. He didn't seem too sure."

"That's interesting."

"How's that?"

McNulty sighed. "I know the place you're talking about."

"You do?"

McNulty nodded before drinking some of his coffee.

"You mind explaining how you know about it?"

"I applied for a job there just after it opened a few years back, shortly after I graduated from college. They must've thought with my

45

military history, medical degree, I'd be a good candidate. So I headed up there and was there for three days. Sat test after test—psychometric tests—to see if they thought I'd be a good fit. I thought I would've aced it, but apparently not. During my time there, I asked questions, wanting to know more about their work there with veterans, but they weren't very forthcoming. I'd assumed it was just medical confidentiality, that kind of thing. But anyway, the long and short of it is I didn't get the job."

Reznick nodded.

"Friend of mine did get a job there. But she left after a couple months."

"Why?"

"I don't know why."

"So this place is legit?"

"Far as I know. I understand there might be a public perception from people in the area that, because it's delving into the memories of veterans, there are ethical issues involved. But no, far as I know it's highly regarded, pioneering work. I think I remember reading somewhere that they're using methods to erase bad memories and reestablish the positive ones."

"So you think Jerry's in good hands?"

"Sure, why wouldn't he be?"

"Your friend—do you think she'd mind speaking to me about the place? Just to put me at ease that Jerry's OK."

"I think that's unlikely. She got a severance package which stipulated she couldn't divulge details about her employment after the contract was signed."

"So they're pretty big on secrecy."

"Jon, can I offer you a word of advice?"

Reznick lifted up his cup of coffee and took a large gulp. "Sure."

"This place is held in high esteem. From what you describe, Jerry was probably in a frightened state of mind. So my advice to you is, just let it go and get on with your life."

Reznick nodded, deep in thought.

"Since you're an old friend, I'll tell you what I'll do. I remember I met a guy like you trying to find out more about the facility. He might know more about the place than me."

"Who's that?"

"A reporter who was pestering my friend who'd worked there. He seemed to know a lot about the place. Probably keen to write a big article on it what with the cutting-edge research."

"You got a name?"

"No, but I can get it for you if it'll help." McNulty looked at his watch. "Sorry, Jon, got an appointment in ten minutes and I need to do a bit of reading before then."

Reznick wondered if he had leapt to the wrong conclusions about the Wittenden Institute. He felt better having spoken to McNulty and clapped him on the back. "Appreciate that."

"You're probably reading too much into things. Jerry's in a good place. Trust me on that."

Eleven

It was a short drive from McNulty's house in Owls Head back to Reznick's home on the outskirts of Rockland. When he got inside, his landline phone was ringing. He picked up. It was Jimmy Gonzales.

"I just heard about Jerry's old man. That's tough, man. Terrible."

Reznick blew out his cheeks. "Yeah. How's your sister taking it?"

"She didn't much care for Hank, and lately Jerry too. But she still feels bad for them. Jon, the reason I'm calling is I've ended up organizing the funeral, since no one else was willing to do it. You know, communicate with the undertaker on behalf of what remains of Jerry's family."

"Has Jerry been told?"

"That's just the thing. I tried calling them, but there's no answer on the main number. I must've tried a dozen times. Nothing."

"Leave it to me. I'll deal with it."

"Jon, you've gone over and above what I'd expect. And by the way, for what it's worth, I'm real sorry I asked you to head up to Bar Harbor. I think you've probably got enough on your plate without witnessing that."

Reznick didn't fill Jimmy in on how he had been questioned by Bar Harbor police as a suspect or that he believed Hank had been murdered. He knew the cops weren't buying the suicide theory. Which begged the question, who had killed Hank? Had someone wanted to silence him? But why? Then again, was it somehow connected to Jerry's escape from the hospital? The more he thought about it, the less he understood. "Seen a lot worse, Jimmy. Anyway, I'll give the doctor a call, find out if she's aware Jerry's father is dead or if Jerry has been notified and that you'd presumably want him to have the chance to attend the funeral."

"Absolutely. He might be crazy. And it might be upsetting for everyone. But on compassionate grounds, that's a no-brainer. He deserves to say farewell to his father."

"They might argue that he's in no fit state."

"They can say what they fucking like. But he should be at his father's funeral, end of story."

Reznick ended the call. He pulled out the business card Dr. MacDonald had given him. He dialed the number. He tried calling several times but there was no answer. The rest of the day dragged as he thought of Jerry White at the hospital. About the death of his father. Jerry needed to know. That night, he called Dr. MacDonald's number again. It rang for nearly a minute before it was finally answered.

"Dr. Eileen MacDonald."

"Sorry to bother you, Dr. MacDonald, Jon Reznick. Can I have a couple minutes of your time?"

"It's very late, Mr. Reznick."

"It's about Jerry White. It's quite urgent."

A silence echoed down the line. "Mr. Reznick, I'm very sorry. Jerry White regrettably cannot, at this moment, receive visitors."

"Listen . . . the thing is . . . Jerry's father died."

A beat. "I'm sorry to hear that."

"I'm requesting, on behalf of Jerry's family—his brother-in-law and wife—that Jerry be allowed to attend his father's funeral. It'll be sometime over the next few days, maybe a week or so."

"I'll certainly consider that, Mr. Reznick."

Reznick thought her tone was very offhanded. Dismissive and cold.

"We have to think of the patient first and foremost. What will be the impact on his mental health, which is already in a perilous state?"

"Dr. MacDonald, I'm not telling you how to do your job, but I think Jerry is entitled to attend his father's funeral. That's just what I think, for what it's worth."

"So do I. But that final decision is made by the Wittenden Institute board of governors. And only with all the facts on the table can they make an informed choice about what is best for Jerry."

"So can you tell me when that will be?"

"Let's see . . . The board meeting is tomorrow evening. I will be attending. And I can certainly reassure you that I will be recommending that Jerry be escorted out of the hospital—remember, he is not a well man; this might be under mild sedation—and be allowed to attend his father's funeral."

"OK, fair enough."

"How about I call you tomorrow night as soon as I hear?"

"I'd appreciate that. Thank you."

An awkward silence stretched between them. "Anything else, Mr. Reznick?"

"Yeah, do you mind me asking how Jerry is? What's the latest on his condition?"

MacDonald sighed. "Last I heard, Jerry was sleeping. And I know he's attended music therapy classes. We find that in some patients it can alleviate the symptoms of post-traumatic stress disorder. Helps relaxation. It provides a useful distraction for those in pain but also stimulates parts of the brain."

"And he likes that?"

"Very much. Along with his new medication, we are seeing some promising signs."

"OK, I appreciate the heads-up."

"I should be able to get back to you by nine tomorrow evening. If that's all, Mr. Reznick, good night."

Twelve

Early the following morning, Gittinger was in a separate room behind the one-way Plexiglas, watching as Jerry White was awoken by the beguiling, hypnotic sound of the traditional Vietnamese stringed instrument *dàn tran*. It reminded Gittinger of his years in Hanoi. He thought it was sublime and soothing.

He sighed as he gazed at the patient. Like a frightened animal, he was looking around him, unsure of his surroundings. Gittinger saw how heavily sedated he was.

Suddenly, the voice activation kicked in, with harsh lights all around. White looked alarmed as he struggled to sit upright in bed.

This time it wasn't a recording. The woman's voice was calm, authoritative, and clear.

"Good morning, Jerry. Did you sleep well?"

White's eyes were roaming all over the room. "Who's saying that?"

"It's Nurse. I said good evening, Jerry. Did you sleep well?"

"Yes, thank you."

"You seem a bit calmer than yesterday, don't you?"

"Yeah, I guess so."

Gittinger watched closely as Jerry's eyes got heavier.

"What day is it?" Jerry asked.

"Why is that important, Jerry?"

"I don't know. I don't know what time it is or what day it is."

"Are these things important?"

"I don't know. I can't remember. I can't remember . . . My thoughts are being changed. This is not me."

"Jerry, can you see the new plants at your bedside?"

Jerry nodded.

"Aren't they lovely?"

"They're very nice."

"Do you know they have a lovely fragrance?"

"There's a really nice smell in the air. Is that where it's coming from?"

"Why don't you find out yourself? The plant is right there."

Gittinger watched as Jerry got out of bed in a trancelike state, bent over, and sniffed the plant.

"Take your time, Jerry. Do you smell that distinctive aroma? That perfume?"

Jerry's head hung loose, as if he was struggling to stay awake.

"Just lie down in your bed, Jerry, why don't you?"

Jerry took a couple steps and slumped on the bed, eyes rolling back in his head.

"Repeat after me, Jerry: 'I must do as I am told.'"

Jerry opened his mouth but said nothing.

"Repeat after me, Jerry: 'I must do as I am told.'"

The lights went off and the voice continued.

"Repeat after me, Jerry: 'I must do as I am told.'"

"Jerry, punch the air," the woman's voice said.

Gittinger was transfixed as Jerry began to punch the air.

"And again, Jerry."

Jerry lashed out at nothing.

"Scratch your arms, Jerry."

He began to claw at his forearms with his nails. Blood seeped onto the bed.

"Good, Jerry, that's better."

He was clenching his teeth. His chest was rising up and down as if his breathing was getting more labored; perhaps he was just becoming more anxious.

"You're making great progress, Jerry," the woman's voice said. "We're so happy with your efforts. And now, I can see quite clearly you are allowing yourself to absorb the messages and let them wash over you. Do you feel them washing over you?"

Gittinger watched as Jerry White began to stare into space, the voice and the lights ever present.

Thirteen

It was a short drive for Reznick across to Achorn Cemetery. The orange tinge from the setting sun glinted off the hundreds of headstones, throwing long shadows across the graveyard. He picked up the flowers he had bought on Main Street and walked solemnly to the plot for his mother and father.

His mind flashed to images of their funerals. First his mother. He was just a boy. A freezing cold day, standing, shivering, holding his father's hand. He'd never seen his father like that before. Memories of his father's funeral still hurt him deep down in his soul. He remembered the eyes on him. Carrying the coffin past the same headstones until they reached his father's resting place, in the same plot as Reznick's beloved mother.

Even when they had lowered his father's coffin on top of his mother's, Reznick hadn't shown any emotion. It was the way he was. His father, by contrast, had been far more emotional. Heart on his sleeve. Reznick had learned how to conceal his feelings. He didn't want people to know what he felt. That was his business. His deepest memories were for him alone. He held his love for his parents in his heart and in his soul. Every time he breathed, that was them. They had given him life.

Reznick saw the alabaster headstone with both their names inscribed. *Beloved father and mother of Jon.* He thought back to his father's darkest days. After Vietnam. The days, weeks, and months of drinking himself senseless. His wife's death had almost tipped him over the edge.

But he had hung on. He had worked the shittiest job in the sardine-packing plant. He had cursed out the foremen. But he knew they were just there making ends meet too. It was a living. If you could call it that.

Reznick had grown up fast. He had watched and learned. He had been taught how to hunt and fish by his father. He had listened as his father patiently explained how to bait the hook. They had spent weekends out in all conditions. His father's weathered face withstanding wind, rain, hail, and snow. He had learned not to moan. He was taught the importance of patience. But also of doing the right thing. His mind flashed to a hazy memory of his mother as she lay dying. She was looking up at him on her deathbed, smiling. Her hand was going cold. He remembered that. She knew she didn't have long. But even then, even at that moment, she was thinking of his father. Her husband. *Look after him, Jon, when I'm gone,* she said. It was like she sensed her husband needed support. There was a selfless quality to his mother he revered. He could only imagine how it must have been to cope with the crazy guy who had returned from Vietnam. He had bottled everything up. Drank to forget. And she was always forgiving. *When you've walked in his shoes, then and only then, Jon, can we judge what a man does.*

He leaned over and picked up the dead, shriveled flowers he had left a couple of months back. And he put in their place the fresh lilies his mother would have loved. He remembered his dad had said that.

He sat down on the grass, facing their headstone, dead flowers by his side. He leaned forward and touched their names, inscribed on the stone, as he always did.

He sat for quite a while as the last remnant of the sun dipped beyond the far horizon.

He thought of their lives. Ordinary men and women. People who toiled. And endured. Nobodies. But they weren't nobodies. Far from it. They were, in his eyes, giants. Quiet, unassuming, hardworking, upstanding, strong, and honest. The real America. The unsung. They were the people who worked for very little. The backbone of a country. The people who had built America. The people who had fought for America. And its values. Through hard work, sacrifice, and love.

The light was fading as he left the cemetery.

Reznick dropped off the dead flowers in a trash can nearby, got back in his car, and drove back to his house. He arrived home to find a message on his voice mail. He played it. It was from Dr. Eileen MacDonald.

He returned the call and waited for nearly a minute before it was answered.

"Thanks for calling back, Mr. Reznick." Her voice was brittle, as if she was trying to conceal her annoyance.

"No problem."

"The board of governors has decided that it would not be in Mr. White's best interest to attend his father's funeral. He is in no fit state."

"Doctor, we're talking about his father's funeral. You're going to deny him that?"

"It wasn't me, Mr. Reznick. As I said, it was the board. And it was a unanimous decision after having access to all the facts and medical data on Mr. White."

Reznick stared out over the dark waters of Penobscot Bay. "So no one can visit *and* he can't leave for the funeral?"

"That's the decision laid down by the board. We must adhere to it."

"One final question, Doctor."

"Certainly."

"Has he even been told that his father died?"

"I'm not in a position to answer that, Mr. Reznick."

"Do you want to clarify what you mean by that?"

"If that's all, I have a patient to attend to."

The line went dead.

Reznick was slightly taken aback at her curt response and the call's abrupt end. He couldn't shake the feeling that something wasn't right.

He headed out onto the rear deck of his house, overlooking the water. The sound of the waves crashing over the rocks in the cove below. The smell of salt water in the air.

He thought of Jerry in a psychiatric hospital, who couldn't leave and couldn't get visitors. Whose father had died. Most likely murdered.

The more he thought about it, the more he wondered why the level of secrecy. He wondered about the work going on at the Wittenden Institute. They claimed to be helping veterans with post-traumatic stress disorder. But not allowing even visits home on such occasions left Reznick cold. It didn't seem right.

Then again, maybe Jerry was so damaged he was a risk to himself and others. Hadn't he proven that when he'd come out of the house holding a knife? Was that it?

Reznick thought about his meeting the day before with Tom McNulty. He took his cell phone out of his pocket and dialed his number.

"Jon, I was just about to call you."

"Hi, Tom. Sorry to disturb you."

"Hey, not a problem. What's going on?"

"You mentioned a reporter who had looked into the workings of Wittenden. I was wondering if you'd managed to get a name."

McNulty sighed. "I think you're on a wild-goose chase . . . The place is highly rated. Trust me, the place is bona fide."

"I'm sure it is, Tom. I'm simply curious, that's all. You know, just trying to find out a bit more about this place."

"OK, fair enough. The guy's name is Kevin Houlihan."

"Who does he work for?"

"He was a freelancer, used to work for the *New York Times*, occasionally the *Washington Post*."

"And he knows stuff about Wittenden?"

"I believe so. My friend Cindy, who used to work there, said he bugged her all the time. Said he was going to write a major feature on the place."

"Was it written?"

"I don't think so . . . Anyway, he knows a bit about the place, apparently."

"You got a number?"

"I put in a call to a few people yesterday, thinking about what you said, but the *New York Times* and the *Post* have no current number for him. No cell phone number. His last byline was a couple of years back. No one knows what's happened to him."

Fourteen

Reznick headed up to his study and sat down at his laptop. He googled the reporter's name and it brought up numerous articles Houlihan had written. But no recent bylines. The pictures showed a smiling, full-faced, middle-aged guy. Reznick tried to pull up social media profiles, but nothing matched.

He wondered what had happened to the guy. Was he writing a book? Had he dropped off the radar? Was he leading the simple life in a Buddhist retreat somewhere?

Reznick racked his brain and tried numerous other online searches, which all brought up nothing. Not even a LinkedIn profile. He drummed his fingers on the table, feeling frustrated.

He considered calling Meyerstein and asking for help, drawing on the resources and expertise of the FBI. But he knew what she'd say. This wasn't their case. And it wasn't. It was his. It was personal.

He made himself coffee and trawled the Internet for hours trying to find out if Houlihan owned a business, a house. All he got was a previous address in Midtown Manhattan. But that was five years ago.

How could Houlihan just have disappeared? Unless he didn't want to be found. Was that it? Or was he a guy who had simply retreated from the ever-flagging newspaper business? It was quite possible, maybe even highly likely, that his story about Wittenden had never seen the light of day. It was quite possible the story just wasn't strong enough.

Reznick searched the Internet for *Wittenden* and *Houlihan*, and it didn't bring up one single article. He was beginning to wonder why he was wasting any time on this. He then began searching for the Wittenden Institute. No website. Only a blurred image on Google Street View.

Reznick stared out the upstairs study window. While it was slightly uncommon to have such a small digital footprint, he figured the hospital would be keen to protect the privacy of the veterans inside. Which made perfect sense to him.

His thoughts began to drift. He couldn't help but think of Jerry. He could only imagine the demons Jerry was fighting in his head.

He wanted Jerry to know he was not alone, that people were thinking of him. Rooting for him to get better.

Reznick closed his eyes as he began to realize he was obsessing too much. He needed to let his old friend go. Let him have the time and space to get better. His mind flashed on a memory of the fear in Jerry's eyes. The panic. The sheer horror, as if he were being engulfed by demons.

Just as he was about to pour himself a beer, he remembered someone who might be able to help.

A young Miami hacker. Former NSA computer genius. A guy who had helped him before. But for a price. Why hadn't that occurred to him?

He pulled up the guy's number on his cell phone.

The hacker answered after two rings. "Well, well, if isn't my old friend Mr. R. What are you looking for, man?"

"I'm looking for a reporter."

"As in a journalist? What's he done?"

"He's done nothing."

"You're not going to harm this fucker or anything?"

Reznick smiled. "Absolutely not. I'm hoping he can help me."

"You want me to find him, pure and simple?"

Reznick sighed. "I've searched online, and I can't seem to find out anything about this guy in the last few years. Not even one hundred percent sure if he's still alive."

"OK, what's the guy's name?"

"Kevin Houlihan. Previously worked for the *New York Times*, *Washington Post*, and the *LA Times*. All I want is a number. Or failing that, a current address."

The sound of keys tapping in the background. "It'll cost you. My prices have all gone up."

"How much?"

"For you, Mr. R, three thousand dollars."

"You should be wearing a mask."

The hacker laughed. "How do you know I'm not?"

"Good point. Fair enough, you got a deal."

"I'll give you a call back as soon as I can."

A couple of hours later, Reznick's cell phone rang.

"Yo, Mr. R, this guy was ridiculous to find. I mean, who the hell is he?"

"You got him?"

"He's been trying to cover his tracks. Pulled all his social media pages—Facebook, Twitter—a few years back, deleted his WordPress website, moved house fifteen times in the last three years."

"How many?"

"Fifteen."

"That's a lot."

"No kidding. Yeah, the guy does not want to be found."

"How did you find him?"

"Data mining. Face recognition technology. And through that I've traced him."

"You got a number?"

"Nope."

"No landline or cell phone?"

"Nothing. But I have got an address."

"Where?"

"Small town in Massachusetts."

Fifteen

The following morning, Meyerstein was gazing out of the seventh-floor-office window of the Hoover Building, in Washington, DC, when her phone rang. She swiveled in her seat and picked up.

"Meyerstein."

"Lieutenant Jackson, Bar Harbor Police."

Meyerstein looked at her watch, knowing she had a meeting to prepare for with the Director. "What can I do for you?"

"I hope you don't mind me calling out of the blue. You gave me your card. I thought—"

"Not a problem, Lieutenant. So, how can I help you?"

"It's just that I wanted you to get a heads-up on this, what with that Reznick connection and all."

The mere mention of Reznick's name piqued her interest. "Yeah, go on."

"We've got a few aspects of this case which are troubling us here."

"Like what?"

"We believed from the outset this was homicide, hence our interest in Reznick."

"Do you want to get to the point, Lieutenant?"

"The medical examiner has carried out a full autopsy. According to the report, Hank White's face was congested, tongue bitten. Ligature just below the thyroid. But on dissection, the neck muscles showed signs of trauma. The medical examiner found that the tracheal cartilaginous rings were fractured."

Meyerstein listened intently, scribbling some notes. She knew exactly what that meant.

"The trachea, the report said, contained bloodstained froth. Assistant Director, there were numerous abrasions and contusions on the chin, both arms, and abdomen."

"Which would suggest a struggle," she said.

"Precisely."

Meyerstein closed her eyes for a moment as she contemplated the scenario. She knew it couldn't be Reznick. But he was squarely in the frame for this.

"Now that I've laid that out there on the table, I think it is important that we have cooperation. We believe Reznick might be involved in some way."

"Lieutenant, this is your call. Your case. If you believe this is a homicide, then that's something for you to investigate. The only reason I intervened on behalf of Mr. Reznick was that he occasionally does work for us. I would say, though, that in all the years I've known Reznick, he is—"

"A trained killer?"

Meyerstein was taken aback at the sharpness of the response. "Lieutenant, this is not his doing, I can assure you."

"Then why is everything pointing at him? Forensics has his prints all over the place."

"Why were your guys called, Lieutenant?"

"We got an anonymous tip-off and discovered the body. Then we found Reznick in the woods right below where Hank White was hanging from a tree. And we've subsequently learned that Hank White's son nearly ran Jon Reznick off the road with a stolen car a few days back. Did you know that? There's probable cause right there. That's motive."

Meyerstein kept quiet, allowing the lieutenant the time and space to get to his point.

"He's our number one suspect. And I'm giving you the courtesy, after your previous intervention, of letting you know that we are going to be interviewing Jon Reznick for a second time about this murder as soon as we find him."

Meyerstein couldn't believe what she was hearing. "This is crazy."

"The only problem is that he wasn't home in Rockland. We turned up at his place, but he's gone. But when we find him, you need to know he will be questioned about this homicide. And as it stands, he is the only person we want to speak to in connection with this."

Sixteen

After a flight down from Owls Head to Boston, Reznick took another flight across to Albany. Then he rented a car and drove for forty-five minutes. He pulled up a block from a tidy colonial house in Stockbridge, Massachusetts. He wondered what the hell he was doing. Did he have too much time on his hands? The bottom line was he wasn't in any way responsible for Jerry White. But deep down Reznick was beginning to think that maybe, just maybe, there was more to the Wittenden Institute than met the eye.

He walked down the street toward the house, the events of the past few days still swirling around his head. Outside, a man was smoking a cigarette. He turned and stared as Reznick approached.

"How's it going?" Reznick said.

The guy squinted in the sun, hand partially shielding his eyes from the glare. It was clearly Kevin Houlihan from the last photograph Reznick had seen, only puffier around the face and thicker around the middle. "I'm fine. Do I know you?"

"I don't think so. You're Kevin, right?"

The guy stared at Reznick but stayed silent.

"I didn't catch your name."

"Reznick. Jon Reznick. I'm looking for some help."

"Who sent you?"

"No one sent me. Look, I'm not here to give you any grief or hassle you."

"How the fuck did you track me down?"

Reznick sighed. "A hacker with advanced technology gave me a helping hand. I don't mean you any harm. I just want to talk to you."

The guy took a few moments to answer, as if deciding whether he could trust Reznick. "You're not from some crime family that has a contract out on me?"

Reznick showed his hands. "Not as far as I know."

The guy dragged hard on the cigarette and threw it onto the gravel path. "Do you always turn up on people's doorsteps unannounced?"

"Not usually."

"What's this about?"

"It's about a friend of mine . . . I'm trying to get to him. He's not very well. My friend is a veteran. He's being cared for at Wittenden."

The guy closed his eyes for a moment. "Fuck."

Reznick's gaze wandered around the affluent neighborhood. "Nice place to disappear to."

"It was until you turned up, man. Who are you?"

Reznick cleared his throat. "Do you want to go inside and discuss this in private?"

Houlihan sized Reznick up for a few moments. He cocked his head and Reznick followed him inside. Houlihan showed Reznick into a large open-plan kitchen with a laptop on a wooden table, scribbled notes adjacent, and the dregs of coffee in a mug beside.

"Welcome to my humble abode. Supposed to be off the grid, but I guess not."

"You're more off than you realize. I don't think anyone will find you, unless it's a government agency."

"That's not very reassuring. Is that where you're from? A government agency?"

Reznick shook his head. "I'll be up front. In my work as a military specialist—"

"Oh shit, man, I knew it. Now that makes me very uncomfortable."

Reznick smiled. "Just relax. I'll be completely upfront: I have done some consulting work for the FBI. But this case has nothing to do with them. This is about an old friend of mine. Ex-Delta."

"Oh shit, don't say stuff like that to me." Houlihan began to pace the room. "You see, that's the kind of stuff that unsettles me. Delta. Delta. That's like, trained killers, right?"

"Kevin, you need to calm down. You're going to give yourself a heart attack."

Houlihan sat down at the table. "Sorry, it's just that I'm permanently wired. Fucking wired all the time."

"I think you can help me. You know about the Wittenden Institute."

Houlihan nodded. "Go on." He took out a cell phone and placed it on the table and a red light came on. "I want to know everything. Tell me from the beginning what this is all about."

Seventeen

Reznick took a few moments to gather his thoughts. He thought the guy was being unduly secretive, perhaps even paranoid. "This conversation is not for public consumption," he said, looking at the light on the cell phone.

Houlihan nodded.

"Do not identify me. That might be problematic."

"You got it. So let's start at the beginning. I need to know how this came about."

Reznick gave him a succinct version of the events to date, interspersed with an occasional "Oh shit" from Houlihan. When he got to the part about finding Jerry's father, the color seemed to drain from Houlihan's face.

"Holy fuck."

"So it's all pretty messed up."

"And you want to know what?"

"Jerry White is still in Wittenden. Another friend of mine, a psychologist, said he had gone for an interview there. Psychometric tests. Didn't make the grade, apparently. But a friend of his, a woman, did, but she resigned after only a few months."

"That is very interesting."

Reznick leaned forward. "Kevin, I was told you had been in touch with this woman, trying to find out what happened. Were keen on writing a story."

Houlihan sighed. "I know the woman you're talking about. Top psychologist. But she didn't say a word. Not a damn word. I think she was scared. Do you mind me asking, why exactly are you here?"

"I've got the number of a psychologist who works there. And I can call her and she can call me. But it's Jerry I want to speak to. And I'm wondering if you knew how I should address this. Maybe you've had the same experience, I don't know. Should I write a goddamn letter asking to see Jerry? But since I'm not a relative, why would they allow that?"

Houlihan sighed long and hard. He got up to fix himself and Reznick some coffee. "So you're concerned that he's in there. Are you not a little concerned about why they're so secretive?"

"Yes I am if I'm honest."

Houlihan went quiet for a few moments, as if trying to find the right words. "Jon, you don't know the half of it. You're only scraping the surface. I'm still only scraping the surface. Most people have no fucking idea what that place is like or what it does to the patients."

"I don't follow. I was told it's a highly respected hospital. Pioneering work."

"I've spoken to dozens of people who have worked there. I won't beat around the bush—the stories they told unnerved me."

Reznick shrugged. "Are they maybe disgruntled former employees?"

"No."

"How can you be so sure?"

Houlihan leaned closer. "Jon, the Wittenden Institute is an experimental lab for crazy veterans."

"I thought it was a hospital."

"That's what they say. But it's not. It's headed up by a guy called Robert Gittinger. Does that name ring a bell?"

"No, should it?"

"I'm estimating that he's in his late seventies. Canadian. Used to work at McGill University, in Quebec, at the Allan Memorial Institute under the tutelage of a brilliant psychiatrist, Dr. Donald Ewen Cameron."

Reznick shrugged. "What relevance is that?"

Houlihan scratched his head. "I'll get you a photograph. Because this relates to everything. The beginning, the middle, and the end of this story." He headed upstairs and returned with a black-and-white image showing two bespectacled men standing in the snow. "This was taken outside the Allan, in Quebec, in 1962. The younger man is Robert Gittinger, a science genius. The older man, the Scottish psychiatrist and his mentor, Cameron."

"So Gittinger was trained by this guy Cameron in Canada?"

"Yes, at McGill. Cameron was working on a program to erase the memories of those with schizophrenia."

"Erase memories?"

"He wanted to in effect reprogram the human psyche. They used drugs like LSD and electroconvulsive therapy. Crazy stuff."

"That doesn't make sense."

"Jon, like I said, you don't know the half of it. You know what they did? Played tapes with phrases or commands for weeks at a time, and all the time the patient was in and out of insulin-induced comas. Psychic driving. That's what they called it."

Reznick wondered if Houlihan was making it all up—it sounded very far-fetched. "How do you know that?"

"I spoke to people who worked there. People who were damaged by what they saw. It's well documented what happened up there."

"I don't understand how, if this is true, it's allowed. What's the point of doing such horrible things?"

"Wiping memories and implanting trigger words."

"What?"

"Try to imagine how horrific that would be, trapped in what they called the driving room. Voices repeated, phrases repeated, instructions, mantras repeated, words, phrases again and again and again. And with drugs? These are vulnerable, psychotic people who are put in this most terrifying environment. They were being driven out of their minds. Deliberately. You can only imagine. They were, in effect, being brainwashed. Their memories erased. But what is happening now is that you also have trigger words and phrases being implanted at Wittenden—that's what I've heard—to make the subject obey orders."

Reznick wondered what to make of this. "I don't know . . . It sounds pretty out there."

"It's completely out there."

"OK, that was at McGill under Cameron in the early sixties. What about Wittenden now?"

"That is Wittenden now. In the twenty-first century. The same as before, except they're now using trigger words and phrases."

"That sounds like a nightmare. Are you sure about this?"

Houlihan held up his hand, as if wanting Reznick to listen closer to what he had to say. "Ten years ago, I was working for the *New York Times* and the *Washington Post*, freelance, whatever. Crime. Politics. Whatever took my fancy or the editor's fancy. Then one day I got a call. From a woman who used to work at the Wittenden Institute. I had never heard of it. She was a cleaner. A humble cleaner. And she told me about this basement. Actually, it was a subbasement. And she had to clean it. It had three rooms, audio equipment hooked up, medical beds, leather straps. She occasionally saw patients wheeled down there on a gurney. Unconscious. She told me that she was seeing a male nurse who worked there. His name was Frank Perino. And he had told her about everything. He suffered nightmares because of what he'd seen. So did some of the other nurses and doctors. And they were all on various types of medication. Frank killed himself with an overdose."

"And that's what got you interested in this place?"

"Yeah, the *Times* was very keen on the story. And then they just got cold feet after a few months. Said it didn't feel right, that kind of thing."

"That's quite a turnaround."

"They got spooked. Or someone got to them. I think."

"Do you have any proof?"

"No."

"So what did you do?"

"The *Washington Post* wasn't interested. I was working full-time freelance. But suddenly I wasn't getting hired. No one wanted to touch me. Then it wasn't long before I began to get calls in the middle of the night. Threatening me. Saying I was being watched."

"Watched? By who?"

"They didn't say. Then they began to call saying I was going to be killed."

"Did someone know you were working on this story?"

"Absolutely. And they were trying to scare me. And they did a pretty good job too."

"So you began to move around?"

"Wouldn't you?"

"And this Wittenden Institute . . ."

Houlihan held out his hands, a slight tremor. "It's taken over my life. It's kind of destroyed what I had. I had some savings. But they're nearly gone. Flat broke. I intended to write a book about the place. But . . ."

"But what?"

"The two publishers that were interested got cold feet too."

"Why don't you publish it yourself?"

"I might. I don't know. I've written about three hundred thousand words. I need an editor. I don't know. It's turned into a monster."

"OK, let's back up for a minute. This Gittinger was working under this Cameron guy?"

"Eminent psychiatrist. Used to be the president of the American Psychiatric Association in the early fifties. But here's the interesting thing. Who was covertly funding all of Cameron's work?"

Reznick shrugged.

"The CIA."

"You're kidding me."

Houlihan shook his head. "Swear to God. One hundred percent correct. Very well documented. Cameron didn't even know it was the CIA that was plowing all this money into his research. He was living in Albany, and he was commuting across to Montreal a couple times a week."

"Why Canada?"

"It's illegal for the CIA to operate on US soil. So research funding through Cornell made its way to McGill and Cameron and his team. There was funding coming in from the navy, army, you name it."

"And Cameron didn't know about the funding?"

"He didn't know exactly where it was coming from. The money was delivered through grants from charities which were in fact CIA fronts. He thought it was legitimate."

"Tell me about Gittinger."

"He won a CIA medical scholarship to McGill. He learned everything there under Cameron. But when Cameron left under a cloud in 1964, Gittinger completed his studies. He became a CIA psychiatrist. Deployed in Vietnam. Laos."

"Hasn't he retired?"

"Very interesting point. Apparently, he was brought out of retirement for this special project. He was put in charge of it, on the ground, special access program, above-top-secret classified. You heard of SAPs?"

Reznick nodded. He felt overwhelmed by the revelations. His friend was being treated inside such a hospital? Was he being experimented on?

"So you'll know that it's restricted only to certain people. People with the highest level of security clearance."

"What's the purpose of this program?"

"I have my suspicions."

"What do you think is happening there?"

"It's interesting that it's on US soil. I believe it's a wholly privately funded project, but with 'oversight' from the CIA."

"Almost certainly illegal."

"Yeah. Getting back to your question, what do I think is happening there? If you'd asked me a couple of years back, I'd have said the purpose was to develop procedures to be used in interrogation and torture."

"Sleep deprivation, constant sound, right?"

"Yeah, but now? I think the Wittenden Institute is about more than just that. A hell of a lot more."

"Like what?"

"I don't know for sure. But the hellish conditions you saw in Abu Ghraib—constant white noise, music, humiliation, breaking down the personality and human being—these are well established. I find it hard to believe that Wittenden is undertaking the same tests for the same purpose. I believe there's more to it."

"Do you have any proof—written proof—of this?"

"Oh yeah, I got stuff alright." Houlihan went to a safe hidden in the floor and pulled out a sheath of papers. He handed them to Reznick. "The full details of the special access program and the architect's schematics when Wittenden was built."

"How did you get your hands on this?"

"Sources." He pointed to a paragraph. "The drawings? Other sources." He pointed to the various levels of the hospital. "On the outside it seems like a three-story facility. But there are two sublevels below ground."

"You think this is where the tests are being carried out?"

"Bet your life they are. See what they call them? Intensive therapy rooms. And trust me, you won't see these plans on the Internet. How do I know? I checked. There's nothing."

"Shit."

Houlihan pointed to other aspects of the plans. "What does that say?"

"Access tunnels."

"They have tunnels underneath. You fucking believe that?"

"For what purpose?"

"I have no idea."

"Have you had verification of these basements and tunnels?"

"One guy. A former priest."

"Ex-priest? What's that all about?"

"He was excommunicated after writing to a local newspaper talking about 'sinister forces' at work at the Wittenden Institute. But he told me there was a subterranean world going on there. His sister worked at Wittenden. But she killed herself, apparently, on the day the letter appeared in the paper."

"What's his name?"

"Father McNamara. He lives in Ithaca."

Eighteen

Three days after Jerry White had been returned to the facility, Gittinger made his way down to the hospital's basement.

His job was to determine when Jerry White would be ready to be *released into the community*. The phrase was code for the patient being activated.

He headed into the special observation room, where doctors and nurses could watch patients through special one-way reinforced Plexiglas. He observed through the glass as Jerry White sat up in his bed, looking around his room blankly. The haunting, ethereal sound of the traditional Vietnamese instrument the *đàn tran* breezed out into the room. Gittinger always loved the juxtaposition between the calm and peaceful music and the nightmare the patients were enduring. It was a signature element of the program he had introduced. It reminded him of his sweat-drenched days and nights in Vietnam in the late 1960s. The smell of rice cooking, the kerosene in the sticky air amid the chaos. The look in the captured Vietcong kids' eyes as they were locked in a windowless basement room, awaiting their fate.

The woman's voice coming through the speakers snapped Gittinger back to the present. "Jerry, how do you feel today?"

White looked around, as if unsure where he was. "How do I feel? I feel good."

"Can you describe why that might be, Jerry?"

"Why do I feel good?"

"Yes, what do you believe is contributing to your happiness?"

"Things seem clearer now. I'm beginning to feel more focused. I think I'm beginning to understand that you're here to help me. I didn't understand that before."

"That's very good, Jerry." The woman continued: "When you returned to us, you seemed very agitated. Now . . . Well, I think you can see for yourself what we're achieving together."

"I was scared. I'm not scared anymore."

"That's very pleasing to hear, Jerry. Tell me, are you still having nightmares?"

"I see things very clearly in my dreams. I see people. And they're afraid. But I'm not afraid. I can see them cowering in fear. From me."

"How do you feel about that?"

"I feel fine. That doesn't bother me."

"Do you feel calm during the dream?"

"I remember watching the events, shooting them, and it's almost like I had to do that."

"Do you mean you felt compelled to shoot them?"

Sitting on a dresser at the bottom of White's bed was a picture of him as a boy. "I absolutely had to do it."

"And is that a good thing?"

"It's a really good thing. I was smiling in my dream. No one was smiling. Apart from me."

Gittinger watched as White closed his eyes and began to hum a tune. It was as if he was in a trance. Which he was. A deep trance. Locked in. A little part of Gittinger felt sorry for the poor bastard. But at his time of life, he was beyond caring.

The woman's voice said, "Jerry, why don't you lie down? Do you want to sleep?"

Jerry nodded blankly, eyes still shut.

"Are you ready to begin? Do you want to feel that way again? Do you want to feel calm again?"

Jerry began to rock back and forth for a few moments, then lay down on the bed in the fetal position.

The voice began on the loop again. *No past. No future. No now. No past. No now. No future.*

Gittinger could see that Jerry White would soon be ready. He caught his reflection in the glass. He was smiling.

Nineteen

Later that day, Reznick touched down in Ithaca after catching a flight from Albany with a one-hour layover in Newark. He paid cash for a rental car and headed out to Father McNamara's address; the GPS indicated it was right beside Ithaca College. He pulled up outside a modest home, a faint light on inside.

Reznick had been wondering why he was pursuing this. He wondered if he was losing all sense of perspective. He was reacting to events. It was almost like he was being drawn into the story. But why? What was the story?

A psychiatric hospital was using controversial practices? Was that it?

The more he thought about it, he saw that he simply wanted to know that Jerry was being looked after. What he'd heard had aroused concerns. Deep concerns. He had doubts about Houlihan. He was the archetypal loner turning his back on the world. But he had documented proof there was something suspicious going on at the Wittenden Institute.

Then there was something deeper inside Reznick that had been awakened. This quest of his was more than simply helping a friend, ex-Delta and all that. It wasn't just that he had a real connection with Jerry. Or that Jerry had propped him up in his dark days after his wife's terrible death on 9/11.

He was starting to see there was something more.

Reznick knew firsthand how intense and punishing Delta Force was. It was only for the fittest, toughest, and most resilient but also the most robust, armed with critical thinking skills and the ability to see the big picture and not get bogged down in detail. It required a complex mixture of physical, psychological, and physiological attributes.

Was Wittenden experimenting with how Special Forces soldiers would react under certain types of psychological torture? So they could resist under such conditions?

He remembered the Rockefeller Report in the 1990s, which revealed that the Department of Defense had used military personnel—hundreds of thousands of them—in human experiments. The files covered everything from deliberate exposure to mustard and nerve gas, hallucinogens, all the way up to drugs used during the Gulf War.

His own father had told him all about Agent Orange. A close friend of his father's in Vietnam had been part of a massive lawsuit by veterans against the drug manufacturers. The friend eventually died, and his wife was entitled to only the most miserable of pensions. Her lawyer had fought on and, against her and her husband's wishes, settled out of court.

She received a settlement of $3,700. If her husband had lived, he would have received $12,000, paid over ten years.

Reznick remembered being told and being outraged. His father never said a word. He just stared off into the dark waters of Penobscot Bay, as if the whole thing was too painful, perhaps content to remember the sacrifices of those who had served. But also of the people on the ground. His father always told Reznick that the Vietnamese suffered the most.

The US government, through the DoD's Defense Advanced Research Projects Agency (DARPA), had used herbicides as military weapons, following the lead of the British in Malaya. But the cost was incalculable.

Reznick remembered reading about a $43 million project to clean up dioxin hot spots in Vietnam. While it sounded like a step in the right direction, Reznick was under no illusions: the only reason the US government was forking out some money was to forge closer ties with a country that could help it counter China's growing power and influence in the region.

All those thoughts were going through Reznick's head as he got out of the car. He walked up the overgrown path, strewn with weeds, and knocked on the door.

A minute or so passed and he was about to knock again.

The door cracked open, and a silver-haired man with rheumy eyes stared at him. "Yeah?"

"I was wondering if you could help me, Father."

"I'm not a father anymore."

Reznick smiled. "I know."

"You part of the faculty?"

"No."

"Like I said, I'm no longer an ordained priest."

"I need to talk to you, sir."

"Listen, I don't do confessions, and I don't do Hail Marys or whatever else you might want to hear."

"I want to talk about you. About your sister. And about the Wittenden Institute."

The old man stared at him, eyes filling with tears.

"I hope you can help me."

"In the name of God, son, why do you have to bring that up?"

"My friend is now in Wittenden. I want to visit. But I'm being told I can't. I'm hearing stories about the place. I thought you might be able to help me. Point me in the right direction, if you will."

The old man stood and stared, as if unsure what to do, before tentatively opening the door. "Come on in."

Reznick headed in and stood in the narrow hallway. The old man shut and locked the door, then ushered Reznick into a living room.

The old man slumped down in an easy chair and pointed Reznick toward the sofa opposite. "I don't get too many visitors. None actually."

Reznick nodded.

"Where you from?"

"I'm from a small town in Maine. Rockland."

"Long way from home."

Reznick smiled.

"So do you mind me asking who you are?"

Reznick patiently explained the sequence of events and how he had ended up in the small house in Ithaca.

"This brings back a lot of painful memories for me. Talking about it is difficult."

"I'm sorry to rake over this. I came all this way. Kevin Houlihan. I spoke to him."

"How is he?"

"I don't know him personally. Didn't know him until yesterday. But I'd say he's been very affected, damaged even, professionally and financially after investigating Wittenden. That's what I know."

"He did his best. But they get to those papers. And they didn't want to know anything about Wittenden after that."

"And you spoke to Kevin confidentially?"

"Yes, I did. But I also wrote a letter to a local paper."

"Kevin mentioned that."

Father McNamara's hand was trembling slightly. "Let me tell you this, I am not afraid. I will not shut up about Wittenden."

Reznick smiled, admiring the defiance of the vaguely broken man in front of him.

"Tell me more about your friend inside Wittenden," McNamara said.

"Jerry? We were in Delta together. We drifted apart, as you do. And then the other day, a few days ago, he's suddenly back in my life, running for his life. He was petrified. Never seen him like that before."

"How do you mean?"

"I don't just mean because he was skeleton thin. Which he was. And I don't mean how scared he was. But it was as if he was out of it too, almost like in a trance. I don't know if it was because he was undergoing a psychotic episode, but he seemed real strange."

"The Wittenden Institute is a dangerous, horrible place. I know, because my sister used to work there, God rest her soul. She'd been depressed and on medication for years afterward. And her deterioration matched that of quite a few other people who worked there over the years and who I counseled or took confession from after seeing what they described as bedlam. They were talking not about a Victorian asylum system but a twenty-first-century hospital, only built about a dozen years ago, on the site of an old brickyard. My sister's husband left her. He thought she was crazy. But she wasn't. She just didn't know how to comprehend what she was witnessing, seeing, or hearing about. Men being strapped down, put into drug-induced comas for days and even weeks, and crazy taped voices being piped into their rooms at high volume twenty-four hours a day."

"Why was no one interested?"

"They're scared. Scared they'll lose their jobs, their children will lose their jobs. All the newspapers, no one is interested."

"What about politicians?"

"What about them?"

"Isn't anyone interested in what happens in there?"

"I've lost count of the number of senators or congressmen I've tried to raise this issue with. They all think I'm crazy. Eventually, the lack of any progress, or any idea that anything will be done, meant we lost hope. That's what they want us to do. Just forget. But I can't forget. How can I? My sister was driven crazy inside that place."

"Father, Kevin Houlihan told me about the experiments down in the subbasement."

"That's where my sister worked. She was scared. She began to wake up in the night screaming. She thought she heard whispers in her head. On and on and on it went. There was no respite for the poor, demented souls in there. But the people who worked there, the impact was also terrible."

"Kevin said he had compiled a dossier on the place and wanted to write an exposé. What I can't understand is how a hospital can exert pressure on major newspapers to pull a story."

"No one knows if that's what happened. It might have been pressure. It might have been the threat of legal action against the papers. Possibly they didn't think they had enough to put it out there."

"Father, if what's going on inside that place is as you believe, and as Kevin alleges, that would be unethical, surely."

"Not only unethical but immoral. Torture—and that's what it is— is against the Geneva Conventions, which we've signed on to. That prohibits torture. But there's also the American Convention on Human Rights, the International Covenant on Civil and Political Rights . . . We have signed up to show we are not a country that tortures."

Reznick sighed. "Tell me, Father, do you have any pictures of this place?"

Father McNamara went upstairs and returned a few minutes later with a photo album. "This has all the photos I have of the Institute." He handed it to Reznick.

Reznick flicked through the pages. It showed a low-rise brick building ringed by high-security fences, with cameras high up on poles scanning the entrance. He checked out angle after angle. Then he saw a long-lens photo of a top-of-the-line red Lexus driving through the gates. "What's this?"

"Have a close look at the driver."

Reznick squinted to see the grainy image of the elderly driver. "This is Dr. Robert Gittinger. What about footage inside the hospital?"

"Nothing. Several cleaners and one nurse were fired and the cameras they'd smuggled in confiscated."

"So no one knows where these experiments take place."

McNamara sighed long and hard. "It's in the basement. It's a huge area . . ."

"I've seen some drawings. Acres of space. A person could get lost there."

"I think that's the plan. The area that takes up the vast majority of the space is underground. And that's where all the bad stuff happens."

Reznick nodded. He felt anger begin to build up within him at the thought that Jerry might be undergoing some of those terrifying experiments there.

"In addition, there are five huge rooms where the patients live, and those are underground too. Out of sight. Out of mind."

Reznick shook his head. He couldn't understand why the hospital hadn't been shut down.

McNamara smiled. "You look like you could do with a drink."

"I could. But coffee will do for now, thanks."

"OK if I fix myself a Scotch?"

"Go right ahead."

Twenty

McNamara made coffee for Reznick and poured himself a double Scotch on the rocks. It was just after 6 p.m. He sipped the drink and closed his eyes. "My last remaining vice. Gave up smoking five years ago."

"Tell me, Father, how many entrances and exits are there to the Wittenden Institute?"

"Only one going in, and the same one going out. But there were, when it was created, underground tunnels that led out into the countryside. And that's all been integrated into the new three-story building."

"How do you know that?"

"Schematics I got my hands on."

Reznick wondered if they were the same ones Houlihan had shown him. "You got them?"

"Yeah, but I know what you're thinking."

"And what's that?"

"You're trying to figure out if you can gain access via the tunnels."

"It's a possibility. Not without its risks."

McNamara took another sip of his whisky and sighed. "Let me tell you a story about one time, just before my sister left. There was a young man, believed to have been in the Marines, and he got down into one of the tunnels. He was a patient."

"What happened?"

"The guy managed to get the key from one of the charge nurses, got out of his room, and then disappeared down a service tunnel. And from there he headed out a door within the tunnel, which led to a road that in turn led to the outside world."

"Shit."

"He was very close, by all accounts. Maybe one hundred yards down until he got to a hatch that led to a country road."

"What happened?"

"He was being pursued, and according to my sister, who had this verified from two nurses, he was shot by a tranquilizer rifle before he made it. Collapsed on the ground. And the poor kid was carried back into the facility."

"So that exit route is still available?"

"Two days after this happened, building contractors began work sealing up the tunnel exits. Concreted the whole thing. Then put a steel door in front of it, which was welded shut. That way in is now well and truly blocked. Unless you are prepared to go in with sticks of dynamite."

Reznick felt frustrated, his stomach knotting with anger. "What about cameras in this place?"

"All over the place. There were quite a lot before. Now? I heard from a former security guy that worked there that it's wall-to-wall." McNamara looked at Reznick while he finished his whisky. "Let me tell you something about this place. Partly from what I've learned, partly what I've pieced together, and partly from speaking to Kevin Houlihan. The Wittenden Institute is no ordinary psychiatric hospital. Far from it."

Reznick rubbed his face as he struggled to take it all in.

"The red flag is the secrecy. The payoffs to those who have raised concerns or even—get this—just been overheard talking in the community. You believe that?"

"Sounds like the East German Stasi, not America."

"Absolutely. There have been, by a conservative estimate, dozens of employees whose silence has been bought over the years. Others live in fear. The Institute pays on average seventy-eight percent higher salaries than for comparable work on the outside."

"I've been told by a psychiatrist who went for a job out of college that they do psychometric tests to determine what sort of personality they want working there."

"They do it for every member of staff, including my own sister, God rest her soul. Theresa passed the psychometric test. But working in such conditions clearly took its toll."

Reznick nodded. "Dr. Robert Gittinger's involvement is interesting."

McNamara smiled. "You won't believe the shit he's been linked to."

Reznick nodded, trying to absorb as much information as he could. He was sorely tempted to start taking notes.

"He was one of the postgraduate students who worked up at the Allan, in Montreal. You know, part of McGill, all those years back with Cameron."

"Kevin told me about him."

"The CIA was funding the project. Funding a torture project. And this went on at dozens of hospitals and facilities across North America, all paid for by front charities run by and financed by the CIA."

"Gittinger was CIA, Houlihan said."

"One hundred percent. Cameron we don't believe was. But Gittinger, his medical scholarship was paid for by the CIA. Gittinger's father was a CIA physician. The personal physician of Allen Dulles. Under Dulles, the CIA began MK-Ultra, the mind control project. This was early in the Cold War. Dulles was so close to Gittinger's father, Gittinger had Dulles as his godfather."

"Jesus Christ."

"He is inextricably linked to the original trials and what's going on now. He's the golden thread between it all."

"Houlihan said Gittinger was still part of the CIA after Cameron left under a cloud."

"You're not listening. Of course he was! Gittinger was always around. He wrote the manual, which became the methods used at Abu Ghraib. Learned a lot in Vietnam. But he was the one who was chosen to head up this project. No one should know about it. You wouldn't have known about it if it wasn't for your old Delta friend breaking out."

Reznick was quiet for a few moments.

"I know what you're thinking."

"And what's that?"

"'How do I get my friend out of there?'"

"It had crossed my mind."

"There are vested interests at work. Military-industrial complex."

Reznick felt a mixture of anger and sadness that his friend was being kept in such a facility. He scribbled down his name and cell phone on a scrap of paper and handed it to McNamara. "Here's my number, if you have to contact me."

"Thank you."

"I thought my friend was just psychotic, acting crazy when the staff from Wittenden arrived to take him back."

"The poor man must have been out of his mind with fear."

"So you think this begins and ends with Gittinger?"

McNamara smiled and arched his eyebrows. "That's where I'd start."

Twenty-One

It was just after 8 p.m. when Gittinger returned to his huge lakefront home in a gated community a few miles from Ithaca. His wife, as always, fixed him a single-malt Scotch and had Debussy playing in the background. He sank into his easy chair and loosened his tie.

"You're a bit later tonight, darling. Everything OK?" Dorothy asked.

Gittinger sipped some whisky and enjoyed the warmth in his belly. His mind was racing, and he knew his blood pressure was hiking higher than his doctor would have liked. He felt intense pressure at his work, and White's escape had introduced serious complications to the project. He was in charge. And he alone shouldered the responsibility. "Just a rather trying day, that's all."

His wife tenderly touched his shoulder. "I'm concerned, at your age, what this job is doing to you."

"I have obligations. Besides, I signed the contract. And I will honor the contract."

"How much longer is the term?"

Gittinger sighed. "The next couple of years, I guess."

A silence stretched between them as he thought back to the original pioneers, of which he was one, of the project MK-Ultra. It still rankled him that the program had needed to be scrapped.

It was outrageous that he and his former colleagues had all been demonized. The press hounded good scientists and portrayed them as power-crazed ideologues, more intent on keeping the funding rolling in than considering the moral implications. He had lost count of the number of colleagues and scientists whose careers had been wrecked by their involvement in the original project. He, by comparison, had been lucky in the sense that he had been moved by the CIA to a host of "mind control" projects they were working on. Vietnam, Cambodia, and Laos were rich pickings. He'd had numerous subjects—both captured Vietcong and traumatized American GIs. The knowledge gleaned over those years had greatly improved his understanding of the darkest fears of man.

He relished the role. And yes, it turned him on. The power over man. Or woman.

Then he spent a few years in Central America.

The CIA were keen to have his insight during interrogations. He found himself not feeling anything after a while. The screams only echoed in his dreams. But he could deal with that.

The last assignment before his retirement was the Middle East. Bahrain.

His links with that tiny archipelago of thirty-three islands made him the perfect choice for the assignment. Bahrain, a former British protectorate, was ruled over by a Sunni monarchy who used fear to govern the majority Shia population. Its links with Saudi Arabia and close ties to America and the United Kingdom gave it clout beyond its size.

"Bob, are you OK?" his wife asked.

Gittinger briefly snapped out of his reverie. "Yes, sure. Just thinking over the work I've got to do."

Gittinger felt very lucky. The pioneering years of MK-Ultra had been invaluable to the project he was doing now. Jerry White's scans had shown there were new neural pathways being created in his brain. His research was changing thought processes.

His wife sighed. "I thought your assignment would be complete well before now."

"That was the plan. But we're behind schedule with the diagnostic tests on some of our patients. So the original timescale is going to be very challenging."

Dorothy sat down beside him in her chair, the fire blazing nicely. She was drinking a gin and tonic. "Can I be frank, Bob?"

"Sure."

"You're getting on. And your job is incredibly demanding. Twelve hours every day might be fine in your forties. But in your seventies, you're looking your age."

Gittinger smiled. Dorothy was so sweet, always looking out for him. She had been with him since they'd met at McGill, when she was a classics student specializing in ancient Greece. They had spent countless vacations visiting places like Knossos and the Acropolis, in Athens. They were inseparable. But she was unaware of the true nature of his work. She thought it was for the humanitarian psychological services of US veterans. The truth, and his work in Langley and at secret sites across the world, could never be revealed. Even to his beloved, devoted wife.

He was prepared to drive himself and those who worked at Wittenden hard until the project was complete. He knew what awaited Jerry. And it was going to take people's breath away.

"Once I'm done with my research, I promise we can retire to the Greek islands."

"Can you imagine living in Crete? Chania and the Venetian heritage is amazing. I would love to live out our final days there. The children could come and visit in the summer. And grandchildren. Imagine."

Gittinger sipped some more whisky. "What about the house I like?"

"In Elounda?"

"I like it."

"I'm not fussy, darling. Elounda or Chania would be amazing."

Gittinger's cell phone began to vibrate in his pocket and he groaned. He checked the caller ID.

"This is what I'm talking about, darling," she said. "This is so tiring for you. Can't someone else deal with it?"

"I need to take this in the study."

Dorothy shrugged, resigned to the demands of his job. "We'll have dinner in fifteen minutes."

Gittinger smiled and headed upstairs to his study, where he locked the door. He sat down at his desk. "Gittinger. What is it, Laurence?"

"I'm hearing from a police source that Reznick has dropped off the radar. He hasn't been home for the last twenty-four hours."

Gittinger felt his stomach tighten. Knots of tension began to form in his shoulders. "Do we have anything to worry about? Bearing in mind the trip to Bar Harbor to visit Jerry White's father."

"This Jon Reznick is a wild card. I don't like it. And his involvement with the FBI is not good. Anyway, I thought you'd want to know, especially in light of the escape."

"Laurence, you did the right thing. I appreciate that. We need to double down on our security. And I don't care about the costs. Am I clear?"

"Crystal."

"I want to know the moment Reznick resurfaces. Do you hear me?"

The line went dead.

Twenty-Two

It was just after 10 p.m. as Reznick peered through the binoculars and past the guardhouse at the entrance to the gated community. He could see Gittinger's car. He tried to make out the license plate, but it was partially concealed by the huge oak trees surrounding the property. He needed more information. He pulled away and headed to a downtown diner, where he got a steak sandwich, fries, and a black coffee. When he finished, he dialed the number for the computer hacker in Miami. He passed on Gittinger's name, the community where he lived, as much information as he could.

"What sort of things would you be looking at?"

"His cell phone. I can't gain access to his car as it's either in a garage within the facility or in his gated community."

"When do you need this?"

"As soon as possible."

Reznick ended the call and got some more coffee. He went to the bathroom and popped a couple Dexedrine. It would keep him awake and sharp for as long as he liked. He splashed some cold water on his face and stared at the reflection staring back in the mirror. Pupils like pinpricks. Slightly unshaven. Shadows under his eyes.

He got back to his booth and drank some coffee. His gaze wandered around the rest of the patrons of the diner. A lot of college kids on their cell phones, a couple with MacBooks punching away at the keys as they enjoyed their coffees and fries. He couldn't help thinking of his daughter up at college in Vermont. He wondered if she would be hanging out at a diner. Perhaps at a friend's dorm. Then again, with a boyfriend, maybe she was in a bar drinking, forgetting her studies. She said she was snowed under with essays and assignments, so hopefully that would keep her busy. She was a very smart girl. But Reznick couldn't suppress the doubts that surfaced when he thought of his daughter.

He was overprotective to a fault. Lauren teased him about it. But that was his job. That was the deal. A father looked after his flesh and blood no matter what.

He thought back to when he had sent her away to boarding school. He missed her like crazy when she wasn't around. But his work dictated when he had to leave town. And with no mother, Reznick thought it was the only way to give her a great education without having the day-to-day worry. He had thought about sending her to New York to be with Elisabeth's parents. But they had already done more than enough to help her as she grew up. He wanted her to be independent. Or as independent as she could be. He remembered the first letter she had written home telling him how homesick she was. She wanted to come back to Rockland. She missed her friends in her hometown. His heart had sunk. He wanted her to be happy. But he had written back explaining how much he loved her, but that without Mom to help out, he needed her to be looked after. It took her months to overcome her homesickness. But eventually, after making friends in the school, the pain of separation began to abate. Her letters started to talk increasingly about what she was doing at school that week. The trips to museums. The sports. Lacrosse. Tennis. She threw herself into life at the school. When he saw her next, during Thanksgiving, she was no longer that frightened little girl, afraid of her own shadow. She seemed more relaxed with herself. More self-assured. As the years rolled on, Reznick couldn't help seeing she was more and more like her mother. The way she rolled her eyes if he suggested something. The way she smiled. The way she curled her hair behind her ears. The mannerisms were all there.

He was tempted to call her, but since he was waiting on a call, it might be better to speak to her later.

The minutes dragged as he waited for the hacker to get back to him. Reznick ordered another coffee refill and some pancakes with maple syrup. He felt famished despite the sandwich and fries.

He wolfed the food down in minutes.

Fifteen minutes later, his cell rang.

"Yeah, any luck?" Reznick said.

"I tried everything I had at my disposal and I didn't see any phone registered to Wittenden. That doesn't mean the phone wasn't registered by someone else or bought by someone else."

"Fuck."

"Don't worry, man. All is not lost. You're dealing with the best in the business."

"What've you got?"

"His wife has a cell phone, and I've remotely activated it."

"Interesting."

"And it's picked up the wireless signals of their Wi-Fi router and a cell phone that isn't hers. It was registered by a company called Twenty-One Consultancy in McLean, Virginia. Formed three years ago. Can't find anything else. No tax returns or anything."

Reznick thought it sounded like a CIA special project, especially as the company was based in the town of McLean.

"Interesting. What else have you found?"

"The cell phone and the provider. And I hacked into the provider and got an itemized billing of every call he's made from the phone. Also the geolocation of where he's been."

"Now that is interesting. Can you message me that information? Encrypted of course."

"Who is this guy, if you don't mind me asking?"

"Just a person of interest."

The hacker gave a throaty laugh. "Don't tell me any more, man."

"Bill me and you'll have your money when I get a moment."

"Don't sweat it."

The hacker ended the call.

Reznick paid the check, left a nice tip, and headed out into the night.

Twenty-Three

Reznick checked in to a nearby hotel for the night, showered, and put on a fresh set of clothes. He got himself a Coke from the minibar, pulled out his cell phone, and began examining where and when Gittinger's phone had been used.

He scanned the long list of locations.

Gittinger was a man of fixed habits: a two-mile drive from his gated community in Ithaca to the Wittenden Institute. He left his house at 5:30 a.m. every day and returned at 7 p.m., apart from today, when he had arrived home an hour late. Otherwise, he was as regular as clockwork.

Reznick scanned the list, until he saw a visit to DC three weeks earlier. The location? A CIA satellite office adjacent to Langley.

The more Reznick looked at the timeline and the locations, the more he was struck by the regularity. Nothing changed. Two visits in six months to the CIA office. The rest of the time, Gittinger headed to or from work. Nothing was allowed to intrude on his world.

The problem was there was no chink in Gittinger's armor that Reznick could see.

He lay back on his bed and thought of Jerry White across town, deep in the bowels of Wittenden. He closed his eyes and imagined Jerry shut off from everyone, undergoing some shit-crazy experiments devised sixty years earlier as a method of torture. A guy who had laid his life on the line for his country. And who now was being treated like a guinea pig.

And for what?

What was the purpose?

Was it just for the military to observe how far they could push psychologically fragile soldiers? Was that what this was about?

The problem was he didn't have proof of this happening. All he had were assertions from a reporter who was clearly paranoid. And a priest who claimed his sister had witnessed what was going on inside.

It was just their word.

But Reznick's gut told him that both these men weren't lying. That Gittinger had visited a CIA office twice in the last six months confirmed their stories. Gittinger was indeed heading up a program, a top-secret classified program.

Houlihan had shown him details. That was pretty compelling.

Reznick headed out to his rental car. He drove across town to the Wittenden Institute. It was only three minutes away, according to the GPS.

He negotiated the quiet downtown streets and headed to a tiny town a couple of miles away. On the outskirts, he saw for the first time the floodlights of Wittenden.

Twenty-Four

Reznick peered through binoculars as the employees arrived. He watched as security guards scanned their ID badges. He glanced in his rearview mirror as an SUV pulled up right behind him. The front passenger door opened and out stepped a familiar-looking figure.

Reznick put down the binoculars. He saw it was Laurence Cray, director of security at the Wittenden Institute. Out of the back seat, two other rather imposing guys stepped out, both carrying batons.

A sharp knock at his window.

Reznick opened it.

"Jon, how are you this morning?"

"I'm well. How are you, Laurence?"

Cray leaned into his window. "Do you mind me asking you a question?"

"Sure."

"What are you doing here?"

Reznick smiled. "Just looking around."

"You're a long way from home, Jon."

Reznick glanced in his side mirror as one of the security guards spoke into a walkie-talkie. He wondered if they were calling in the license plate. "Guess so. Nice town."

"Do you mind me asking exactly what you're hoping to achieve, Jon?"

Reznick got out of his car and eyeballed Cray. "I want to see my friend."

"I'm sorry, but as we explained before, this is not an option just now. We don't have an open-door policy. And I don't think it will be looked on very favorably you just turning up outside, knowing full well you can't visit."

"When I spoke to Dr. MacDonald, she seemed a reasonable person."

Cray sighed. "She is a reasonable person, Jon."

"Can I speak to her?"

Cray winced and looked off toward the workers arriving for the shift. He turned to face Reznick. "That's not going to happen."

"Look, I've got her number on my cell phone. Why don't you explain to her that I'm outside and want to speak to her?"

Cray shook his head. "You're killing me, you know that?"

"Let her know I'm here. Let her decide."

"Do you think I'm making this up? We have a very strict policy for a good reason. The rehabilitation of our patients is our top priority."

"I don't want to disturb the workings of the hospital. I just want an opportunity to speak to Dr. MacDonald."

Cray shrugged and pulled a cell phone out of his pocket. He turned away and spoke into it. "Dr. MacDonald, very sorry to bother you, we have Mr. Jon Reznick . . . Yes, that one. Mr. Reznick has been observing the entrance of the hospital. He wants to see his friend Jerry White."

He nodded as he listened to her answer. "I've explained that, but now he says he wants to speak to you." He nodded. "Are you OK with that?" He nodded. "Will you require us there?" He cleared his throat. "Very well, I'll pass that on." Cray ended the call and turned to face Reznick. "Guess you're in luck."

Reznick said nothing.

"East Green Street. Ithaca Coffee Company. She can see you there in thirty minutes."

Twenty-Five

The coffee shop was deserted apart from Dr. Eileen MacDonald, who was speaking into her cell phone in a corner, sipping her coffee.

Reznick walked in, ordered a latte, and sat down beside her.

MacDonald gave a cold smile. "I'll get back to you this afternoon. Gotta go." She ended the call. "You're up early this morning, Mr. Reznick."

"Appreciate you seeing me on such short notice."

"I'm surprised at you, Mr. Reznick."

"How do you mean?"

"You don't strike me as a stupid man."

Reznick said nothing.

"For the life of me, I do not understand what on earth you thought you'd achieve by turning up like this."

"I'm concerned about Jerry."

"And that's to be applauded. I'm delighted you care about him so much. But you've got to understand, by taking time out of my schedule, I'm not attending to the care of another patient. So while I fully understand your desire to see your friend, your actions put us in a difficult position."

Reznick gulped some of the frothy latte. He contemplated revealing a little of what he knew. He wondered if he should show his hand.

"I'm at a loss to understand the obsession with secrecy. What is that all about?"

"We don't see it as secrecy. We see it as creating a culture for our patients which is free from outside influence, be it relatives, albeit well-meaning ones, or friends, who may resurrect negative feelings."

"I've been asking a few people about Wittenden."

MacDonald flushed. "And?"

"It appears to be operating almost as a law unto itself."

"Is that what people are saying?"

"No, that's what I'm saying. The people I've spoken to have very definite views on what goes on inside Wittenden. And I would not be exaggerating to say they believe that psychological torture is being pursued on highly vulnerable patients, all veterans suffering from PTSD. I'm interested in what you have to say about that."

MacDonald sipped her coffee but stayed quiet.

"Don't you have anything to say?"

"We are a pioneering institute, and whatever people say about us, for whatever reason, it's just not true. We view what we do as intensive therapy. And we have seen the majority of our patients make great strides."

"Why do you think people would say such things then? Are they making it up?"

"People don't like what they don't understand. Disaffected former staff are something we have to contend with, like any organization."

Reznick sighed and leaned closer. "I just want to know that my friend is OK. If I can see him and see that he's being cared for, then that's all I need."

"I think you're being somewhat disingenuous, Mr. Reznick. I don't think even getting a personal tour of the hospital would change your fixed mind-set on what we do at Wittenden. And that's perfectly fine. But I think you have to understand that we operate to the highest possible standards. Ethical standards. I wouldn't operate in a hospital that wasn't humane, caring, and working for the betterment of the patients."

Reznick stayed silent, allowing her to talk.

"I want to help. And I'd hoped that by meeting you face-to-face you would see that we are reasonable people. Professional people. I take pride in the work I do. And I ensure that Jerry and all my other patients are looked after and given the appropriate psychological support in addition to the rehabilitation therapies we offer."

"Can I ask you a question, Dr. MacDonald?"

She shrugged and sipped her coffee. "Go right ahead."

"It's no ordinary hospital, is it?"

"No, we're not. We are an extraordinary hospital. Pioneering fantastic new treatments for some of our most damaged veterans."

"Can you tell me how many have undergone treatment at the Wittenden Institute and been integrated back into society?"

"We have numerous success stories."

"So how many?"

MacDonald sighed. "I'm sorry, but I think I have been quite open with you."

"Is that it? Is the discussion over?"

"Mr. Reznick, I'd appreciate if you didn't use that tone of voice. Now, I've been patient. But I've got a very busy day ahead."

"So when will I be able to see Jerry?"

MacDonald stared at him. "I know who you are and what you've been involved in. But you are close to crossing the line."

"And what line is that?"

MacDonald picked up her bag and briefcase and got to her feet. "I'd strongly advise you to leave town and let us get on with our work undisturbed."

"Strongly advise? And if I don't?"

"Let's not find out."

Reznick returned to his hotel room, showered, and changed. Over the rest of the day, he contemplated his next step. He wondered if he should cut his losses and leave, head home. That would be the best thing for a quiet life. And he liked his quiet life. He liked his own space. His own way of doing things. He didn't like to get caught up in things that weren't strictly his business.

But the more he thought about it, the more he realized he couldn't just turn and walk away. He knew there was something wrong with the Institute. And everything he'd heard from the journalist and the priest, plus the evasiveness of Dr. MacDonald, pointed to a facility with a lot to hide.

The knee-jerk reaction would be to make a move and get inside. He knew that would not only be complicated but also need a hell of a lot of thought. One thing he'd learned in Delta was the need for first-class intelligence. No use just turning up and hoping some firepower would suffice. It required brains. And time. But that wasn't something Jerry had the luxury of.

Reznick lay back down on the bed and felt himself drifting away. The exhaustion and lack of sleep was finally catching up with him, even with the Dexedrine in his system. He felt himself floating downstream on a dark river. Tiny stars in an inky black sky.

One a.m.—he must have nodded off. He awoke in darkness, his cell phone vibrating in his shirt pocket.

"I might have something for you." The hacker.

"What?"

"I don't know if it's anything crucial."

"Go on."

"I'm monitoring everything that's happening on the cell phone you asked me to get into."

"And?"

"Ten minutes ago, the guy who has the phone had a meeting in his office with a Dr. MacDonald. That name mean anything to you?"

"Sure. What was discussed?"

"They mentioned moving a guy."

"What guy?"

"I wrote his name down . . . Jerry."

"You kidding me?"

"Nope."

"What other details?"

"They're going to move him tomorrow night."

"Got a time?"

"Not so far."

Reznick ended the call, headed to the bathroom, and splashed water on his face to wake himself up. He began to pace his dark room. Moving Jerry tomorrow? Where to? And why? Was this a move to the second hospital? Was this some sort of endgame for them? What did they have in store for Jerry?

"Fuck." He clenched his fists, getting angrier and angrier. The reassurance and warm words from Dr. MacDonald had just been a smoke screen. He needed to figure out a plan. And fast. Whatever the consequences.

Reznick's mind began to race. He got his binoculars, crouched down behind the blinds, and peered through the wooden slats. Farther down the street, he noticed two men in a black SUV, lights off.

One of them was Cray.

Twenty-Six

It was a sleepless night for Reznick as he tried to figure out the best way to rescue Jerry. He had begun to formulate a plan. A plan that involved getting himself noticed. He checked the bedside clock, which said 5:09 a.m. He needed them to know he was not disappearing.

He cracked the blinds. No vehicle there. He put on sweatpants, a T-shirt, and a sweatshirt, and pulled on his socks and running shoes. He did some stretching exercises for a few minutes. Then he headed out into a cold, crisp morning, his breath turning to vapor under the streetlights.

He headed through the eerily quiet Ithaca streets, only a handful of cars driving around.

He felt his heart rate hiking up a notch as the adrenaline began to flow. He ran in the direction of a sign pointing to Cass Park. He was getting his bearings. He was on the western shore of Cayuga Lake. He picked up his pace. The first tinges of a tangerine dawn washed over the upstate sky.

Reznick ran farther on the trail, feeling himself getting stronger and sharper. He began to think of Jerry again. His plight. He crossed over the trail, which led to Stewart Park on the eastern shore.

He felt the blood flowing as he contemplated what moves he could make. He knew he was seriously restricted. But one thing he was sure of was that being here in Ithaca had allowed him to be seen, and in turn the people at the Institute had had to react to him. And it was that reaction, or any future reaction, he was counting on to open up an opportunity for him.

The more he thought about it, the more he knew he couldn't walk away from Jerry even if he wanted to. He was a blood brother. Was that it? He had an obligation, maybe even a duty, to look out for Jerry White's interests. After all, no one else would.

Reznick turned around and headed back the way he came, through Cass Park and toward downtown. A cop car pulled up across the street and in front of him as he pounded the sidewalk.

Reznick slowed down as a thickset cop got out of the passenger seat. He wondered who had tipped the police off. He had a good idea. But that was his plan. To needle them. To let them know he wasn't slinking away. And then, perhaps, just maybe they would give him a chance.

"Excuse me, sir, you mind me seeing some ID?"

"Not at all, Officer."

Reznick reached into the back zip pocket where he carried a wallet with fake ID for emergencies. He handed it over to the cop.

The cop looked him up and down. "You like running in the dark?" he said.

"I usually start early."

The cop scrutinized the card and called in the details. While he waited for confirmation of the name, he eyeballed Reznick. "Mr. Greer, says on your ID you're from Camden, Maine."

"Yes, sir."

"You in town on business?"

"Thinking about moving here."

"Is that right? What line of work you in?"

"Real estate. Property. Some buying, some selling."

The voice on the cop's radio said, "Yeah, that's clear. Mr. William Greer, Alden Street, Camden, Maine." The cop smiled and handed back the ID. "Sorry for bothering you, sir. Enjoy the rest of your stay in Ithaca."

"Appreciate that, Officer."

Reznick watched as the cop got back in his car. They pulled away, and Reznick continued the rest of his run until he got back to his hotel. He showered and changed. His mood was hardening. And the final straw was the Institute's security guy parked outside the back of the hotel the night before.

He got in his rental car and headed onto the streets of Ithaca, only one thing on his mind.

Twenty-Seven

Reznick picked up a coffee and a box of donuts at a Dunkin' Donuts and headed farther down the road from the Wittenden Institute, with line of sight of the entrance. Cars pulled up and the employees piled out. A few vehicles, possibly senior management, were in a separate line.

He popped a Dexedrine and washed it down with the scalding, sweet coffee. He felt it buzz his system to life. He fully expected to get company. And he wasn't disappointed.

A few minutes later, he glanced in his rearview mirror and saw the SUV pull up again, Cray in the front passenger seat. Cray hauled his bulk out of the SUV and strode toward Reznick's car. He tapped on the window. Reznick let the window down, the cool air rushing in.

"Morning, Laurence," Reznick said, taking a gulp of coffee. "How are you today?" He handed him the donut box. "Try one. They're delicious."

Cray stared down at him.

"You OK? You look stressed."

"I'm not so good, Jon. You're going to give me an ulcer with all this hanging around outside the hospital."

"As you were checking me out at my hotel, I thought, why not? Let's return the favor."

"You're a real smart-ass, aren't you, Reznick?"

"I have my moments. Not too many to be fair, but yeah, one or two moments. I guess this is one of them."

"Jon, you have no business being here."

"I'm not obstructing you. I'm not obstructing your hospital. Just hanging out."

"You're not hanging out. You're pestering people. We're a peaceful community here."

"I'm just curious. Besides, I've got nowhere else to go."

Cray sighed. "Jon, we had this talk yesterday morning. This can't go on. You're clearly a nuisance and upsetting employees of the Institute."

"Like who?"

"Me? Dr. MacDonald? Look, I don't want to call the cops on you. You seem a decent sort."

"I actually was stopped by the cops when I was out earlier."

Cray said nothing.

"Was that you, Laurence? You calling in a favor with the local cops?"

"Jon, pulling a fake ID trick with the cops is not a smart thing to do."

"News certainly travels fast in upstate New York."

"I know the cops around here. They know me. I used to be a cop myself. I also used to be in the military."

"Army?"

"Yeah. Look, Reznick, this is my town. I know my town. And the people in it. They're good people. But they don't take kindly to people from out of town coming in and causing aggravation."

Reznick took a couple of gulps of his coffee and shrugged.

"We're reasonable people, Mr. Reznick, and had hoped to reassure you that your friend is being properly looked after."

"Well, I'm pleased to hear it. Except you didn't reassure me."

Cray leaned in closer to Reznick. He caught a whiff of cigarettes on his stale breath. "My patience is wearing very thin. As it stands, you might leave us with no choice but to use other means to prevent you from harassing the people who work at the Institute."

"Are you threatening me, Laurence?"

"Perhaps. Maybe go down the legal route. Maybe not. You know where I'm coming from, Mr. Reznick?"

Reznick was tempted to wipe the stupid smile off Cray's face. Nothing would give him greater pleasure than knocking the fucker out. But that was exactly what Cray wanted him to do. So the cops would be called again. But this time he would be charged. "Appreciate the feedback, Laurence. And send my regards to Dr. MacDonald. Very nice lady."

"Stay away from the Institute. Stay away from the staff. I think you've overstayed your welcome."

Reznick smiled.

"What's so funny?"

"I've got to disagree with you, Laurence. I like it here. So much so that I'm thinking of moving here. I like the Finger Lakes with all this fresh air and outdoor stuff."

"You've got a problem with authority, don't you, Jon?"

"You reckon?"

"Yeah. But sometimes you've got to know when you're beaten."

"You're absolutely right, Laurence. Good to talk."

"Take care now, Jon." Cray eyeballed him until Reznick put the window up. He watched Cray saunter to the rear of his car.

Reznick glanced in the side-view mirror. Cray had stopped and appeared to be examining the rear of Reznick's car. He walked up to the window again and tapped it twice.

Reznick wound it down.

"You might want to check out your rear left light. It's broken or something."

Reznick smiled. "I'll check it out, Laurence. But it was working fine earlier."

He wound up the window again and glanced in the rearview mirror.

Cray pulled a baton out of his jacket and casually smashed the left rear taillight. Then he walked back to his SUV.

Twenty-Eight

Gittinger was standing at his office window at the Wittenden Institute, staring out at the ash-gray skies shrouding Ithaca.

The door opened and in came Laurence Cray.

"This Jon Reznick character is being more than a nuisance, isn't he?" Gittinger said.

"I don't think he's going anywhere," Cray said. "I think he's going to become a bigger problem for us. I believe he might become a threat to our operation."

"That's very emotive language, Mr. Cray. Did you manage to find out if our hidden camera has identified anything at the priest's house?"

"As we suspected, Reznick turned up there."

"Now that is interesting."

"I'm hearing that Hank White's death is being treated as suspicious. And only Reznick is in the picture for it."

"So why haven't they arrested him?" Gittinger said.

"They're waiting for him in Maine. The only thing stopping them is the involvement of the assistant director of the FBI, who he's worked for in the past."

"How very cozy."

"Sir, I've got a plan that would take Reznick out of the equation. And I'm not talking about getting him arrested for flashing the false ID this morning."

"The easiest thing in the world is violence, Mr. Cray. Reznick is used to violence. And he's very good at it."

"I'm not talking violence. I'm talking about taking him out of the game."

"Do you want to elaborate?"

"Just leave it with me. I got this."

Twenty-Nine

Reznick got his smashed taillight replaced at a garage before he returned to the area around the Institute. He cruised the perimeter. The chain-link fence was topped by barbed wire, glinting in the morning sun. Beyond the perimeter was a secondary defense, an inner barrier, cameras on high poles dotted all around.

He remembered what Father McNamara had said. The tunnels underneath had been blocked up.

Reznick wondered if he was missing something. He took out his cell phone and dialed the Miami hacker.

"Back again for more, Mr. R," he said. "You still haven't paid me for the last time."

"You'll get your money."

"Yeah, that's what they all say."

"Listen, I was talking to a guy who mentioned schematics. Plans of a building in Ithaca. The Wittenden Institute."

"You want me to dig them out?"

"That's just the start. I want you to tell me the access and exit areas for this facility."

"What do you mean exactly?"

"I've been told there are tunnels."

"Tunnels?"

"Yeah, leading into and out of the facility. First, if you can get the schematics from the architect who designed the building. It's relatively new, and I've been told that the tunnels have been concreted in, enclosed. There are cameras watching the tunnels. So I want you to tell me first if there are tunnels, to ensure that the person I was speaking to was telling the truth. But also I want you to find out if they're concreted over. And I need to know today."

The hacker sighed down the line. "Well, let's see. I'd get that from Wittenden's surveillance cameras. I can do that, man. For you. But it will cost you big."

"How big?"

"Ten thousand."

Reznick didn't balk. He had perhaps a couple million in the bank, earned from numerous black ops over the years since he'd left Delta. He had lost count of the number of wet jobs he'd carried out. In London, New York, Riyadh, Paris, Dubai, wherever. It was invariably jihadists masquerading as businessmen. His job was to take them, and their cell, out of operation.

"You OK with that?"

"Not a problem . . . although your hourly rate seems to be increasing."

"This will take me away from my other work. So when will I see my dough?"

"You'll get all your money if you get me what I want by three today at the latest. A minute later, you get nothing. Deal?"

"Deal. Leave it with me."

In the hours that followed, Reznick collected his belongings from the hotel, checked out, paying his bill in cash, and then drove to an out-of-town diner near the freeway and had lunch. He returned the rental car to Avis and swapped it for a Chevy Suburban.

Once the paperwork was complete, he drove to a downtown motel and checked in under a fake name.

Reznick made himself a coffee with the Nespresso machine in the room.

The afternoon hours dragged. It was interesting that they had plans to move Jerry tomorrow night. He wondered if they would risk it knowing Reznick was still hanging around. Then again, they were assuming he wouldn't make a rash attempt to get to his friend. But Reznick knew such a plan, if they were indeed going to move Jerry White, would be doomed to fail.

He didn't know if Jerry would be in a protected vehicle. He assumed so. And he wouldn't know exactly which vehicle Jerry would be in. Would it be the ambulance he'd seen before? It would likely be flanked by security cars, no doubt with armed guards, marshaled by Cray.

It was not beyond him. But the end result—almost certainly multiple deaths—couldn't be justified. They probably knew that.

Reznick would stand a far better chance if he had a team with him. Six capable guys would be able to exploit the situation. A seemingly rash crash by a truck into the side of the convoy and, in the ensuing chaos, they could locate and retrieve Jerry. Then get him to a bone fide psychiatric facility.

However, the price would be high.

He could be risking not only his own life but also Jerry's and those of any Special Forces operatives he could muster. The reality was he would be the bad guy in this situation. The outlaw.

He pictured himself being hauled out of bed by Feds in the dead of night, maybe at some motel. And for what exactly?

Reznick pondered on that for a few moments. He needed to get inside somehow. He had contemplated getting a Wittenden Institute ID made up by a guy he knew in Manchester, New Hampshire. But that posed multiple risks.

They would be watching for him. They might even have facial recognition software in play.

His cell phone rang, snapping him out of his thoughts. He didn't recognize the caller ID.

"Yeah, who's this?" Reznick said, half expecting it to be the Miami hacker.

"Mr. Reznick, I was hoping to catch you." Dr. Eileen MacDonald. "Sorry for bothering you, and I hope you don't mind me calling out of the blue like this."

"Everything OK?"

"Yes, everything is fine. Are you still in town, Mr. Reznick?"

"Yeah."

"I'm with Father McNamara. He is, as you might know, a long-time critic of the Institute. He called me over to talk. And I've listened, just like I listened to you."

Reznick wasn't buying the line she was spinning.

"And I've been reflecting, after speaking with him, about what you were saying. I've only been in the post for about a year, and my objective was simply to follow the same position we've always taken, which is, perhaps, very rigid."

"What are you saying?"

"I'm saying I'd like to talk things through—just me, you, and Father McNamara—over coffee. And I hope we can come up with a way of accommodating both you and Father McNamara on a visit to see your friend Jerry, and hopefully that will reassure you, so we can get on with doing our job. But first, I think it's important we lay out some ground rules."

Reznick sensed right away that it was a trap. Maybe a ruse to lure him inside. But why? "You want me to go around to Father McNamara's house?"

"Yes, it's just opposite Ithaca College."

Reznick weighed the offer, his antennae switched on and alert to any traps. This couldn't be anything else. "And Father McNamara is fine with this?"

"Oh yes. He's just getting some tea and coffee ready as we speak."

Thirty

The GPS helped Reznick negotiate the tight roads of Ithaca as he headed back to the priest's little cottage. He pulled up outside but didn't see any other cars. He wondered if MacDonald had parked farther away, perhaps in the grounds of the college.

He got out of the car and headed up the path to the front door. The curtains were drawn inside, as before.

Reznick knocked three times. He stood and waited as he had earlier. "Father, it's Jon Reznick." He knocked again and rang the bell.

Still no answer.

He tried the handle, but it was locked.

Reznick knocked again, pacing the front of the house. He waited again for an answer. But still nothing.

He went around the side of the house, climbed over a locked gate, and headed around the back.

Reznick tried the back door and it was open. Alarm bells were going off in his head. He went through the utility room, past a washing machine, and into the kitchen. The smell of coffee, pot still hot.

"Father, you want to shake a leg?"

Reznick heard water from upstairs. "Father, are you on the john?" The water was still running, but no response. His senses were all switched on.

He took his gun out of his waistband and pulled back the slide.

He got to the upstairs landing and pressed his head against the door where he heard the water. Inside, it sounded like the faucet was still running.

Reznick crouched down, began to turn the handle, and pushed open the door. Water, turning red, was spilling onto the bathroom floor.

Lying naked in the overflowing bath was Father McNamara, wrist and neck slit. Blood stained the water and the beige carpet, where a bloody knife lay.

Thirty-One

Just before dawn, Meyerstein's plane touched down at Ithaca after a hurriedly arranged flight up from DC. She was met at the airport by two local Feds and driven straight to Ithaca Police HQ. The chief of police, Rod Berger, filled her in on the details.

"So what's the position?" she asked.

"The position is, Assistant Director, Jon Reznick says it wasn't him. He said he was told to head there by Dr. MacDonald, from the Institute."

"Have you checked that?"

"Just finished checking her cell phones. She has a private cell phone and work cell phone, and there are no calls at all."

"Chief Berger, you know as well as I do that Jon Reznick is wanted for a suspected homicide in Maine about forty-eight hours ago."

"That for us was very compelling."

"Can I be frank, Chief?"

He shrugged. "Sure."

"Reznick didn't do this. And he didn't do the Maine homicide either. That's what I think."

Berger displayed his palms, as if finding it hard to believe what she said.

"Here's the thing. I know him. I know him pretty good."

"Can I be frank, ma'am?"

"Of course."

"Are you perhaps—and I don't want you taking this the wrong way—letting your professional friendship with this guy cloud your judgment somewhat?"

Meyerstein felt her stomach tighten with anger. "I beg your pardon?"

"Is it possible that you want him to be innocent?"

"Let's be clear. That's not what I'm basing my judgment on. Over time, you get to know people. I've gotten to know Jon Reznick very well."

The chief leaned back in his seat. "Maybe you do. But I've been in this job a long time—maybe too long—and we have footage of him captured from yesterday outside Father McNamara's house."

"Do you mind me asking how you came to be in possession of the footage?"

"A source within the Institute."

"Were they spying on the priest?"

"I believe it was filmed by an employee who lived nearby."

Meyerstein said nothing.

"So this is the second time he's turned up at a location. Twice. Two victims found dead. One in Bar Harbor and now Ithaca. It's quite a coincidence, don't you think?"

Meyerstein took a few moments to compose herself. She had decided on the flight up that she would defend Reznick. Her heart and soul and every fiber of her being told her Jon Reznick did not kill Hank White in Bar Harbor or Father McNamara in Ithaca. But her head said the evidence didn't look good. "Where is he now?"

"He's being interviewed by two of my most experienced detectives."

Meyerstein nodded.

"They might be some time."

"Have you had Reznick's cell phone examined?"

"The SIM card was copied and electronically sent across to the Forensic Investigation Center, in Albany."

"When will you hear back?"

"Within the hour."

"I'd like to speak to Jon Reznick."

"Don't go throwing your weight around. Why do the FBI always do that?"

"Listen to me, Chief, and listen closely. I am here at the behest of the Director of the FBI." He showed her a letter confirming this. "And as you can see, it gives me authority to speak to Jon Reznick if I see fit."

"If you see fit? Are you kidding me? On what grounds?"

"If what you're saying is true, Reznick could be a serial killer. And as such he would come under our jurisdiction if we have reason to believe that he crossed state lines, which in this case we most certainly do."

"You're not going to pull that, are you? This is our patch, you know that."

"I need to talk to Jon Reznick. Just me and him. One on one. You understand?"

Thirty-Two

Reznick was lying back on a hard bed in an Ithaca Police HQ cell, hands behind his head, staring at the ceiling. The sound of keys and locks turning, metal doors slamming shut. Then the clacking of heels.

An officer opened the cell door. Meyerstein walked in holding two mugs of coffee.

Reznick got to his feet and took the black coffee off her. She waited until the cell door was locked again before she sat down on a chair.

"Well, this is becoming quite a habit, Jon," she said.

Reznick sat down on the edge of the bed and gulped some of the coffee. "Thanks."

"For what?"

"Turning up, I guess."

Meyerstein sighed. "We got a problem, Jon."

"No kidding."

"Now, this is the second occasion when you've been found at the scene of a murder. Two people dead. Two different towns. And I'm hearing you say you had a call from Dr. Eileen MacDonald at the Institute."

"One hundred percent correct. She was talking about allowing me in to visit Jerry, along with Father McNamara. She wanted to meet up first to lay out the ground rules before the visit. I thought their security goons might be there, worst-case scenario. I was wrong."

"Why would she do this if she had already explained that you weren't getting access?"

Reznick shrugged. "Maybe the Institute didn't like me hanging around town, asking questions."

"What if I told you the cops have already examined Dr. MacDonald's cell phones—she has two, business and personal—and both have no calls today. And also the number that called you was located in Florida."

"Listen to me, I did not do this. You've got to believe me."

"But this isn't about me, Jon. This is about police in two separate states. And another thing, you were caught on camera visiting the priest two days before he died."

"What?"

"His house was being watched."

"By who?"

"The Institute."

"They were spying on McNamara?"

Meyerstein nodded. "You were caught on film visiting on both days. This is not good, trust me."

"Don't treat me like a suspect."

"But you are. Number one suspect."

"Can't you see what's happening?"

"What's that?"

"This is a frame-up."

"By who?"

Reznick said nothing.

"You have no evidence of this."

"I have reasonable belief."

"I don't think you do. You say you got a call from a doctor at the Institute, which you seem to have become completely obsessed with, and then you arrive at the house, the priest dead in his bath. And coming only days after you found Hank White hanging in the woods near his home. I mean, come on, Jon. How the hell do you think that looks? Do you want to try and explain this to me?"

"I've been told this is a CIA project—off the books, so to speak. Led by Dr. Robert Gittinger."

Meyerstein contemplated this. "I can't speak for the CIA."

"You know how they work."

"They have their way of doing things."

"Have you established if this is their little operation?"

"The FBI have reached out to various levels within the CIA, and they are denying this has anything to do with them."

Reznick shook his head. "They would say that, wouldn't they? That's why it's plausible deniability. But Gittinger is ex-CIA."

"So he's not currently employed by the agency."

"Technically, that's correct. But you know as well as I do that this has their fingerprints all over it."

"And you know as well as I do that the CIA aren't allowed to conduct surveillance of US citizens on American soil. We'd have a hell of a time proving they're violating those guidelines."

"Meyerstein, you know better than I that since 9/11 the FBI, CIA, NSA, Department of Defense, and Homeland Security have all been engaged in intelligence activities on US soil. So this Institute, while it won't have "CIA Operation in Progress" on the sign outside, is an Agency operation."

"I don't want to get drawn into interagency turf disputes. Let's get back to talking about you. *You* are the one in the frame."

Reznick sighed. "The common thread is the Institute. Hank White was a loose cannon. Talking about going to the press so he could see his son. And the priest has fought a long campaign against the Institute. Lost his job over it. Communicated with a journalist over the issue. His sister used to work there and took her own life, apparently. This is a very clever frame-up, pure and simple."

Meyerstein looked at him. "I got you out before. But I can't do it again."

"Are you kidding me? This wasn't me."

Meyerstein stared at him long and hard. "The way you're heading here, there, and everywhere seems out of character. I'm worried you've lost perspective. You're taking this personally."

"I'm trying to look out for the interests of Jerry White. We were close."

Meyerstein looked around the bare cell. "And how are you doing that?"

"Listen to me. What I've found out about the Wittenden Institute concerns me a great deal. I don't think this is an ordinary psychiatric hospital for veterans."

"You have no proof of that. All you've got are the ravings of a defrocked priest and some journalist, you say, who claims that he found unethical practices."

"This goes way beyond unethical practices."

"You have nothing. Jon, listen to me. You have not given me one concrete piece of evidence that there is anything untoward about that place. It's all anecdotal."

"Maybe it is."

"Maybe it's what you want to believe."

Reznick stared at the floor. "I thought you knew me better than that."

"Jon, you're a very hard-headed, serious person. Someone I've trusted. Someone who has risked his life for me. But I cannot understand how you've gotten yourself in this predicament. This is not good."

"You think I did this, don't you?"

"Jon, I never said that."

"You don't have to. I can look into your eyes and tell you exactly what Martha Meyerstein is thinking."

"Jon, you've gotten too involved."

"Look at me."

"What?"

"I tried to resolve this. I tried to engage with the people from the Institute. I met with Dr. MacDonald yesterday for coffee, goddammit. And then, because she called me to meet up, I headed to Father McNamara's house. Do you see what I'm saying?"

"Go on."

"I smelled a rat. But I was more concerned about seeing Jerry and making sure the hospital where he's being looked after isn't as bad as they say it is. And when she reached out, offering me the chance to visit Jerry, I took the opportunity."

Meyerstein put down her coffee. "What if you're wrong?"

"What do you mean?"

"What if you're completely wrong about this whole Institute?"

"Perhaps I am. But until I'm convinced otherwise, here's what I know: I'm innocent. And that psychiatric hospital sure has a lot to hide."

Meyerstein got up from the chair and stared down at Reznick. "Don't go anywhere."

"Where are you going? Are you bailing on me?"

"Not quite yet. I'll be back in about an hour. Sit tight."

Thirty-Three

Reznick was put in plastic handcuffs and taken into the interview room. Sitting down at a table in the corner of the room was the chief of police, taking notes.

A detective pointed at the chair.

Reznick sat down.

The recording machine was started. "OK, Mr. Reznick, we've got a few more questions. That OK?"

"Sure."

"You're mighty popular with the FBI's assistant director."

"Natural charm, I guess."

The detective stared at him. "Mr. Reznick, we've got a man who's dead. A former priest. Do you think that humor is the best course of action for you?"

Reznick shrugged.

"You seem very unbothered by this."

"Quite the contrary. I'm very bothered by it. I want to find out who the hell did this."

The police chief gave a rueful smile.

"Whoever did this was very professional," Reznick said. "The knife was clearly arranged to make it look like a suicide attempt."

The detective scribbled down some more notes, as did the chief. "That's interesting. So you're saying that's what happened."

"I'm saying whoever killed Father McNamara set it up. Like I said, very professional. Made to look like a suicide."

"Tell me about your experience in Delta Force, Mr. Reznick."

Reznick leaned back in his seat, arms folded. "Detective, what the hell do you think we do in Delta?"

"I'm asking the questions. This is a very straightforward question. Are you refusing to answer?"

"We did everything. Hostage rescue, counterterrorism, reconnaissance against high-value targets, that kind of thing."

"And you kill people, don't you?"

"We performed complex, dangerous, and sometimes borderline crazy missions. And it's usually classified."

"You didn't answer my question. I'll ask it again. Have you ever killed people? Are you trained to kill?"

"Of course I'm trained to kill. And yes, I have killed people. In Iraq. In Afghanistan. Somalia. And some other places too. But I did not kill this poor priest."

"And yet we have evidence that you were a visitor, twice in forty-eight hours, to his home."

"That is correct."

"Can you see where the problem lies, Mr. Reznick? No alibi. And proof you were there. Prints. Photographic evidence."

"Detective, I didn't kill the priest."

"Tell me again, why are you in town?"

"My friend is in Wittenden. I wanted to visit."

"But weren't you told quite specifically that your friend was not allowed to have visitors?"

"That is correct."

"Do you think Dr. MacDonald is lying when she says she doesn't know anything about this? Her phones have already been checked."

"You'd better ask her that. I can only tell you what I know. She called. The fact she's denying it is bizarre."

"It's more than goddamn bizarre. It's not a credible story. Isn't it more likely that you concocted this whole scenario, putting the Wittenden Institute at the heart of this problem?"

"Good try, but no."

"You think this is funny?"

"Have you questioned Dr. MacDonald in this room?"

"No, we have not."

"Are you planning to?"

The detective slammed the palm of his hand down onto the wooden table. "That's quite enough. We're doing the investigating. And frankly, as it stands, you are up to your neck in it. You haven't given a credible reason why you were there."

"What do you mean, not a credible reason? It is what it is. On the second occasion I went to visit Father McNamara, it was only after a call from Dr. MacDonald."

"Except there was no call, was there?"

"There most certainly was a call."

"Dr. MacDonald is a highly respected international psychologist who has won numerous awards."

"Well, good for her."

"Tell me about your relationship with Father McNamara."

Reznick gave a wry smile. "Detective, there was no relationship. He was a guy I wanted to speak to about the Wittenden Institute. That's all."

"So you're saying you have no sexual motive for visiting his house."

"Detective, you'll have to try a little harder to rile me. Insinuations might work well in the locker room. But trying to establish a motive? Not so much."

The detective flushed. "So you're saying you didn't have a relationship with him?"

"You're a quick learner, Detective. Now have you got any other questions?"

Thirty-Four

It was plain as day to Reznick that the cop was trying to get underneath his skin. He took it in his stride. And that response seemed to be agitating the detective. He flushed.

"Do you know Daniel McNamara is known to police?"

Reznick shrugged. "How would I? I never met him until I wanted to find out more about Wittenden."

"McNamara had a very close association with Ithaca over a number of decades. But probably more so with a section of its community."

"You want to stop talking in riddles?"

"McNamara's homosexuality was an open secret in Ithaca and the diocese."

"Not exactly a shocker saying that a priest is gay."

"Did you know he cruised for men?"

"Detective, I didn't know this former priest until two days ago."

"You might be interested to know that Daniel McNamara was blackmailed by a young friend of his about six years ago. They were caught in the act, at some truck stop."

"And how exactly does that relate to me, Detective?"

"He had a penchant for young toughs."

"Well, you'll be pleased to know that this aspect of his life was not known to me, nor is it of interest."

"You were married and you have a daughter."

"That's right. I was married. My wife died. 9/11. But I'm lucky, I have a great daughter."

"That's nice." A sarcastic tone in his voice annoyed Reznick. "Are you in a relationship, Mr. Reznick?"

"Not since my wife died."

"Wow. Not in a relationship since then?"

Reznick nodded.

"Why is that?"

"Why have I not been in a relationship?"

The detective nodded.

"Listen, I thought you were interested in finding the person who killed Father McNamara."

"Oh, we are. And we will find them, don't worry about that."

"So why the fuck are you asking these questions? You get a kick out of this?"

"Do you have a problem with me asking such questions?"

"Detective, I don't know if you think this is a smart way to get to the truth, or maybe it's how you've been taught to interview suspects, but it's got to be the dumbest set of questions I've ever heard."

"You've got a bit of an attitude, Jon."

"Damn right I have."

"I'm going to let you in on a little secret. Just me and you."

"Cut the bullshit."

"Daniel McNamara was obsessed with a guy from Ithaca, a married man, with a happy, stable family. A Christian man, like himself. A practicing Catholic. And this man had been having a relationship with McNamara on and off for the best part of a decade, but six months ago he broke it off. And McNamara took this very badly."

Reznick said nothing.

"He tried to make contact with this man repeatedly, he was so distraught."

"Is there a point to this?"

"Motivation. This man was terrified he was going to be exposed for conducting this relationship. And we have reason to believe he contacted an individual, who is on the periphery of a New York crime family, and explained his situation and said he was wondering if his connections could make his problem go away. The mob associate, some street thug with family connections to Ithaca, said no can do, and that was that."

"Is this all supposed to mean something to me?"

"So the motivation for McNamara's murder might involve this married gay man—let's call him Simon—desperate to put an end to any chance of him being outed by Daniel McNamara. And that's where you would fit in."

"Nice story. You got a lot of time on your hands to think up that stuff?"

The detective smiled. "You have the skills to do this. This man Simon is very wealthy, so money would be no object. Fifty thousand? Not a problem. Two hundred thousand? He's worth twenty times that amount. So money is no object. You see what I'm getting at?"

"You really need to get out more, do you know that?"

"Wise guy, right?"

"Listen, I'm not the guy you're looking for. You're so wrong it's almost funny. Except I'm not laughing."

"You see, Jon, the more I get to know about you—and I've been reading a file on you—wow, now that is interesting."

Reznick said nothing.

"Delta. Assassin. Hired to kill. You're a specialist in assassination. Interestingly, I believe you are familiar with the phrase *suicided*. A murder is made to look like a suicide. Father McNamara found in the bath naked after slitting his wrists and neck. Knife on the carpet."

"I went over this with the chief." The chief of police, in the corner, kept on writing notes.

"There is an interesting aspect to all this, Reznick."

"And what's that?"

"Your involvement with the FBI. We have had confirmation from Assistant Director Meyerstein that you have worked with them on several classified operations."

"I can't discuss anything like that. I'm sure you can appreciate that."

"This is a helluva résumé. You kill for a living. Tell me, Reznick, how did this approach from Simon happen?"

"You really going down that route?"

"Did he offer you a lot of money? Everyone needs money, right?"

"I'm fortunate. Money is not a problem for me."

The detective leafed through a few papers. "But you have some seriously hefty outgoings, and you have had for many years."

Reznick said nothing.

"We've been doing some checking. And you're paying quite a bundle in tuition fees for your daughter."

"You're scraping the bottom of the barrel now."

"Private college. Now that would make a dent in anyone's bank balance, right?"

"Good try, Detective, but a cursory look at my bank account would show no money going in that can't be accounted for."

The detective smiled. "You think this is a joke, Reznick?"

"I think your powers of deduction are a joke. A man has died and you're pointing to the guy that discovered the body. It's absurd."

"Imagine this scenario: You're contacted by Simon, or someone who knows Simon. Maybe a bar. Maybe a visit to your home in Maine. And you agree, for a significant fee, to wire-transfer money offshore.

Maybe the Caymans. Switzerland. Panama. Take your pick. And all you have to do is kill this frail old gay guy. He'll be dead in a few years anyway. So what the hell? And the fact is he's blackmailing someone. So you wouldn't be killing an innocent."

"You ever thought of writing books, Detective? Terrific imagination you've got."

The detective stared long and hard at him. "Reznick, you need to stop the smart-ass comments and realize you are in a whole lot of trouble."

Thirty-Five

An hour later, Reznick was doing push-ups in his cell when he heard the clanking of keys, doors slamming shut.

A tall man in a smart suit was standing outside. A cop opened the cell door, and the man stepped inside. "Jon Reznick?"

Reznick got up and wiped his hands on his jeans. "Yeah, who are you?"

The man stepped forward and gave a firm handshake. "Nice to meet you, Jon. Robert Friedman. General counsel for the FBI. I'll be your lawyer."

Reznick took a few moments to get his head around what was happening. "And . . . if you don't mind me asking, who got you involved, sir?"

"You have the assistant director to thank. Oh, and the Director himself."

"The Director himself . . . Have you been briefed?"

"I know enough." Friedman sat down slowly on the edge of the bed as Reznick remained standing. "Here's what's going to happen. You are going to be released without charge but with several conditions. These include forfeiting your driver's license. And you have been put on notice that they will be interviewing you again once the forensic tests are completed."

"But I haven't been arrested."

"Not yet. But that is almost certainly their next step. And that's when things get messy. Media, press, all that bullshit."

Reznick shook his head, folding his arms. "That's not a good thing. At least for me."

"I understand that. And that's why I've become involved. I've spoken to the district attorney, and he has communicated with the Ithaca Police Department, and they have agreed that as long as they have your driver's license and your passport, and if the FBI vouch for you—I'll spare you the legal stuff—then you can leave here."

Reznick nodded. "What else?"

"There are other conditions we have provisionally agreed to. I'd strongly advise you to agree to them too."

"What are they?"

"The FBI has a resident agency office in Ithaca. And they have agreed to oversee your stay."

"When does that come into force?"

"From the moment you walk out of here."

"So I can't leave Ithaca?"

"Until this matter has been resolved. The cops might decide to arrest you, and then, if we're lucky, we would have to post a three-million-dollar bond to keep you out of jail."

"I'm assuming this matter is not up for discussion."

"You assume correctly. It's a good deal, Jon. It might annoy you. But it means you don't have to stay cooped up inside."

Reznick nodded.

"We have pulled some serious strings for you. And you've got Martha Meyerstein in particular to thank."

Reznick cleared his throat.

"But here's the thing. You need to keep away from trouble. Otherwise, you'll be on your own."

Thirty-Six

The FBI legal counsel checked himself and Reznick into the Marriott in downtown Ithaca. He handed Reznick a key card for his room. "Change of clothes inside your room, courtesy of the assistant director."

Reznick smiled. "Where is she?"

"You've got ten minutes to freshen up, get your new clothes on, and head across to see her."

Fifteen minutes later, Reznick was in the tiny FBI office in Ithaca. Martha Meyerstein was sitting on the edge of a desk. He was introduced to a couple of agents. Then Reznick, Meyerstein, and Friedman went into a separate office.

Friedman spoke first. "I've been in the legal business a long time, and this situation is not to my liking. Anything which attracts focus on the FBI, especially pertaining to illegality or alleged illegality of those who work for it or have an association with the Bureau, is absolutely not what we want in this or any climate."

Meyerstein nodded. "Jon, I've got to be frank. I don't know why you've gotten yourself in such a mess. This is very unlike you."

"So why didn't you just let me face the consequences?"

"If you had been arrested, without any FBI counsel or any FBI input the leaks from the police would be that an FBI contractor, freelancer—whatever they wanted to call you—would be splashed all over the papers. We can't have that. We need to protect the organization. The backlash against the FBI would sorely damage us. But there's another reason."

"What's that?" Reznick asked.

"Myself, the director, and Counsel Friedman believe you are wholly innocent."

Reznick felt somewhat relieved. "Appreciate that. Look, once this is over I'll understand if you decide not to proceed with allowing me to work for you again. I get that."

Meyerstein said, "That's for another day. For now we need you to take a few steps back."

Reznick sighed.

"What is it?" Meyerstein asked.

"You genuinely don't think I did it?"

"No, I don't, Jon," Meyerstein said.

Friedman said, "We know you're not to blame. But persuading a judge that you're innocent, if it makes it to trial, might be altogether trickier. Wrong place, wrong time, and all that circumstantial evidence."

"So if," Reznick said, "we agree I didn't do it—and trust me, this sure as hell wasn't me—I would appreciate it if FBI forensics could be called in, like in Bar Harbor."

Meyerstein nodded. "As part of this deal, we offered the services of FBI specialists and forensics officers, and they are going over the Ithaca crime scene in minute detail."

"They good?"

"They're the best. They're already hard at work going through what the cops have, but also crucially what the cops have not gotten or thought of."

"I sure hope so," Reznick said. "The question then is, well, if it wasn't me, then who was it?"

Friedman furrowed his brow, as if deep in thought.

"I'm not an investigator or expert in your kind of work, but what was the motivation? What was the link? Was Hank White, who was always shooting his mouth off, apparently, going to go to the press to see his son? And then the priest? Neither of these two had been taken out before I showed up. I get that. But was Jerry's escape the catalyst that prompted someone to take an action that would neutralize the threat to the Wittenden Institute? And by getting these two out of the way, I would also be in the frame. I'm the patsy."

Friedman rubbed his face with his hands. "Then, if what you're saying is true, this is a conspiracy. Not just a murder and conspiracy to murder but a web of deceit."

Meyerstein held up her hand as if to get a word in. "We're reaching. And we don't know any of that."

Reznick said, "I'm telling you, this is what happened."

Friedman said, "I don't want you going within a half mile of the Institute, do you hear me?"

Reznick felt frustrated. He nodded. "Sure."

"Your cell phone and gun have been confiscated."

"You kidding me?"

Friedman shook his head. "That was part of the deal."

"Shit."

"Be thankful you don't have to sleep in a cell tonight. We give Wittenden no excuses if they are in some way involved. The Institute is on the eastern outskirts of the town, so you have no reason to go there."

Reznick, Meyerstein, and Friedman returned to the hotel, ate dinner, and enjoyed a quiet drink in the bar afterward. They made small talk. It transpired that Friedman had to catch up on some paperwork.

Reznick waited until Friedman was out of sight. "Am I OK to stretch my legs and get some fresh upstate New York air?"

Meyerstein looked at him as if trying to establish his true motives. "Stretch your legs . . ."

"I need exercise."

Meyerstein sighed. "Do I look like a stupid person, Jon?"

"Quite the contrary."

"Well, don't treat me like some schmuck. I'm looking out for you."

Reznick nodded. "I know you are."

"I have your back. And time and time again I've blocked people within the Bureau who wanted you out on your ass."

"I know that."

"I don't want your thanks. And I don't want your gratitude. Just a bit of respect."

Reznick said nothing.

"I know you're not going to let this go. I know you too well."

Reznick felt conflicted. He knew she was going out on a limb for him. And if he took things further, he would be throwing all her hard work back in her face. But much as he liked, respected, and admired Meyerstein, he couldn't just abandon Jerry. "This isn't easy for me."

"I appreciate that. But I don't think you realize what you're facing."

"Trust me, I do."

"You think you do."

"What does that mean?"

"Friedman has your cell phone and Beretta. What do you think you're going to prove?"

"I believe that my friend is still in there. I also believe they're going to move him later tonight."

"You heard what Friedman said. He's a good man. And a smart man. He told you in no uncertain terms you will be on your own if you go within a mile of that place." Meyerstein leaned forward, her voice now a whisper. "You are in danger, grave danger of being hauled in front of a court and charged with two homicides. That's the reality of what you're facing. This time if you head out there, no one will have your back."

Reznick leaned closer and lowered his voice. "I plan on getting into that facility."

Meyerstein looked away and shook her head. "Your friend is not the only one who's going to be in danger if what you say is true, and the Institute, or people linked with it, have had two innocent people killed. You will be at risk. And for what?"

"Jerry White is a brother. We fought together. And I was the one he ran to when he escaped from there. He was pleading with me. Begging with me not to let him be taken back. But I let him down."

"You never let anyone down. But fine, let's say they're treating him involuntarily. Why not contact a lawyer and go down that route?"

"Listen to me. There isn't enough time. I believe they're trying to control his mind. And take away his ability to think for himself."

Meyerstein said nothing.

"I have to do this."

After an excruciatingly long pause, she nodded. "Your friend the hacker called you."

"What?"

"He called and I answered it. Remember, I have your cell phone."

"Shit."

"He seemed a bit reluctant to talk. But I explained what had happened to you and asked if he had any message to pass on."

Reznick raised his eyebrows.

"He said there are two tunnels underneath. One leads out. And the other leads into the facility."

"I had heard they had been concreted over."

"Definitely not the case. Your friend said he had surveillance images of the tunnel which showed they had clear access into the facility."

"I'd imagine there'd have to be surface access for emergencies. And I'd imagine that it would be concealed."

"You imagine correctly. Just over two miles northwest of the facility there's a manhole shaft, brick and cylindrical in shape, which leads down two hundred feet underground. The steel access covering is in a field."

Meyerstein showed him a message on his cell phone. It gave coordinates, latitude and longitude. "You got that?"

Reznick nodded.

"You got your wallet?"

"Sure."

"That means you can buy any provisions you think you might need."

Reznick looked at her for what seemed like too long.

"I must say, me to you, I don't want you to go. I don't think it's a smart strategy."

"But you're not going to stand in my way."

Meyerstein nodded. "Just remember you'll be on your own."

Thirty-Seven

Gittinger was watching from his window as the headlights of Laurence Cray's SUV pierced the darkening gloom on his approach to the illuminated Wittenden Institute gatehouse.

The guards ran a scanner over everyone's ID and waved the SUV through to the inner security fence. More checks and then the steel electronic gates opened, allowing them in.

Gittinger left his office and knocked on the conference room door. Inside was his CIA contact. The man who was controlling things. He didn't know the man's name. He had asked. But all the man said was "You don't need to know that." He wore a navy suit, white shirt, a mauve tie, and highly polished black shoes. He exuded a sense of power. Menace.

The man, like Gittinger, had to be fluent in Arabic or else he wouldn't have been posted to Bahrain. He had alluded to Gittinger's "cover" job the first time they met. Did he know more about Gittinger's cover story than he was letting on? Gittinger always assumed he did. He believed the man was well aware that his work at the fake charity had appealed for other reasons. The crop of willing patients he'd cultivated was not just for his carnal desires. The end result was several highly compliant individuals who could also be activated. He had groomed them. And he, and he alone, could unleash them.

Gittinger's mind flashed back to the unbearable heat of Bahrain. His cover was as the director of a humanitarian charity that helped traumatized youths. He was given a small office in downtown Manama. His work, he claimed, focused on the sons and daughters of those who had been tortured and killed by the regime.

And so began a stint which would reap a rich harvest.

He would compile reports on the damaged youths he interviewed. He used psychotherapy techniques to help them address their fears and anxieties. He talked to them about the intimate details of their lives and how they had been affected after their father or mother or sister or brother was tortured and killed.

Gittinger began to grow attached to several of the girls, all of whom were suffering flashbacks and panic attacks. He came to be trusted by them. Then he began to hypnotize them.

Putting them under his spell, he began to use trigger words and phrases on them.

He loved watching them relax on his "magic couch." And it wasn't long before he was indulging himself in anything he wanted to do with them. All while they were under his spell.

The CIA spook was deep in conversation and waved him into the conference room.

"Let me know if they move out of there, you understand?" the man said. He ended the call and leaned back in his seat.

Gittinger pulled up a chair and sat down.

"Bob, that was one of Cray's guys. They've staked out the Marriott. Apparently, that's where the Feds are. This whole thing looks like it's going to fuck."

"I hadn't envisioned anything like this taking place."

"Anything like what?"

"The deaths of Hank White and Father McNamara."

The spook sighed. "You know how these things work. This is the sort of fallout we have to deal with if this project is to be kept off the radar and allowed to come to fruition."

Gittinger nodded.

"Jerry White will be moved after midnight," the man said. "No one will know he's gone."

"What about Reznick?"

"He's at the Marriott, according to our sources in the police."

"He worries me."

"You sound like you want out."

The man's steely gaze lingered on him long enough for Gittinger to feel uncomfortable and shift in his seat.

"Once Jerry White is activated and carries out the operation, you are free to go."

Gittinger felt conflicted. Retirement would be easy. But did he want to spend the rest of his life under Dorothy's thumb? He'd expected to pursue this project for at least another year. And he still had work to do if he wanted to see the fruits of his labors. There was, though, the matter of the hundreds of photos the man had. Shots of Gittinger in Southeast Asia. With girls. Young girls. Sometimes boys. He wasn't fussy. But his weakness had allowed them leverage. When they came calling, wanting Gittinger to work for them, he couldn't say no, even if he'd wanted to. He would be ruined. They had that on him. And he knew they would use it if he didn't comply.

"Did you hear what I said, Bob?" the man said. "Once the operation is done, you can go."

"Very well," he said.

"He'll be out of here by two in the morning at the latest. What stage are we at?"

"He'll be woken thirty minutes before he leaves. And then he'll be shipped out to begin final preparations."

Thirty-Eight

The first thing Reznick did was head up to his room, grab his backpack, and leave through the staff entrance at the back of the hotel, baseball cap pulled down low.

He walked a few blocks and caught a cab. He directed the driver to a Home Depot across town. The cab waited as he bought some supplies. A couple knives, a pay-as-you-go cell phone, a shovel, a large backpack, rope, bolt cutters, and some portable steel- and metal-cutting equipment which would allow him to cut and weld, contained within a carrying case. Included was a welding hose, welding goggles, torch, cutting attachment, oxygen regulator, acetylene regulator, and flint striker.

Reznick loaded the gear into a cart and took it to the checkout. "No flashlights?" he asked the kid behind the desk.

"Getting them in tomorrow, apparently."

Reznick paid for it all and was out within a matter of minutes, the cab still waiting. He loaded his booty into the trunk.

"Where to, buddy? You work nearby?"

"Bought a small plot of land outside town. Just getting some new equipment."

The cab driver nodded.

Reznick started up his cell phone and tapped in the GPS location. "So we need to head to McCallum Farm Road."

"You living up there?"

"No. Just a shack until I build myself a house."

"Good for you."

After a ten-minute drive from the outskirts of town, the driver pulled up at an intersection of an asphalt road and field.

"You find your way back?"

"I got this."

Reznick gave the guy the fare and tipped him twenty dollars. "Appreciate your help, bro."

"Take care."

Reznick unloaded the contents from the trunk and watched as the driver turned around and drove off. He checked the bearings on the cell phone. He reckoned he was about a fifteen-minute walk from the location. The map on the cell phone showed a dirt road that led to a dirt path.

Reznick loaded the gear into the backpack and carried the welding bag with his left hand. He felt naked without his Beretta. He had contemplated heading to Walmart to try and buy one. Or even steal one. But he knew that would attract way too much attention.

The cool evening air felt good. It was beginning to revive him.

He loved solitude. Time to think.

He headed off. Down the dirt road toward the woods, glancing occasionally at his cell phone to confirm his position.

Thirty-Nine

The fecund aroma of the forest carried in the breeze and reminded Reznick of home. He felt at one in such surroundings. The outdoors, fresh air, dead leaves, fishing, trees, hunting, woods. He felt sharper after being cooped up in the police HQ. But he was starting to feel the magnitude of what he was about to attempt.

The more he thought about it, the more focused he got.

Meyerstein was right. He was on his own. She thought he was being reckless, crazy, and unfocused. Maybe it was true. It was a high-risk strategy. But bottom line, he couldn't let Jerry be the subject of whatever crazy experiments they were doing.

The deaths of two people and his setup were the final straw. He was involved now. He had become the whipping boy. One of the first things he had been taught in Delta was how to take the fight to the enemy, even if the odds were stacked against you. Sure, he could avoid the fight. But he felt he was at risk if he didn't go after these bastards. He wanted Jerry out. And he was prepared to do whatever it took.

It was the way he was wired. The way he was. His father had been the same. He hadn't cared how high the odds were stacked. He had hunkered down and fought. And clawed his way out of whatever shitstorm he was in, whether in Vietnam or in a back alley in Rockland. Once people knew that about him, they always left him alone. He didn't have to show anyone what he was made of. They knew.

Reznick sensed there were powers at work that he hadn't envisaged from the outset. Would he have done anything differently if he'd known? Almost certainly.

He began to focus on the task at hand. He checked his GPS. He was heading down a path that had veered off north from the road. An old, old trail through fields, the full moon offering much-needed pale light in the darkness.

He stopped for a moment and decided to call the hacker.

A few moments later: "Who's this? Don't recognize your number."

"It's Mr. R."

"Mr. R. You OK, my friend?"

"I've been better. But I believe you talked to a woman from the FBI."

"She was nice."

"She passed on the details you had."

"So glad. Listen, she's not going to try and get a fix on me? Because if she is, I'm out of here."

"You're fine, relax. She was more interested in the info you had. I'm en route to that spot you mentioned."

Reznick kept on walking.

"OK, now that I got your cell phone pinpointed, I can guide you the last mile or so if you want."

"Appreciate that."

"So she gave you the location of the vertical access point?"

"Can't believe it's way out here." Reznick wondered if Jerry was going to be shipped out through the tunnel. But to where and for what purpose? "Look, this all might mean nothing, but it might be more important."

"Jon, sorry to interrupt. You are two hundred and twenty yards away if you move a fraction more north-northwest."

Reznick adjusted his direction and headed forward.

"You're not far now," the hacker said. "Jon, you mind me asking you something? You gonna be OK doing what you're doing?"

"I don't know."

"Man . . . You've got me worried."

"Just focus on your work."

The hacker sighed. "Don't know if this is the right moment to ask for payment."

"Probably not. But you'll get it."

"But what if something happens to you? What then?"

"I'm sure Assistant Director Meyerstein will gladly pick up my tab."

"FBI? Jeez."

"You worried they might be listening in?"

"Not a chance. I've set up the most advanced cell phone protocols and firewalls in Florida. Perhaps in the whole of the United States."

Reznick took the cell phone away from his ear and checked the location. He was within forty yards or so, according to the GPS. He put the phone to his ear. "I'm close."

A sigh down the line. "Thirty-two yards north-northeast."

Reznick adjusted his position and was closing in on the red dot on his cell phone. He walked on for a few more yards.

"Thirteen paces straight ahead and you'll almost be on top of it, Jon."

Reznick walked on as his eyes adjusted to the low light all around, pale moonlight on the red-brown soil.

"A few more yards and . . . stop! You're on top of it."

Reznick took a few more steps. He put down the bag with the welding equipment and took off the backpack. He unzipped the backpack and took out the shovel. He began digging, lifting the earth. He dug down for a foot or so, but nothing.

"Hey, Reznick, you OK?"

Reznick put the cell phone to his ear. "I'll find it."

"What if I need to contact you and there's no reply?"

"Then you call the other number—the FBI have that one. And ask to speak to Martha Meyerstein and no one else. Classified. You're ex-NSA, right?"

"Don't remind me."

"Then you know the drill. Need to know."

"Anything else?"

"I'm going in by myself. Have you tried to gain access to their network?"

"I'm working on it. Probing. But this one will take time."

"Thought you were the best there was."

"I am."

"Then prove it. Ideally, I want the surveillance networks to be remotely disabled. Just leave a frozen image so it appears it's working, if you get me."

"Could be tricky."

"I don't want to hear it could be tricky. I need a break. And I need it done like in five minutes."

"Are you kidding me?"

"Nope."

A sigh down the line. "Why did you not let me know earlier?"

"I didn't want you testing out their computer defenses and inadvertently alerting them ahead of time. Besides, I didn't know if you'd do it."

"Yeah, I'll do it. Not that you left me a lot of choice. And I've just sent you all the schematics, so you've got them on your new phone."

"I owe you one, man."

"Be safe."

Reznick ended the call. A ping sounded on his phone and he checked the message. He opened it up and it showed the design, layout, and infrastructure of the building. Corridors. Control room. Rooms marked "Driving Rooms." Was that where they had Jerry?

He studied the plans for a few minutes, trying to get his bearings. Winding corridors, which led from the tunnels, and the vertical shaft down which he would have to climb. No backup.

Reznick made a mental note of the plans. And then flicked through the different levels of the building. Entry points. Exit points. Ventilations systems. Internal generating facility.

And up top the offices.

Reznick could see one of the tunnels headed off in an odd direction, but it wasn't labeled, as if it wasn't complete.

Reznick put the cell phone back in his pocket.

He began to dig around the original hole. Twenty minutes became thirty. Then he struck metal. He dug the earth away and brushed dirt from the steel access hatch.

Reznick kneeled down and examined the metal. Welded shut, as he suspected it would be.

He quickly assembled the cutting and welding equipment, put on the goggles, and got to work. Ten minutes later, he had taken off the steel lid.

Reznick peered down into the darkness. He pulled on the backpack, knife through his belt, and tied a military knot around the metal step near the top. The steps went all the way down. He looked around the dark field; no one in sight. He stared down again into the total darkness.

Then he began to descend, feeling his way, gripping tight, deeper and deeper down the brick walls, not knowing what lay ahead.

Forty

Meyerstein felt one of the two cell phones she had on her vibrating in her pocket. She checked and saw it was Reznick's, the one he had given up as part of the deal.

"Yeah, who's this?" The hacker.

"We spoke before," Meyerstein said. "You're in Miami, right?"

"I wanted to talk to you. Pass on what I know."

"I'm listening."

"I've lost contact with Reznick's cell phone."

"What cell phone?"

"He got a new one. And we talked."

"OK, I'm listening."

"Just . . . I'm a bit freaked out by all this."

"Listen, relax, no one is coming for you. Besides, it sounds like we wouldn't be able to find you even if we wanted to."

"That's true." A long sigh. "Reznick's signal has dropped. The last location was the GPS location I passed on to you."

"Vertical access shaft, right?"

"Precisely. I lost touch with him three minutes and twenty seconds ago."

"Shit." So he had managed to get into the facility. "What else do you know?"

"I've been looking over the plans again. Thoroughly. The tunnels underneath the Institute head out of Ithaca to an area one mile due west."

"And what's there?"

"That's the problem. On the surface there's nothing. Nothing at all."

Meyerstein waited for the hacker to elaborate.

"I mean there are no buildings on that site. Torn down, leveled, flattened, and turned into farmland. Cattle graze on it."

"You said on the surface. What exactly do you mean?"

"I mean there is nothing to see on the surface, but I've detected data traffic flowing across various networks directly from that area."

"Are you saying there's something underground?"

"I'm saying one hundred percent there's something underground."

"How you can be sure?"

"The routing and transferring of packets of data are occurring directly under this locale. And the origin is an underground tunnel situated at the Wittenden Institute."

Forty-One

Reznick felt firm ground below him. He'd made it. He pulled out the knife from his belt and cut the rope. He took a few moments to get his bearings. He felt his way to a cold brick wall, felt faint vibrations. His mind's eye saw the schematics and plans and he headed left along the tunnel for a couple hundred yards, breathing hard. He stopped for a few moments, the only sound his heart pounding, a low humming noise as if from a generating plant.

He pressed on farther down the tunnel. A pinprick of light up ahead. He headed toward it and spotted a tunnel access door. He peered through the keyhole. He ran his fingers over the lock. Damn. It was a barrel lock.

He took out a knife and tried to pry it open. But it wouldn't give.

Reznick opened up the welding bag. He popped on the goggles, lit up the flint, and set the torch to tearing a hole in the lock. A minute later, he had gained access.

He zipped up the bag of welding equipment and pushed on through the door. Behind it was a cavernous space, dimly lit, like a corridor. He could see. He reckoned he was about two hundred feet underground. But he was very exposed.

His senses were switched on. His eyes were getting used to the dim light.

Reznick edged left again. He checked his cell phone. No signal. He checked the downloaded plans and refreshed exactly where he was. Phone back in his pocket. He headed catlike down the tiled subbasement corridor, adjacent to the tunnels. Deeper and deeper into the facility.

The sound of footsteps behind him. He turned around and faced a security guard with a flashlight shining on him.

"Who the hell are you?" the guard asked. "No one's supposed to be down here."

"Maintenance. Gas leak, apparently."

"No one is allowed down here. Rules are rules."

"Gas leaks need to be fixed, buddy. Can't you smell it?"

The guard sniffed the air. "Nothing."

Reznick took a step forward. "Here, I'll show you my instructions." He reached into his pocket and pulled out the knife and pressed it hard against the man's neck, drawing blood. "Not a fucking word!"

The security guard nodded slowly.

Reznick grabbed the flashlight and shone it in the man's face. "On your knees! Hands on head!"

The guard complied.

"Take your clothes off!"

The guard stripped off down to his boxer shorts.

Reznick pulled on the man's shirt, jacket, and dark trousers and hung the ID badge around his neck, making sure the photo was tucked inside his shirt. Then he tied up the guard with duct tape and wrapped it around his mouth. Then he tied his wrists to his legs with some climbing rope. He took the guard's walkie-talkie and the set of keys in his hand.

The guard was shaking on the ground, clearly in shock.

"Do not move. Do not set off any alarms. Because I'm coming back."

Forty-Two

Reznick headed down the tunnel as his mind flashed details of the layout. He saw a door up ahead with a scanner on it. He swiped the ID bar code across it and it clicked open.

He was carrying the backpack.

Down the corridor to a set of stairs, ignoring the elevator. The lights were brighter here, but he was still deep underground.

Reznick headed up the stairs to level minus two. He saw a sign for X Wing and Driving Rooms.

Up ahead he saw a thickset female nurse with a white uniform on.

"Only nurses have access to this area, sir," she said.

"Sorry, report of a gas leak. Chlorine. You not been told? We have to evacuate this whole section immediately."

The nurse grimaced. "I don't think so. Hold on, what's your name?"

Reznick stepped forward and pressed the knife to the nurse's neck. "Don't worry about that. I want to know where Jerry White is. What driving room?"

The nurse cocked her head. "He's not here."

"What do you mean?"

"He's not here."

"Where was he?"

"Fifty yards away. X Wing. But they've moved him again."

Reznick frog-marched the nurse down a dark corridor. A sign for the reorientation unit. He peered through thick Plexiglas. Inside was a man lying on the ground in virtual darkness having a seizure as a voice boomed out slowly time and time again. *No past, no future, no now.*

"Jesus Christ. Where's Jerry?"

"Jerry was moved three hours ago."

"To where? And don't fucking lie to me."

"He's no longer in the X Wing. He's on the next level up, waiting to be transferred."

"Who's the guy in there now?"

"He's another patient."

"What sort of fucking experiments are you doing on these people?"

"We're doing research."

"Bullshit. This is torture. Don't you understand that?"

The nurse began to shake and weep.

Reznick pressed the knife to her cheek. "Show me where Jerry is!"

She led him out of the ward through sliding doors and up some stairs. Pressed her thumb against a biometric scanner and they entered a soundless, windowless space.

Reznick edged down the huge room covered in Plexiglas. In the middle booth—some sort of glass pod—was Jerry White sitting on a seat, glassy eyed, still, looking drugged out of his brains.

"Open it up."

The nurse pressed her thumb to a pad by the door and it swung open.

Reznick turned to her. "On your knees for five minutes, and not a word."

She fell to her knees and began to pray, moaning and crying.

Reznick edged toward Jerry. "Hey, man, how you keeping?"

Jerry stared ahead, mouth agape.

"Jerry, it's Reznick."

Jerry stared ahead as if in a catatonic state.

Reznick had seen enough. He picked up Jerry, who was painfully light, and draped him over his shoulder. He kicked the nurse. "You, open the doors!"

She got to her feet and opened the automatic doors again. They headed up the stairs from the driving rooms, then out a side door, and then they were in the corridors, the light getting dimmer.

Reznick took the nurse's keys and ID badge.

"On your knees. Now. Count to two thousand nice and slow. And don't do anything dumb."

The nurse did as she was told.

Reznick felt a surge of adrenaline and began to jog down the corridor and past the security guard, who was still on his knees. He headed through the door he'd opened and then he was into the tunnels. It was darker here.

His heart was pounding as he raced down the darkening tunnel. Blood pumped through his body as Jerry moaned.

Reznick slowed down—they were suddenly in pitch darkness. The backpack, Jerry, and the welding bag were weighing him down. He considered ditching the backpack and decided that was a good idea. He kept the welding bag. He felt his way to the vertical access route. Every second his eyes grew a fraction more accustomed to the pitch blackness. But he knew he couldn't hang around.

He sensed he was close to the opening. But how close?

Jerry moaned. "No today. No tomorrow. No now."

Reznick felt a faint chill on his cheek, as if from a breeze. He trudged up the ladder yard by yard, knowing they were close. Really, really close.

"No now," Jerry said.

"Hang in there, Jerry," Reznick said.

Reznick pushed on for another fifteen paces until he spotted the faintest bit of light. He turned and looked up and saw the pinprick of inky-blue sky through the darkness. "We're nearly there, buddy. Gotta just hold on." He tied Jerry to him and wrapped the rope around them multiple times before tying the tightest and most unbreakable knot he could. "You gotta hang on, buddy."

Jerry moaned.

Reznick gripped for the metal rails as they began the vertical climb, Jerry on his back. One step. Two steps. And up. And up. Each step closer. And closer. His heart was pounding, ready to explode. But he was in the zone. He would rather black out than fail.

He would get his friend out of the facility and out of harm's way.

Sweat soaked his skin.

Every step became harder.

Jerry was now a dead weight, not even holding on, only the rope keeping him in place.

Reznick began to see the sky.

He climbed another thirty steel rails and hauled his body into the fresh air, Jerry entangled with him.

"We made it, man," Reznick said, breathing hard.

The unmistakable cold steel of a gun was pressed to his neck. "Don't fucking move," a voice said.

Forty-Three

Reznick felt himself moving in darkness. He sensed people were watching him. The sound of talking. A man's voice. A commanding voice. Getting louder. Then lights.

He opened his eyes and he was strapped to a bed. Leather chest restraint, wrist ties, ankle ties, harsh lights all around, mirrors—no doubt two-way. Was he being watched? Fuck.

He struggled to escape, but there was no give. Nothing at all. He summoned every ounce of strength and tried to burst through the straps. But nothing budged.

A man's voice boomed out of the speakers embedded in the walls and ceiling. "So the drugs have finally worn off, Mr. Reznick. I'm sorry we can't make you more comfortable. But we thought it would be best to take every precaution to ensure you are compliant."

"Fuck you!" Reznick struggled hard against the leather ties.

"It's natural to be afraid, Mr. Reznick. Fear is something to be embraced, at least occasionally. You will have been trained to deal with that. But fear is interesting. It's just there to remind us that we are, indeed, alive."

"I said fuck you!"

"You're quite an intriguing character, Mr. Reznick. You really don't know when you're beaten. I've got to say, and speaking personally, I find

those attributes wholly commendable. You look at this current generation, and it's difficult not to conclude they are exceedingly pampered,
selfish, and bratty. Your actions were quite selfless. I admire that in a
man."

"Who the fuck are you?"

A deep sigh. "Very, very impressive, Mr. Reznick. I mean, accessing
a vertical shaft. I think we'd be very keen to find out what you know."

"Go to fucking hell!"

"We believe there was outside help. The question is, was there
inside help too? I guess we'll find out soon enough, won't we?"

Reznick seethed, chest rising hard against the leather straps. He
wondered what was in store for him.

"We've been working on a variety of drug permutations, and I think
we're close to finding the exact strength. First, we'll put you to sleep
for a little while. And then, while you're out of it, unaware and unconscious, we will administer our special Wittenden Institute formula. All
those bad memories will disappear. And you will become a different
person. Over many days, weeks, and months. But you won't recognize
the old Jon Reznick. Can you imagine how liberating that will be? No
more tough guy stuff in your head. You'll be free."

Reznick closed his eyes.

"So close and yet so far, Mr. Reznick. Quite an effort you put in.
And so close to being successful."

"How many others do you have here?"

"Quite a few. Very damaged, like your friend Jerry. Just think, you'll
be part of the remarkable work we're doing here. Helping us to develop
a potentially memory-free future. How does that sound?"

Reznick smelled ether-like fumes in the air. He sniffed. He felt his
eyes getting heavy. He fought it.

"Just a little blast of chloroform, Mr. Reznick. So you can have a
nice, long sleep."

Forty-Four

Time seemed to expand and contract as Reznick felt the needle in his arm. He was powerless to move. Paralyzed. He wanted to open his mouth and scream. Or move. But he couldn't do a thing.

A psychedelic world opened up in front of his eyes. Colors merged, exploded, and erupted out of tiny pieces of dust, floating in the air. He felt tears on his cheeks as the drug began to take effect.

His mind flashed back to his early days in Iraq. When he was gripped by fear. Moving from house to house. Virtually hallucinating from the heat, exhaustion, hunger, and thirst.

He thought he heard music. Very low. He felt the bass vibrate. The sound of pulsating electronic beats. Like a metronome. Then a man's voice.

In the beginning, there was just us.

In the beginning, there was just us.

In the end, there was just you.

In the end, there was just you.

Reznick gritted his teeth as the beat got louder. His heart was pounding hard. He wanted to scream. But he couldn't. The drug was engulfing him. The sound. The drug. Overwhelming him.

In the beginning, there was just us.

In the beginning, there was just us.

In the end, there was just you.

In the end, there was just you.

Reznick tried to block out the voice, but it was too loud, incessant, monotonous, pervasive.

He was tripping. He felt himself trying to snap the leather straps with his chest muscles. He tried to channel the inner torment and anger and fear of the drug to try and break free. Time and time again he tried. Imploring himself to fight harder. To resist. But the words kept coming.

In the beginning, there was just us.

In the beginning, there was just us.

In the end, there was just you.

In the end, there was just you.

Reznick flashed back to his childhood. He thought he saw his father on the Rockland Breakwater. Casting a fishing line. Showing a young child how to put the bait on the hook.

He felt himself slipping into a watery grave, the beat of the metronome and the voice always with him.

Forty-Five

Meyerstein headed to her hotel room and locked the door. She switched on the TV, turning up the volume so those in the next room couldn't hear. Then she dialed the number of the Miami hacker on Reznick's phone.

"We spoke before," Meyerstein said. "What the hell is going on?"

"I managed to get in behind their firewall. And I managed to disable the surveillance just moments before Reznick went down."

"And now?"

"I think he's still in there."

"Reznick told me a while ago about you. He said you're very good. Ex-NSA."

"Yeah. What are you getting at?"

"What I'm getting at, Mr. Hacker, is that my acquaintance, who you seem to know, is in mortal danger, do you understand?"

"Yes, ma'am."

"Now, if you disabled the system before, I think you can do more. A whole lot more."

"Like what?"

"I want you to bring the system down."

"The whole system. It's a hospital, right?"

"It's a private facility. And if Reznick isn't back, then he was right—it's not legitimate."

"My brother's a veteran. Iraq War. And so is my uncle. Vietnam. Both pretty messed up."

"So are you going to help Jon Reznick or not?"

"This is very, very tricky. I can do this. There are various layers to their security. But it will take time. And I'm looking at their network, and it's all being beefed up as we speak. The intrusion spooked them."

"Damn. Listen to me. I don't know what Reznick has promised you in monetary terms."

"That's a private transaction."

"Well, I'm going to quadruple that fee if you do as I say. I want that system brought down in whatever way you can. You've heard of asymmetric warfare?"

"Sure."

"Well, show me what you've got. And do it real, real quick."

Meyerstein ended the call.

Forty-Six

Reznick came to, red lights flashing on and off and an alarm piercing the air. The brainwashing mantra was still playing. He opened his eyes and saw a nurse behind the Plexiglas talking into a cell phone, anxiety creasing her face.

"Get me out of here! Get me out of here!"

The nurse stared back at him and turned away as she continued to speak into her phone.

"Get me the fuck out of here!"

Reznick began to struggle.

He began twisting his right wrist against the leather restraint to create friction. A half-inch give and he began a movement that looked like he was shaking, perhaps having a convulsion. But he was moving the leather up and down and against the steel bedframe he was strapped to. Minuscule movements. He knew what he was doing. He'd been taught the trick by an American guy who'd been in the French Foreign Legion. The friction was causing his skin to chafe. And chafe. The pain was stinging. Then burning as the skin tore away and he began to bleed. The blood was oozing out, but he continued. The pain was now his friend. The worse the pain, the better for him. He tore and moved and jerked and moved. The leather was tearing into his skin, peeling off a layer. And the blood oozing out made the inside of the leather wetter. And wetter.

He felt a fraction more give in the leather. He twisted and twisted, making his fingers tight together, twisting and jerking. Until he felt a bit more give. Blood was dripping heavily from his wrist onto the tiled floor.

Reznick twisted and turned his wrist again and again and again until finally he whipped out his hand. He quickly leaned over and undid the left wrist restraint. Then both on the feet.

He stood on the bed and punched a hole in the air vent and ripped it out with his bare hands.

Reznick pulled himself up into the space. He was crouched, getting his bearings. Then he began to move slowly through the roof space as the alarms rang out.

Forty-Seven

Reznick crawled on exposed steel beams and wooden joists away from the booth. Suddenly, he could see down into an empty booth below. He edged forward, the noise of the alarms deafening. On and on across the structure, flashing red lights washing over the area like a warning light. Danger signal, perhaps.

He crawled on and on until he saw through a crack in a vent. He noticed there was a corridor below.

Reznick kicked it viciously and it gave way, crashing down onto the linoleum floor below. He jumped down, blood dripping from his wrist. He didn't have time to wrap it up.

He headed down a corridor. Then he saw a sign for the driving rooms.

Reznick stopped outside the first driving room and spied Jerry White inside, huddled on the floor in the fetal position. Hands covering his ears, crying and screeching. Reznick banged on the window. He tried the door. But it was shut tight, a bar code scanner and keypad on the side.

He grabbed the handle and tried to yank it out of position, hoping to rip open the lock.

"Fuck!"

Reznick began to bang on the Plexiglas window again and again. "Jerry! Jerry!" He banged repeatedly with the palms of his hands, blood smearing from his wrist on the reinforced plastic.

Out of the corner of his eye, he saw something move.

Reznick spun around and caught sight of the hulking figure of Laurence Cray and two security guards with batons. Behind them was a male nurse with a syringe, obviously hoping to drug him.

He went for the first guard, who threw a clumsy hook with his nightstick as Reznick feinted to the left. Then he grabbed the weapon and smashed it into the kid's face, breaking his jaw. The kid collapsed to the ground, motionless.

Reznick swung the nightstick low and cracked the other security guard's left shin. He screamed in pain. Reznick smashed the baton hard into the guard's balls, and he crumpled in a heap, dropping the baton, which Reznick kicked behind him.

"Only you and me, Laurence," he said.

Cray was flushed red with fury. "Bitten off more than you can chew tonight, tough guy."

"The way I like it. Are you gonna do this, or are you gonna keep up the hard man persona?"

The comments did their job.

Cray lunged forward, and Reznick stepped back and swung the baton hard at his thick skull, cracking bone and drawing blood. He fell like a tall oak, blood spilling from his wound, before he blacked out on the floor.

The male nurse turned and fled as Reznick ripped Cray's ID badge from around his neck. He extricated a pile of keys from his belt and put them in his back pocket.

Reznick swiped the card over the scanner outside Jerry's room, and the door clicked open. He reached in and pulled the screaming Jerry out, holding him tight. "It's OK, man, it's Jon. Jon Reznick."

Jerry was shaking, tears in his eyes. "Jon?"

"Yeah, it's me, buddy. I'm getting you out of here."

"Me?"

"Yeah, you, Jerry."

Reznick could see Jerry was virtually catatonic, staring up at him openmouthed.

"Jon?"

"It's me."

"Hold me."

Reznick hugged his friend tight. He felt Jerry sobbing and crying hard. He was holding on as if his life depended on it. "Jerry, we gotta get out of here." He looked at Jerry's face. "We need to get out of here. Now."

Jerry stared, eyes blank.

"Shit, don't worry. I got this."

Reznick propped his friend up against a corridor wall as he picked up a baton and took away the IDs for the other two guards. He also confiscated a walkie-talkie from Cray, still out of it. In a waistband pouch, he found the man's cell phone, which he stuffed in his pocket.

He took a Zippo lighter from one guard's top pocket.

He flared it up against a smoke detector, and more alarms started going off.

He saw an antibacterial hand wash outside a room and kicked it over. He ripped out some paper towels nearby and placed them on the ground, squirting antibacterial alcohol gel onto them. Then he set them on fire. He pulled out the bed from Jerry's room and used it to block the corridor. He set that on fire. It caught easily.

Reznick hoisted Jerry and slung him over his shoulder and they headed down the corridor. He saw a sign for the office of Director of Security Cray. He kicked open the door, no easy matter with Jerry weighing him down. Inside, he looked around. He saw a safe with a scanner attached. He leaned down and swiped Cray's ID and it opened.

Inside was a Glock with a magazine already in it. He took it and pulled back the slide.

He headed out into the corridor as the noise became deafening again, Jerry moaning and crying on his back. Up ahead, Reznick spotted a sign for parking bay deliveries.

He headed through a door and down some stairs then kicked open a fire escape door, and they found themselves outside.

He saw an ambulance, a driver inside.

Reznick pointed the gun at him. "Out now! Disappear!"

The guy jumped out the other side and ran.

Reznick loaded Jerry into the passenger seat, started up the engine, and hit the gas and accelerated hard. He sped through a chain-link inner gate and then plowed through a metal barrier, the windshield smashing as he motored through, glass raining down on his face and arms.

He ignored the cuts and drove. Jerry whimpered, curled on the passenger-side floor.

"What's happening, Jon?"

Up ahead, a guard pulled out a gun, but Reznick had already pulled his, and he shot the guy in the leg. The guard went down screaming, clutching his thigh.

Reznick drove on hard, head down. A bullet whizzed through the back window, narrowly missing Jerry's shoulder, lodging in the back of the seat.

Reznick powered through another gate, and then they were out and onto asphalt. He drove hard, not stopping for anything or anyone.

Forty-Eight

Reznick dumped the ambulance in the parking lot of a motel on the outskirts of Ithaca and hot-wired a Jeep. He put Jerry in the back and drove into the night. He called the hacker from Cray's phone.

"Hey, you still awake in Miami?" Reznick said.

"Yo, Mr. R, how the hell are you?"

"I've felt better. But I'm out. For now. Listen, need a favor again. The cell phone I'm calling from, can you download the contents?"

"Why?"

"Just can you do it?"

"Sure."

"I'm going to dump this cell phone soon, since I'm sure they'll be tracking me."

"You're a dangerous man to know, Mr. R."

"This ain't over. I just want you to see if there's anything incriminating or interesting in the calls on this device."

"It's uploading as we speak. Three seconds. And. We. Are. Done."

"So that's safe with you?"

"One hundred percent. Keep it like that. And let the assistant director know if you come up with anything."

"You on the run?"

"Damn right I am."

"Take care, man."

The line went dead.

Reznick called his cell phone and Meyerstein answered.

"Who's this?"

"It's Reznick."

"You kidding me? I feared the worst."

"Listen to me, I have Jerry."

Meyerstein took a few moments for that to sink in. "Jon, you've crossed a line now."

"Maybe I have. But I'm willing to hand myself in."

"Don't play games, Jon."

"Listen to me, Martha, that place is not a psychiatric hospital. They're experimenting on vulnerable, damaged people. And they started on me."

"What?"

"That's what happened. I can't begin to describe the place. Deeply unsettling. And that comes from someone who was in Fallujah, for Christ's sake."

"What's the deal?"

"I will deliver Jerry into your hands, and you get Friedman to get a court order to allow an FBI psychiatrist to take him to a safe house to be looked after."

"This is more than irregular, Jon. This is criminal."

"Trust me, I've just witnessed something beyond criminal. If this got out, the American people would burn the place to the ground. Scientific experiments. You wouldn't treat lab rats like that."

"Jon, that may be . . . but we have no evidence with which to bring an investigation."

"I'm going to give you a heads-up. Jerry was down at a veterans' hospital in Florida. I'm guessing there's a patient broker there who gets kickbacks for recommending or facilitating the transfer of patients to the Wittenden Institute."

"You have no evidence of that."

"What if you had a tip-off from a person, a concerned friend of someone who had been inside, who said he believed there was a Medicare fraud scheme? The FBI investigate that kind of thing, don't they?"

Meyerstein said nothing.

"Can you do this?"

"I can do this. The question is, should I do this?"

"All I care about is getting Jerry into safe hands. As for me, I'll hand myself in, with Friedman in tow, to the Ithaca cops."

Meyerstein sighed. "Jon, this is crazy. I mean—"

"Can you speak with Friedman?!"

"Leave it to me. I'll call you back in ten minutes."

"Make it five."

Reznick drove along country roads. Forest everywhere. He found a good place to stop and put Cray's keys in the glove compartment. He got Jerry out of the car and laid him beside the road on some leaves and pushed the car over the edge and down a steep incline into the forest below. He heard it crashing and disappearing in the darkness. He picked Jerry up and slung him over his shoulder. He had knives in his belt, the Glock in his waistband. And a Zippo lighter.

He crossed the road and headed into the woods.

Forty-Nine

Reznick headed deeper and deeper into the woods, the smell of leaves and bark and earth heavy in the damp air. Eventually, satisfied he was well away from trails or dirt tracks, he made a makeshift shelter. He began the process of cutting off branches and twigs. Then he covered the frame with leaves and foliage and branches.

He covered Jerry, who was now shaking, with his jacket.

His cell phone rang.

"Jon," Meyerstein said, "Friedman said no deal."

"What?"

"Friedman has, as I suspected, pulled the plug on that."

"Then we got a problem."

"Jon, don't be like that."

"Jerry is not going back in there. Now, I have answered your call and the FBI's calls on several occasions. I don't ask for much. But I'm calling in a favor now."

"Jon, you're all out of favors."

"I'm asking you to sort this out and do whatever you have to, to get Friedman or the Director to make this happen."

"Or what?"

"Just do it."

"Jon, you're out of control."

"Maybe I am. Get onto Friedman again. Get onto the Director. Have you spoken to O'Donoghue?"

"I don't appreciate your tone. Besides, I'm hearing that not only has Jerry been taken from the hospital but that there were assaults on staff and that you stole a handgun and keys belonging to Cray."

"The keys are in the glove compartment of a Jeep just off Stone Quarry Road, down a ravine, in a deep bit of forest. As for the rest? It's all true. But what's also true is that I don't appreciate being drugged against my will and then strapped down to listen to crazy voices on a loop playing loudly in the background. That happened. Now, I'm asking you once again to go back to Friedman and the Director and also the hacker, get back to the forensics investigating the death of Jerry's dad and Father McNamara. Also, Jerry White was at a hospital down in Florida like I said before. Was there any illegality with a patient broker?"

Meyerstein sighed. "Friedman has made his position clear. We have also been informed by a national security expert who is close to the CIA that we would be well advised to stay clear of this."

"What the hell does that mean?"

"It means this is very sensitive. And that this is not our jurisdiction."

"Make it your jurisdiction."

"You're impossible, Jon, do you know that?"

The line went dead.

Fifty

Gittinger was ensconced in his office, the shock of the escape still raw, when his cell phone rang. He had a mission. And the escape put everything in jeopardy. He was conflicted. He wanted Jerry to be caught and brought back again, alive. But he knew that perhaps more important was ensuring that the workings of the Wittenden Institute remained secret. They could find another Jerry.

"Bob, it's Laurence."

The voice of his director of security filled him with dread. "Talk to me . . . This better be good."

"We've hired a private chopper and have our people spread out all over the area where they headed into the woods."

Gittinger closed his eyes, wishing for the whole mess to be a terrible dream. "I don't want to know about their movements. I want to know where they are now. At this goddamn moment. Do you understand?"

"We have deployed military-grade tracking technology. We will find them."

"I can't stress how vital it is that we not only find them but we neutralize them. Are you clear on this?"

"You don't have to tell me."

"We handle things in-house. That's the way we work. We don't want this whole thing getting into the hands of the Feds or the US Marshals."

Cray sighed heavily.

"So where do we believe they're headed? What are your thoughts?"

"Jerry White won't be driving this. It's clearly Reznick. And I would bet he wants to keep them on the move. But keep out of sight."

"Which would mean?"

"Getting some wheels."

"You need to get a fix on them. And take them out. No questions asked. No more fuck-ups. I want them brought back in body bags."

The line went dead.

Fifty-One

Dawn was breaking, a dark-orange glow peeking over the horizon. Reznick had been watching the road for several minutes, while Jerry lay semicatatonic, curled in a ball. He saw an eighteen-wheeler truck slowly headed out of town. He jumped out, waving his arms, and the truck screeched to a halt.

The driver wound down his window. "Hey, what the fuck? You're gonna get killed, buddy."

Reznick said, "Me and my friend—he's a veteran—need a ride out of town. Can you help us? Yes or no. There'll be no trouble. Just broke, that's all."

The driver shrugged. "I'm going to Burlington, Vermont."

The mention of Vermont triggered Reznick. He thought of his daughter, Lauren, on the Bennington campus. He imagined her wrapped up, chatting with friends, at the foot of the Green Mountains. He had never visited her. He wondered why that was. Did he feel he didn't belong there? He missed her.

His mind flashed back to a time when he had almost lost her forever. The time Lauren was kidnapped. It was a reprisal for not killing a government scientist. He blamed himself. Hated himself. He remembered the depths of dark despair and putrid anger which had boiled inside him. His worst fears of his shadowy world encroaching on his family were being realized. But somehow he had managed to track her down. She had been drugged and kept hostage on a yacht off Key West owned by a Haitian diplomat. He had fought to keep her alive after she had been injected with opiates to keep her quiet. He remembered the moments she had finally come around in the hospital as he had sat watching over her. The hours of not knowing if she would live or die. The agonizing wait to see that she would be OK.

"Where's your friend?"

The question snapped Reznick out of his reverie. "He's just in the woods. We need to get to a friend's house upstate."

"Sure. Get your friend."

Reznick ran back into the woods and picked up Jerry and slung him over his shoulder. He lifted Jerry into the driver's cabin and drew the curtain. "Down on our luck."

The trucker, who was wearing an *I Am a Deplorable* T-shirt, grinned. "So you say you guys are veterans?"

"Yeah, pretty much. You?"

"Vietnam."

"Father was there. Marines."

"Yeah?" the trucker said. "I was a grunt. Infantry. What about you?"

"Bit of this, bit of that. Most recently Delta."

The trucker whistled. "Fuck."

"Yeah."

"Friend of mine once tried to get in. Nearly killed him."

"He make it?"

The trucker shook his head. "Tore his calf muscle on some crazy marathon run up some mountain."

Reznick nodded. "It's a tough gig."

"What about your friend? He doesn't look in a good way."

"He's got some issues. But we're going to get him some help."

"You guys look like you haven't eaten in days."

Reznick smiled. "That bad, huh? Been living rough. Might head down to Florida later in the year."

Just outside Syracuse, Hank Williams was playing on the radio. "Listen," the trucker said, yawning. "I'm going to be stopping off at a diner for breakfast soon. You wanna join me?"

"We have no money, man."

"What's your name?"

"Jon. My friend is Jerry."

"Jon, I'm Steve. I know how it is. When I got back from Vietnam, my wife left me. Took the kids. Lost my job. Drinking. And all that shit. So I know what it's like."

"My friend needs some food and water more than me."

"You both need feeding. And it's on me."

The huge trucker was as good as his word. He treated them to a massive breakfast of pancakes smothered in maple syrup, steak sandwiches, glasses of Coke, coffee, whatever they wanted. Jerry came to but didn't say a word as he ate.

"Doesn't say a whole lot, your friend," Steve said.

"We're gonna get him some help. I know he'll be very grateful for your generosity."

"Forget it. That's what we do. We stick together, right?"

Reznick nodded and gulped some coffee. "So you're headed to Vermont?"

"Yeah."

Reznick was itching to put as much distance between them and Ithaca as possible.

"But I'm going to book into a motel. And then head off early afternoon. If you want to wait until then, fine, but I need to have a few hours. Been driving all night and all evening."

Steve paid the bill in full.

Reznick knew that two strangers in small towns in upstate New York would stick out like a sore thumb. He needed to get Jerry out of sight. The cops would be looking for the two of them, and it was only a matter of time before they found them. He knew what was required. He took off his Tag Heuer watch and handed it to the trucker. "This is worth around fifteen hundred dollars at least, Steve."

"I'm not taking your watch."

"You'll take it." Reznick thrust it into the man's pocket. "This is a small thank-you. But in return I'm going to ask for another favor. I noticed your CB radio. You got any trucker friends that'll pick us up?"

The trucker pulled out a twenty-dollar bill. "Get back in the diner, and I'll have someone pick you up in no time."

"I want sound people."

"I know just the guy. He lives not far from here. Don't know if he's on the road. But I'll check."

Reznick and Jerry went back into the diner and ordered another couple of coffees. A couple of minutes later, Steve walked in.

"He's on his way. Just woke him up, but he's a good friend of mine. He'll take you wherever you want to go."

Fifteen minutes later, Steve's friend turned up driving a pickup. He hugged his friend.

"Look after these guys," Steve said before he left.

Fifty-Two

The guy driving the pickup was a tattooed bear of a man. "Before you ask," he said, "yeah, you can trust me. And if you're a veteran, I'm gonna try to help you out."

"Appreciate that."

The miles rolled by as they headed east.

Reznick popped a Dexedrine and stayed awake as Jerry slept. "I need to make a call," he said. "Any chance of borrowing your cell?"

The man grinned. "No problem, bro." He reached into his jacket and handed Reznick the cell phone.

Reznick considered whether to call Meyerstein on his cell, which she still had, or on her own cell phone. He thought better of it when he considered there was someone who would not be having his calls monitored. Instead he dialed the number for the shadowy Miami hacker. It rang for nearly a minute, but no answer. He ended the call.

"No answer, bro?"

Reznick handed the phone back.

"Just keep it," he said. "I've got two more."

"You kidding me?"

"Keep it."

Reznick put the cell phone in his pocket.

"I don't need to know what the hell you guys are all about. You wanted?"

"Perhaps, yeah."

"You in the Marines?"

"Yeah. And then Delta."

The guy grinned. "Now those are some mean mothers, let me tell you."

"We have our moments. Look, you're probably wondering what the hell we've done. I'm gonna level with you. My buddy was in a psychiatric hospital. And I sprung him. Long story short, he didn't want to be there. And he's only dangerous to himself."

"Don't have to explain, man."

"Just so you know. He escaped and headed to my house. But they brought him back. He needed to be out of there."

"Best man at my wedding, he was in the Marines. Tough fuck. He was in and out of various mental hospitals. So I got a bit of an idea what you're talking about."

The cell phone rang and Reznick answered.

"Who's this?" The husky voice of the Miami hacker.

"You sleep in or something?"

"Late night. Not used to getting woken at this time of day."

"Did you find out anything from the cell phone data you downloaded?"

"Have you heard of the word *trilateration*?"

"I've heard of triangulation."

"Right. That has to do with GPS angles. Trilateration pinpoints the exact distance using satellites."

"And?"

"I've pinpointed the exact route the guy who owned the cell phone took over the last seven days, if that's of interest."

"Can you do me a favor? Send that information and route to the assistant director."

"Not a problem. Do you want me to pass on any message?"

"Tell her I'll be in touch."

Reznick ended the call.

"Assistant director?" the pickup guy said. "Trilateration? What the hell are you guys up to?"

"It's a long story, my friend."

"You a fugitive?"

"I think I've said enough."

The guy grinned. His CB radio crackled to life and he picked up the radio receiver. "Yeah, ten-four, good buddy. What've we got?"

A voice came over the radio. "Hey, Jazz, I think you might be looking at a roadblock ten miles up the road from you know where."

"Copy that. Eyes and ears confirmed this?"

"Sister Girl and her man both got stopped. Don't know what it's about."

"Appreciate that, good buddy. Over and out."

The guy put down the receiver. "You really are a fugitive from justice, my friend," he said, before bursting out laughing.

"You wanna let us out now? Don't want you being hauled in too."

"You need to get you and your friend away off the highway."

Reznick wondered if it was the cops or the US Marshals blocking the road. He knew that if the US Marshals were involved, choppers would not be far behind. But knowing what he knew about the Institute—and who was behind it—he wondered if they would keep the escape strictly on a need-to-know basis.

He considered his options for a few moments. If he headed out by himself with Jerry, they would be caught. If he was alone, he had a chance. He could head up to the hills. But his first priority was not only getting Jerry help but getting him to safety.

If they hid out, it was the surest thing that Jerry would either be caught or not survive. The worst possible outcome was that he'd be taken back. Reznick couldn't have that.

He began to run the options in his head. He needed people who would help him. He'd been lucky so far. But that luck would run out.

He saw a sign for Johnstown. "Where's the nearest small airport? Where small planes could land?"

"Fulton County Airport."

"How far is that?"

"Six miles from here."

"Can you head there?"

"You sure?"

"Yeah."

The driver did a U-turn and took a side road before they got on a minor road to Johnstown. "This'll take us away from the roadblock."

Reznick picked up the cell phone and called the number of Don Bleeker, a former Marine and now an aerial photography expert. "Hey, Don, I need a favor. I'm not going to sugarcoat it. But it's either a yes or no answer I'm looking for. And it's an urgent job."

"You mind explaining?"

"Long story. I need a ride out of Fulton County Airport for a friend of mine."

"When?"

"Couple of hours."

"Man, you're crazy."

Reznick explained the background.

"So he's PTSD?"

"Big-time."

"And then where do I take him?"

"You remember Tom McNulty?"

"Yeah, good guy."

"Take him to Tom. I'm going to sort it out with him. But no mention of this on the radio."

"You think there might be some heat?"

"Always a possibility."

"And this guy . . . he's not going to try and take down the plane, is he?"

"The guy's a mess. He seems to sleep most of the time. Put a blanket over him, give him a coffee, some chocolate. And then take him over to Tom."

"You owe me a bottle of Scotch for this, buddy."

"I'll buy you a case. And that's a promise."

"That, my friend, is a deal."

"Not a word to anyone."

"I know the way it works, Jon."

"One final favor. We're about the same size. Can you bring a North Face fleece jacket, Cat boots?"

"I'm a size nine."

"Perfect. And thick wool socks and a wool hat."

"You're not asking for much."

"You have no idea what sort of week I'm having."

"Take care, Jon. See you in a little while."

Reznick ended the call before he contacted McNulty. "Tom, serious favor."

There was silence down the line before Tom spoke. "Jon, what the hell? That's twice I've heard from you in the last few days. You in trouble?"

"Very well might be. Remember the guy I told you about, Jerry White, that escaped and headed over to my house?"

"Yeah . . . sure."

"I broke him out."

Silence.

"That hospital is not an ordinary psychiatric hospital. Trust me, Tom, it's a sham. It's a hellhole. I know, I experienced it."

"Are you kidding me?"

"No. So I need a serious favor. And I need it today."

McNulty hesitated. "I don't know, man."

"It's a big ask, I know. But I need an answer now."

"What do you want?"

"I want you to take care of Jerry White for a little while."

"Jon, that's illegal. Almost certainly. And I could lose my license."

"I'm begging you. Tom, this guy needs help. He was being tortured, swear to God. Crazy stuff."

McNulty was silent.

"Tom, don't leave me hanging here."

"Jon, this is difficult for me. You're putting me in a tough situation."

"I know I am. And I wish I wasn't. But it is what it is. Look, I'm trying to protect my friend from psychological torture. That's what he was undergoing. I saw it with my own eyes, Tom. That place is so fucked up it's not real. And I am literally begging you, and I know what I'm asking puts you in a difficult position, but I've got a friend of yours, Don Bleeker, picking up Jerry from Fulton County Airport, in New York. And he will take him back to Maine in that Cessna of his."

"Don's doing that?"

"He is."

A long silence opened up down the line. "What do I have to do?"

"Care for him. Shelter him. Nurse him."

"I can't do it as an open-ended commitment."

"I understand."

A long sigh. "I will look after him for forty-eight hours. Not a minute longer. Take it or leave it."

"I'll take it. And, Tom?"

"Yeah."

"Thanks, bro."

Fifty-Three

The disappearance of Jon Reznick from the hotel sparked angry exchanges between Meyerstein and the Ithaca police chief. It was claimed she had been duped. She had to listen to accusations of incompetence and "losing perspective." But also to accusations that she had colluded with Reznick.

The FBI's legal counsel, Robert Friedman, tried to keep a lid on things for nearly two hours.

Meyerstein realized she might come to regret her decision to not stand in Reznick's way. She knew the police were right to be angry. By allowing Reznick to walk out of the hotel and take matters into his own hands, she was culpable. But she sensed that, while Reznick's actions had been illegal, rash, and downright dangerous, deep down there was so much more to the story than that.

FBI forensics were still scouring the murder scenes but had yet to come back with anything concrete. And to compound matters, Meyerstein had also had calls from the hacker in Miami who lived "off the grid." Not exactly standard behavior for an assistant director of the FBI to engage with a cybercriminal. Reznick's crossing of boundaries was starting to affect her own behavior and decision-making.

"Gentlemen," she said, "we've been to-ing and fro-ing for quite a while. Can we start on areas where we are in agreement? Namely, that we must find Jon Reznick and bring Jerry White back into psychiatric care."

Her magnanimous tone only seemed to inflame their annoyance and fury at the turn of events.

Meyerstein wasn't used to being on the receiving end of such a torrent of abuse. She was more accustomed to the measured tones in the FBI or the intelligence world as a whole. While there could be sharp differences of opinions, usually they were expressed in less industrial language.

The more she thought about it, the more she wondered if this might not be the final black mark against Reznick's name. Reznick was a wild card. And this proved it. It seemed the chance to make him a formal part of the FBI had come and gone.

Meyerstein's cell phone rang. "Excuse me, gentlemen," she said. "Have to take this."

A few nods and murmurs from those around the table.

Meyerstein went outside into a corridor. She recognized the number of one of the FBI's forensic experts, Special Agent Dennis Fox. "What is it, Dennis?"

"Ma'am, sorry to bother you."

"You still at the priest's house?"

"We're still conducting forensic operations, but I wanted to give you a heads-up."

"What kind of heads-up?"

"Cops missed it or never thought of it. Father McNamara was, according to a neighbor down the street, concerned about his house being burgled."

"I'm listening."

"He had cameras around his house. Including one hidden in the light outside the house."

"You kidding me?"

"Gets better. He also had a camera inside the smoke detector outside the upstairs bathroom, which is beside his study."

"Have we found anything so far?"

"Just started looking over it in the back of the incident truck. But the footage is high quality."

"Let me know as soon as you get something."

Fifty-Four

The Cessna was waiting for them at Fulton Country Airport.

Reznick escorted Jerry on board, strapped him in, and attempted to reassure him that everything was alright. Don Bleeker tried to make him feel comfortable, but Jerry just look frightened.

"Tom's waiting for him," Reznick said.

Bleeker handed him a huge rucksack. "It's got clothes, some snacks, water, a new cell phone, and a knife just in case."

"Phenomenal, Don."

Bleeker shut the plane's door and gave the thumbs-up out of the window as Reznick took the huge backpack, headed into the terminal, and changed in a bathroom. The rest of the stuff was in the bag.

Reznick headed out to the parking lot and saw the pickup truck was still waiting.

"Just wanted to make sure you got what you needed."

Reznick shook the man's hand. "My friend, no idea who you are, but I'd appreciate if you could keep all this under wraps. It's complicated."

"No sweat to me, man. You want a lift?"

"I've got this from here. Just get yourself back to whatever you were doing."

The driver grinned. "You take care." He pulled away and headed south.

Reznick pulled up the collar of the fleece, adjusted the straps on the backpack, and strode away from the town. In the flinty upstate sky, the Cessna climbed higher and banked off to the left, before changing course to head back to Maine, eventually disappearing through the clouds. Reznick was grateful to his old friend. And with the clothes he'd brought, Reznick looked like any other hiker or backpacker.

A few minutes later, he tried to thumb a lift. Within a few minutes he was hitchhiking with a guy driving an RV. The man said he was driving across America re-creating a journey he had taken way back in the 1970s with his wife and kids. But this time he was doing it alone.

The RV was perfect cover, although the progress was pretty slow. They made small talk. But it soon became clear they were headed back along the route Reznick had already taken. He asked to be dropped off near a forest just outside Skaneateles. He got onto a trail leading into the woods. He walked for about six or seven miles, deeper and deeper into the trees, way off the trail. He decided to set up camp about fifty yards from a clearing. He made a makeshift shelter with branches and leaves, concealed with only a tiny gap so he could observe if need be.

He tucked into some sandwiches and a couple of chocolate bars, washing them down with a bottle of water.

The sun had begun to set, and he curled up in his thick coat under the shelter. The chill evening air was fresh and clean, scented by pine and the ancient woods.

Reznick felt calm for the first time in days. He knew Jerry was in good hands. He felt himself drifting off and sinking into darkness.

Fifty-Five

The sound of voices roused Reznick from his sleep. He took a moment to get his bearings. He peered through the gap in his shelter. A couple hundred yards away, Reznick could just make out the silhouettes of what looked like two men, both carrying long guns, walking through the woods toward him.

Reznick wondered what the odds were of some random hunters walking so close to him in the middle of a huge, dense forest. He took a few more moments to adjust his sight to the near-total darkness. He had a choice to make.

It could be two perfectly innocent guys out for a nighttime shoot. If so, he needed to get out of their path. Maybe they were shooting deer. But maybe they weren't.

Even if they were, they might inform the local cops that they had found a guy sleeping rough in the woods. And they would find out if there were any missing people or wanted people in the county, or maybe farther afield in New York State.

Reznick knew hunters. His own father had been a hunter. He had shown him how to survive out in the wild if he had to. How to kill for survival. How to gut rabbits. How to kill deer. What plants you could eat. What plants would kill you.

Reznick observed the men getting closer. Maybe 150 yards. Their voices were low. He knew that if he moved they would be alerted to his presence. He decided to hunker down. He listened to the crunching of the twigs and old branches underfoot, the leaves brushing against their clothes, the low voices.

From where he was crouched in his burrow, shielded by the canopy of branches and leaves and twigs, he could see out. His training had taught him that noise discipline was a vital part of operating in an area like this. But also concealment.

The hunters' presence spooked some birds. They flapped out of the undergrowth, above the trees and out of the woods.

In woods like this, he had sat with his father, laying traps for animals, learning how to live off the land if need be. His father often worried that one day there would be a global crash and money would die. He had drilled into Reznick the ability to look after himself under any circumstances. He had also hunkered down a thousand times in ditches in Iraq. Shanty slums in Mogadishu as gunfire lit up the night sky. Surveillance missions in deserts across the Middle East. He had learned at a young age to endure discomfort. But also to use nature to help him, shield him, protect him, and perhaps even save him.

He sensed the hunters were closing in. He felt himself able to switch off, not feeling the tension of mere mortals. He had the capacity to compartmentalize.

The sound of boots crunching through the woods stopped. He watched them standing stock-still. Looking. The glint of a rifle's metal in the pale moonlight as one of the hunters adjusted his position.

The bulkier of the two kneeled down and examined the ground. He gave a hand signal to his colleague.

Reznick wondered if they were looking for human footprints. Maybe broken branches.

The more he thought about it, the more he wondered if these were really just ordinary hunters. Maybe his location had been compromised by the phone. Maybe the truck driver had alerted the cops. But the way they were behaving indicated they weren't cops. And they weren't US Marshals. Dozens of people, some with night-vision goggles and others with dogs, would have scoured the woods if it was cops, Feds, or Marshals.

The bulkier of the two stood up and looked around. "Jon . . . we know you're out there. We just want to talk." Reznick recognized the voice. It was Wittenden's security chief, Cray, booming out in the darkness of the forest.

Reznick felt his heartbeat hike up a notch.

"We don't mean to do you harm. We just want to help you and your friend Jerry."

Reznick contemplated reaching for the Glock he'd taken from Cray's safe. But it was in his waistband. Any move, the slightest move, and he would be given away. Pulling back the slide. Flicking off the safety.

He wondered why the Feds or US Marshals or cops weren't after him if they had realized he had the cell phone of the pickup driver. Had Steve talked over the CB radio about him and Jerry, alerting eagle-eared security personnel working for Cray? Then again, maybe they were using a Stingray, or a handheld version of the cell phone surveillance device. He'd been taught to use them by an Israeli several years earlier. The device mimicked a wireless carrier cell tower and forced any cell phones in the vicinity to connect to it.

Maybe if Cray had learned that he'd been dropped off at the trail, he could've tracked him down accordingly, just heading out through the trees, hoping the device he was holding would alert them to his position.

"It'll be light in about an hour's time, Jon. And we'll find you then. We'll get the dogs in too. Dogs are great, Jon."

Reznick felt his heart beating hard through his coat.

"We reckon you're within a ninety-yard radius of where I am just now. How does that make you feel? We've got all the time in the world. And here's the thing, Jon. You're already wanted for two murders. So I think trying to take us out would be very foolish. I mean, four deaths? Come on, they'd lock you up forever for that."

Reznick began to work the problem as he had been taught to in Delta. He wondered if he could just get his gun and shoot them. But that would be cold-blooded murder. He could injure them. But that wouldn't look too great either.

"You still there? We know you are."

Reznick's mind began to work out a solution. He was beginning to get a clearer picture of what he needed to do. He looked at the cell phone lying beside him, a Galaxy Note 4. It was an older model. That was good news for his purposes. He prized open the battery and placed it carefully in his jacket pocket. Then he took out the SIM card.

He watched and waited. He wondered if they would notice. If they did, his suspicions would be confirmed. But it would leave them with a decision to make.

Cray's sidekick showed him a handheld device.

Reznick watched and waited, holding his breath.

Cray took a couple steps forward.

"Think the fucker gave us the slip," the sidekick said.

"Not so fast," Cray said.

"We don't have a signal, Laurence. The fucker is out of range. No question."

Cray looked around the woods, as if sensing Reznick was close. "Motherfucker!"

"Let's get back to the others. We'll do a dragnet around the woods. But this time, Laurence, we'll have the dogs ready."

Cray and his friend turned around and walked back the way they had come.

Fifty-Six

Reznick was breathing hard as he slipped deeper into the woods, following a creek farther into the forest. It was still dark in the early-morning gloom as he headed south, away from Skaneateles. Eventually, he was peering out from the forest. A mile or so later, he caught sight of civilization. The creek kept going through surrounding fields. He negotiated through the field to get a better view.

He crouched low and saw a sign for the town of Sempronius.

It looked like a small village.

He got closer.

Reznick saw a silhouetted figure speaking into a cell phone, leaning against an SUV. He decided to approach from the rear flank. He headed back across the field and traversed closer to the village. The man ended the call and lit up a cigarette. The SUV engine was ticking over.

Reznick edged closer, shielded by roadside trees and bushes. He got closer. The rear taillights illuminated the license plate. The same license plate as the vehicle Dr. MacDonald and Cray had arrived in that day in Rockland.

The guy dragged on his cigarette, a talk show playing quietly on the radio.

Reznick moved forward, crouching slightly.

The man's cell phone rang and the guy answered. Reznick wondered if this was one of Cray's goons.

"He's still in there," the guy said, voice low. "He's hiding out. I guarantee it."

Reznick recognized the guy's voice. He was the person who had accompanied Cray through the woods a few hours earlier. He took a few steps, mindful of staying out of the guy's peripheral vision.

"He'll know that it'll soon be daybreak and we'll have him. Right, I'll meet you there in five minutes."

The guy ended the call and put the phone back in his pocket.

Reznick emerged from the darkness and pressed the Glock to the back of the man's head. "Not a fucking word," he whispered.

The guy spun around, but Reznick smashed his fist into the side of the man's neck. The guy fell to his knees in a heap and moaned.

Reznick checked inside the SUV, but it was empty. He hauled the groggy man to his feet. He frisked his waistband and pulled out a Beretta. "Was this a shoot-to-kill operation?"

He said nothing.

Reznick slapped him hard, drawing blood from the man's mouth. "I asked you a question."

"Go fuck yourself."

Reznick grabbed him by the neck and pressed into his carotid artery. "I don't think so." He could see the defiance in the guy's eyes. "Give me your fleece."

The guy winced at the pain being inflicted. "Or what?"

"Or I will put a bullet through your fucking brain."

He took off his Berghaus fleece, and Reznick threw it in the SUV. "Empty your pockets!" Reznick said.

The guy complied, and a couple of twenty-dollar bills spilled out. Reznick picked them up and put them in his pocket.

"I don't think Cray's jurisdiction extends outside the Institute, do you?" Reznick said.

The guy said nothing.

"Why the fuck were you going along with him?"

"Who says I am?"

Reznick slapped him hard again. "Who employs you?"

He groaned as blood trickled from his mouth. "We're freelance grunts. Apart from Cray. He needs help, he gives me a call."

"That's better. Where're the rest of your guys and Cray?"

"They're meeting up in Skaneateles."

"And what are you doing here?"

"Just making sure this southern flank is covered."

Reznick pressed the gun hard to the man's head. "I want you to walk through the field and into the forest. And don't stop."

"Are you kidding me?"

"Listen up. I am not in the mood for any bullshit. Do it or you will fucking die, so help me God."

Reznick shoved the man off the side of the road and down into the field. He kept on walking. Reznick watched for a minute. He took off his heavy coat and put on the fleece. Then he got in the SUV and turned it around and drove due south for Ithaca.

He drove down some back roads for about ten miles, careful not to attract attention, then left the car in a parking garage in the town of Cortland.

Reznick went into a diner and ate a big breakfast. He called the hacker, who picked up straightaway. "Guess who?"

"Are you for real, man? I've been trying to contact you for hours."

"I had to ditch the old phone. This is from one of the crew that were after me."

"Whatever. Listen, the assistant director is desperate to speak to you. She said you needed to call her."

"Why?"

"How the hell should I know? She said it was urgent. Also that you needed to know something."

"I'll give her a call."

"Man, you really owe me."

"Yeah, I know."

"And so does the FBI."

"We'll work something out."

"Make sure you do. Take care."

The line went dead and Reznick keyed in his cell phone number.

"Who's this?" Meyerstein.

"It's Reznick."

"Jon, thank God. I thought something had happened to you. Where the hell have you been? And where is Jerry? This is a serious situation."

"Long story."

"I don't want to hear about long stories. Shit."

"What is it?"

"There's something you need to know. We now know for sure you didn't kill Father McNamara."

"You're telling me something I already know."

"Listen, where are you?"

"Why?"

"I want to talk. Face-to-face."

Reznick said nothing.

"Jon, where have you been?"

"Trying to avoid getting shot by Cray and one of his goons."

"What about Jerry?"

"He's OK."

A long pause. "Well, that's something. Jon, he needs to get help."

"I know that. But not back at the Institute."

"You can't make demands like that."

"I just did. I'm telling you, Martha, he is safe. But he is not going back there. I want Jerry taken into FBI custody and given access to top medical help—psychologists, that kind of thing."

Meyerstein went quiet for a few moments. "Where is he now?"

"He's safe. But I won't be handing him over again so he can go to that Institute."

"Right, this is how it's going to work. Take it or leave it. You know me, and I hope you trust me."

"I trust you one hundred percent."

"That's good. You have my word on this. You hand Jerry over to us, and the FBI will make sure he's looked after."

"The Institute won't like that. And what about Gittinger and his chums in the CIA?"

"I'll deal with that. In the meantime, if you tell us where Jerry is, you have my word he'll get the help he needs. But I also need to speak to you in person. And no, you're not going to be charged with murder."

"You know something, don't you?"

"Where are you?"

Reznick sighed. "Cortland. Do you know it?"

"Can't say I do."

"It's between Syracuse and Binghamton."

"So you could drive to Ithaca from there."

"Sure. Where do you want to meet up?"

"FBI resident office."

Reznick got up from his booth in the diner and left a twenty-dollar bill with the check on the table.

"I'm on my way."

Fifty-Seven

It was a half-hour drive to Ithaca.

Meyerstein and Friedman were waiting when he arrived. A Fed frisked Reznick and took away the Glock, the Beretta, the knife, and the cell phone.

Meyerstein said, "You look terrible."

Friedman frowned. "I'm not going to condone what you've done. Clearly, it is outrageous, illegal, and in violation of numerous laws. That said, there have been developments."

Reznick was handed a black coffee and taken into a small interview room with a large-screen TV. The footage started. It showed what appeared to be a hallway in someone's house. It looked familiar.

Meyerstein said, "This was taken from a hidden camera fitted by Father McNamara in a smoke detector on his upstairs landing. He was worried about break-ins, and he had told friends that his important papers and files on the Wittenden Institute were all in his house."

Reznick nodded.

"That's not all," Meyerstein said. "In the last six months, he had received death threats warning him off investigating anything at the Institute." She pressed a button on the remote control.

The footage rolled in slow motion. Coming into view was a man dressed in black, walking up the stairs. The man was wearing a mask and leather gloves. Eventually, his face was revealed frame by frame.

Meyerstein freeze-framed the image of the masked intruder. "We believe this man killed McNamara."

Reznick said nothing. "Not exactly conclusive who it is."

Meyerstein nodded. "No. But this is. Three minutes and twenty-five seconds later, the lamp illuminating the front of McNamara's house, which also has a camera in it, captured footage of the man leaving."

The footage resumed, showing the furtive figure emerging from the house, mask in his hand. He walked down the garden path to a waiting Buick. The man climbed in the passenger seat and glanced back at the house. Meyerstein freeze-framed the image. "This, we believe, is the man who killed McNamara."

Reznick stared at the image. He couldn't believe what he was seeing. "You're kidding me, right?"

Meyerstein turned and looked at him. "What is that supposed to mean?"

"That guy was the one who was with Cray in the woods, searching for me upstate. That's his Beretta and phone you took off of me. Who is he?"

"Mark Simeone, former US army private. Iraq War veteran. Contractor. Formerly bankrupt."

Reznick shook his head. It was the same guy he had crept up on when he had gone on the run. "Motherfucker. Question is, why did he kill McNamara? On whose orders?"

"The good news is that the FBI are now leading on this."

"What about who killed Hank White?"

"Well, we have Simeone's cell phone. And we will send this to our forensics team to have it looked at."

"And you're hoping this will place him at the scene."

"Very possibly. The Institute is blocking access to the local police, citing national security."

"What?"

"It's officially a classified project they're working on up there."

"So why don't the FBI just storm in?"

Meyerstein smiled. "Nothing would make me happier. But that's not how we do things. We need to consider legalities. Oversight. Jurisdiction. And yes, the CIA if indeed they're involved in some capacity."

"The whole thing stinks. They had me in there. And it's just like McNamara told me. They're experimenting. Trying to drive people crazy. You need to go in there and shut the fucking place down."

"Friedman is working on access. But he's running into some obstacles."

Friedman rubbed his temple, dark shadows under his eyes. "Jon, we've been up front with you. So . . . where's Jerry?"

Reznick said, "I've had a verbal assurance from Martha. And I'm happy with that. But I would like you to give me the same."

Friedman nodded. "My colleagues and I have discussed this matter. He won't be going back there."

"Jerry is with an old friend of mine, Dr. Tom McNulty. Psychologist. He's a good guy."

"Excuse me a moment." Meyerstein made a call and passed on the details. She ended the call and said, "Chopper with two doctors and two nurses along with four special agents will be there in a couple hours."

Reznick called Tom McNulty to let him know. "How's he been?"

"Sleeping most of the time, Jon."

"I owe you, Tom. Above and beyond."

"I'm very concerned about him. He needs 24/7 oversight."

"That's what he's going to get. The Feds will take him off your hands. The main thing is that he gets the help now and doesn't have to go back to Wittenden. And before you ask, you're in the clear."

213

"You're crazy, Jon, do you know that? You probably need some sort of evaluation after this."

"Yeah, no kidding."

McNulty ended the call.

Reznick yawned and began to stretch.

"You really do look like shit, Jon," Meyerstein said.

"Just wanted to check. My hacker friend in Miami—you're not going to hassle him, are you?"

"Quite the contrary. We have a good idea who he is—ex-NSA wunderkind—but apparently no idea where he is."

"So even the FBI and NSA can't track him?"

Meyerstein shook her head. "Hard to believe, right? We think he's masking and rerouting the cell phone signals. The best guess is he's in South Florida. In effect, he's invisible to us."

Reznick smiled, thinking of the brilliant hacker, off the grid, helping his every move. "I owe him some serious money."

Fifty-Eight

Gittinger was summoned into Wittenden's conference room by the CIA spook, who seemed to have moved in full-time, not leaving the building in the last forty-eight hours.

The man was sitting at the head of the highly polished table. "Hard to know where to start," he said.

"I'm well aware of the extent of my failure."

"That's not just your failure. This is a collective failure. We are all responsible. A project that had been progressing so well, and with one outstanding candidate, is now being threatened. We have had our systems hacked. We have had an escape. And then someone breaks in and, quite unbelievably, leaves with our most valuable asset. I mean, whatever way you cut this, Bob, this is a monumental fuck-up. And it's only a matter of time before the Feds are in here."

Gittinger took a few moments to observe the emptiness in the man's eyes. A glassiness. Almost otherworldly.

"The Agency is now asking for the project to be wound up with immediate effect."

Gittinger rubbed his temples. "You can't just pull the plug like that. We have Jerry White to think of."

"That's the least of our problems."

"But if Jerry White is out there not under our oversight, he is a danger."

"I know he is. But we'll deal with that in due course. In the meantime, we have files, thousands of files. Footage we have taken inside the facility over the years. We need to delete everything. And burn every piece of paper in the Institute."

Gittinger felt a deep sense of emptiness. He had envisaged the final chapter of his working life, his swan song, to be finally activating Jerry White for the task all of this was meant to prepare him for. Instead, the project had started to crumble.

"Did you hear what I said, Bob? I want everything burned. Everything. Notebooks. Tapes. Footage of any sort. I want it all incinerated."

Gittinger looked at the man. Didn't the CIA care about the total loss of a black-ops project that had been in the works for so many years? "That's decades of research. Years of vital scientific information. We have begun to understand the trigger points in certain patients. This is valuable work. Work that is in the best interest of the country. That was one of the things you said when you contacted me. You said it was in the American national interest to develop work which would protect us in the future. We can't just end it."

"Yes, we can," the spook said. "I want it all gone. Take it all down to the waste incinerator. And burn it all."

Fifty-Nine

Later that day, Reznick and Meyerstein headed into the FBI's New York field office on the twenty-third floor of the Jacob K. Javits Federal Building, in Foley Square, in downtown Manhattan.

A Fed escorted them down a series of corridors before they were shown into a room with a huge one-way mirror. On the other side was Mark Simeone, sitting alone, smiling and staring. He knew he was being watched and was loving it.

"Interview will begin in fifteen minutes," Meyerstein said as Reznick followed her down a corridor to a conference room. Inside he was introduced to a mustachioed FBI profiler.

Reznick shut the door behind him.

"Sam Tompkins," he said, stepping forward to shake Reznick's hand.

Reznick took a seat beside Meyerstein as Tompkins gave them a briefing. "So, Mark Simeone. What sort of guy are we talking about?"

"This guy is a classic psychopath, in my opinion. Glib, superficial, charming, accommodating, and completely full of himself. He's also very dangerous."

"In what way?" Meyerstein asked.

"He was in Iraq, and when he came back, he tried to strangle his wife. Who is now his former wife."

Reznick listened intently.

"She was rendered unconscious, and he blamed it on alcohol when his wife came to a few minutes later. He was taken away. Put in some clinics. And then escaped and became a panhandler down on the beach in Florida."

Reznick said, "Hang on . . . Florida?"

"Made a tidy living by all accounts, according to his medical file. Told his psychologist he made hundreds of dollars every day on Ocean Drive panhandling around the bars and hotels in South Beach."

"So he was diagnosed as a psychopath and then headed down to Florida?"

"Precisely. He lived rough. He drank. He got into trouble with the law, not surprisingly."

Meyerstein was scribbling notes by now. "So heavy drinking, no address, and acute mental health problems. And trouble with the cops—have I got that right?"

"He got into fights with other homeless people at some hostels he was flopping down in now and again too. Said he was a war hero. And had medals."

"And is he?"

"Complete opposite. Bragging all the time about his exploits with women too. And how he was a great investor."

"Delusions of grandeur?" Meyerstein said.

"Very much. So we've got some interesting character traits. He's got a major problem with women. Cocky, aggressive."

Meyerstein pondered on that for a few moments. "I think I'll take this interview. You think I might trigger him?"

"I think you would. I would caution you that he is an incredibly dangerous, devious individual."

Meyerstein turned to Reznick. "What are your thoughts, Jon? You ran into him twice, right?"

Reznick nodded. "Clearly dangerous. Keep your wits about you around him. He was security inside Wittenden too."

Tompkins said, "What the hell is going on at that place? Is this for real?"

"It's for real. And it's not good. Trust me. I saw it with my own eyes. Experiments. Sensory deprivation."

"A psychopath following orders. Sounds all very familiar." Tompkins smiled. "I think in this case a more nuanced approach might be required."

Reznick shrugged. "How do you mean?"

"What you need is a warm-up act."

Meyerstein said, "Good cop, bad cop?"

"A variation of that, sure."

Tompkins opened up his palms as he got up from his seat and paced the room. It was as if he needed to move to explain the situation better. "We need someone to empathize with him, be impressed. Show admiration. But perhaps more importantly, the interviewer should talk not as an equal but as someone who is beneath the capabilities and intelligence of this guy."

Meyerstein scribbled more notes. "Are we talking about trying to establish a rapport?"

"More than that. Something in common."

Reznick said, "I've got something in common with him. We were both in Iraq."

Tompkins contemplated that for a few moments. "That would work."

Meyerstein held up her hand. "Hang on, we're getting way off base on this. I just wanted to get a handle on where we are with this guy."

Tompkins smiled. "Martha, how long have we known each other?"

"Too long."

"A long, long time. My opinion is that Jon would be a perfect foil. Unless you happen to have any special agents who have served in Iraq."

Meyerstein's facial expression could have turned Tompkins to stone. "No, we don't. We do have exceptionally qualified special agents who are highly skilled in such interviews."

"My opinion? I say Jon does it."

"What? That can't happen. Jon is not authorized to conduct interviews."

Reznick said, "Remember, I signed the paperwork. I am now working for the FBI, am I not?"

Meyerstein said nothing.

Reznick said, "Here's another thing to consider. This guy is crazy, I get that. But who was the one who ordered the killing of Father McNamara? And the probable homicide of Hank White? Who's behind this? Because it sure as shit isn't Simeone."

Tompkins nodded. "Do not let him know that," he said. "Keep that up your sleeve."

"For what purpose?" Meyerstein asked.

"I want you to use that after you toy with him. After Jon has buttered him up, striking up a bond, you will come in and effectively poke him, metaphorically speaking. He wants to be taken seriously. He wants to be admired. You will burst his bubble. And then we'll wait to see what transpires."

Sixty

Reznick was suited up and given new black oxford shoes and a navy tie with his white shirt and entered the interview room alone, carrying two black coffees.

"How you doing?" Reznick said.

Simeone turned and smiled. "I didn't know you were FBI, man. What is this?"

"A long story. You mind if I take a seat?"

Simeone shrugged as if not bothered one way or the other.

"Listen, first I owe you an apology."

"For what?"

"For that altercation. I was out of line. But you know how it gets."

Simeone nodded.

Reznick pulled up a seat and handed him a coffee. "No hard feelings."

"Hey, what happens happens, right? They said you were an assassin. You were friends with Jerry White. That's what they told me."

Reznick shook his head. "Wishful thinking on their part. I was in the army a few years back."

"Yeah? Where?"

"Iraq and other places."

Simeone grinned. "But did you see action?"

"Well, a little. I'm guessing you would've been doing some pretty serious stuff, right?"

"You're damn right serious. Very serious. Covert. All sorts. In and out. Fucking loved Iraq. So what were you thinking, man? Trying to break into Wittenden?"

"I was undercover."

"I get it. I fucking get it."

Reznick gulped some of his coffee. "Look, I'm going to level with you. You're an intelligent guy. I can see that."

Simeone stared at him.

"Here's the thing, Mark. I'm trying to understand how things work with you and the Institute."

"You talking about Cray?"

"Know what I can't understand, Mark?"

"What's that?"

"How a guy like you is taking orders from Laurence Cray. That doesn't make any sense. At least to me."

Simeone sipped some coffee.

"You're clearly smarter than him. So why the hell are you taking orders from him?"

"Good fucking question. Some people get breaks in life, right?"

"Damn straight."

"And that fuck, that fat fuck—who, by the way, is major league incompetent—is telling me do this, do that, go here, go there, you know the shit?"

Reznick nodded. "How's the coffee?"

"It's good. Real good."

"I'm going to be up front. Laurence Cray is being interviewed. In fact, he was interviewed before you. And the thing that doesn't add up for us is why that guy is trying to blame it on the guy on the ground. The guy just doing his job. The grunt."

"Blaming me? For what?"

"The murder of that priest. What was his name again? McNamara?"

Simeone said nothing.

"See, to me it looks like he's pulling the strings, but he's not taking any responsibility for carrying this out. I mean, I just look at that guy and I know, just know, that fuck couldn't have done it. I mean, how could he? He didn't have the chops for it, right?"

"What's he saying?"

"Man, I'm trying to look at things from your point of view. How many times in Iraq did you have to take the heat for someone else's orders?"

"Each and every fucking day."

"Right."

"So is that what he's saying? He's saying I did it?"

"He's saying he knows nothing, absolutely nothing about it."

"Bullshit."

"I said that to my people. They're saying what a cold bastard. You're going to take the fall for it. But even they think it doesn't add up."

"I'm not taking any fall, trust me."

"I said that. A guy like Mark Simeone will not be doing what that guy says or does. Listen, Mark, I want to believe that you haven't got anything to do with this. I really do."

Simeone shrugged but said nothing.

"Someone has to take the fall, and Cray is shooting his mouth off as if he ruled you, and I know that doesn't add up."

Simeone nodded.

"Know the thing about Iraq?" Reznick said. "We always had each other's back. And if you didn't have someone's back, you were in trouble. Everyone was in goddamn trouble. Am I right?"

"If you didn't have a guy's back, you got burned."

"Burned . . . that's it."

"You got burned. You got dead."

Simeone gulped the rest of his coffee.

Reznick got to his feet. "You want another coffee?"

"Appreciate that, bro."

Reznick took Simeone's empty mug and his own. "You need any smokes?"

"I'm OK, man."

Reznick turned and left the room, the door automatically locking behind him.

Sixty-One

Meyerstein watched the whole process through the one-way window.

She could see the arrogance in Simeone. She saw that Simeone had responded to Reznick. He had latched on to their shared bond in Iraq. She knew Tompkins had a valid point about her being the counterpoint. But something was beginning to gnaw at her.

Her experience had shown that striking up a rapport, even with psychopaths, and even if it was surface, was usually better than getting in their face. Getting in their face was the easiest thing in the world. And it worked. Occasionally.

Simeone was different. Complex. Narcissistic. Superficial. Glib. Gave the appearance of being subservient while inside he was probably bursting to scream and shout how he had done it. How he had gotten away with it.

The more she thought about it, the more she wondered if Reznick shouldn't continue doing what he was doing.

A few moments later, Reznick walked in, shutting the door quietly behind him. "This is not going to be easy," he said.

Meyerstein cocked her head and they headed back to the conference room, where Tompkins was going over Simeone's notes. "Here's where I'm at, guys. I think Jon is establishing trust there," she said.

"It might just be an elaborate act," Reznick said.

"Maybe," Meyerstein said. "But I'm not too sure that me going in there smashing his ego to pieces, dismantling his lies, is quite the right play here."

Tompkins looked up from the notes. "The fury in him might play into your hands, but it wouldn't do any harm for Jon to continue doing what he's doing."

Reznick nodded. "He's an arrogant fuck. But yeah . . . why not?"

"I would like you, Jon," Tompkins said, "to go back in, not straight-away, but let him just stew big-time. That will bring the emotions very much to the surface. Then you can return and change the tone. Say you've been handed some fresh information."

"About the footage of him?"

"No. Let's not give that up just yet. Let's start with the vehicle we saw taking him away. Has that been identified?"

"Rental car, hired by Mark Simeone."

"That is interesting. You can go in and let him know you know about that."

Reznick smiled. "You want us to stress Cray was making Simeone the patsy, don't you?"

"Precisely. As it stands, he may or may not take the rap on this. But ideally, we want him to say how this all happened. It's not just him. This is bigger than him. A lot bigger."

Sixty-Two

Reznick let Simeone stew for a full two hours before he went back into the interview room with two fresh cups of black coffee.

"What the hell is going on?" Simeone said, slouching in his chair. "I thought you'd forgotten about me."

Reznick sat down and handed him a coffee. "Relax."

"So what do you want to know now? I thought I told you everything."

"Something's come up. And this has, I'm afraid to say, just been given to us by Cray."

"Cray? What the fuck is he saying?"

Reznick shrugged, allowed some space for Simeone to get worried.

"What he says checks out. And he's acting like the sun shines out of his ass. Real cocky. Squealing like the proverbial pig. Making out you were the dumb guy taking the fall."

Simeone's eyes darkened. "I'm taking no fall. I'm nobody's bitch."

Reznick gulped some of the coffee and stared at Simeone. "Mark, he gave us the details of the car you used to drive to and from McNamara's house."

"Bullshit."

Reznick locked on to Simeone's withering gaze.

"So what sort of car? If you know so much, Mr. Fed. If that fat fuck has told you, what did he say?"

"Gold-colored Mazda. Small car. Cheap to rent."

The color seemed to drain from Simeone's face. "I don't understand."

"Like I said, there are guys like Cray everywhere. Getting people to do their dirty work and escaping the consequences."

"I think it's bullshit what you're saying."

Reznick sighed. "Do you believe in God?"

"What?"

"I said, do you believe in God?"

"What kind of bullshit question is that?"

"Are you a Catholic? Lapsed perhaps."

"Yeah, lapsed, that's me."

"So you believe in God?"

"Yeah, I believe in God."

"So you wouldn't ordinarily harm a man who has dedicated his life to serving God, his church, and the people in his community."

"No, I would not."

Reznick leaned closer. "That's what I can't understand. He's given us the details of the car. And it checked out—you rented the car. That morning. Am I correct?"

Simeone said nothing.

"So what I'm not buying is why a smart guy like you would kill a priest for no reason at all. I don't believe you just woke up and decided to head over there and kill him. But that is exactly what Cray wants us to believe. And he's laughing his nuts off too."

Simeone stared at Reznick, an emptiness in his eyes.

Reznick reached into the pocket of his jacket and showed Simeone the photo of him getting into the gold Mazda. "Cray is telling the truth on that, I have to give him that. That is a gold Mazda and that is you, no question."

Simeone stared at Reznick. "Where did you get that?"

"He thinks he's outsmarted you."

"No one outsmarts me. You understand?"

"It looks like it in this case, Mark. You see, as it stands, you're looking at first-degree murder."

Simeone shrugged.

"You know how we got the photos?"

Simeone just stared back at Reznick.

"We were told by Cray that he had fitted surveillance cameras in and around McNamara's property," Reznick lied. "So what that means is you were walking into a trap. He trapped you."

"Whatever."

"Do you know, one thing Cray isn't aware of is that there's a thing called extreme emotional disturbance? And it's a defense in first-degree murder cases. I know a lot of guys who have suffered over the years. I'm talking psychological damage. You were damaged by Iraq, weren't you, Mark?"

"Yeah, I was."

"Only people who were there would understand. You have trouble sleeping?"

"Yeah. I don't sleep."

"And did you get treatment when you came back?"

Simeone closed his eyes for a moment.

"You OK?"

"When I came back from Iraq, they said I was crazy."

"Who did?"

"Doctors. When I was a patient."

"A patient where?"

"A psychiatric hospital—what do you think?"

"Which one?"

"Does it really fucking matter?"

"It might help us prove you were suffering from an extreme emotional disturbance. And it might mean the murder was committed in those heightened circumstances. You might even—who knows?—get off. Do you think that would piss off Cray?"

Simeone went quiet, as if contemplating making that move.

"Do you think he'll be expecting you to pull that one?"

"I guess not." Simeone gulped the hot coffee in one go.

"I'm looking at you, Mark, and I can tell you just about everything there is to know about you."

"What do you mean?"

"Cray thinks you're his puppet."

"I ain't nobody's puppet. And certainly not that fat bitch's."

"I've shown you we have proof you entered and left McNamara's house. And Cray has given that to us on a plate. A guy who is, as it stands now, the puppet master. He's pulling your strings. And there isn't anything you can do about it."

"That's where you're wrong."

"How?" Reznick leaned back in his seat and shrugged. "You've been played. And I've got to hand it to Cray, he's smarter than I thought. I've got to give him credit for that."

"He's not smart. Him? Gimme a break."

"He's got you by the balls. And he's squeezing. Real hard."

"Nobody's got me by the balls."

"Mark, I'm sorry to break it to you, but he does."

Simeone sat upright, eyes locked on to Reznick's. "Don't say that."

"Did you want to kill the priest?"

"Hell no."

"So who ordered this? And I must warn you, Mark, my colleagues are just desperate to pin this on you. They know you did it. But you and I know it's more complicated than that, don't we?"

Simeone nodded.

"This is not just about you turning up out of the blue in a rental car and killing the priest. You're not that dumb, are you?"

"No, I'm not."

"You can see what Cray has tried to do. And he thinks he'll get away with it. And he's going to get away with it."

"Don't keep saying that!"

"Why will he get away with it? Because he wants you to say nothing. He wants you to maintain the warrior code and say nothing. That's what he's counting on. But you can see that already, can't you?"

Simeone nodded.

"He might think he's smart, but he cannot outsmart someone like you. You can turn the tables on this fuck. And you'll be the one who laughs last, won't you? You're not going to be the patsy on this, are you, Mark?"

"I'm no one's patsy."

"Cray rigged up those cameras, thinking he had you. But he doesn't realize that you have something on him. We don't believe for a minute you just turned up and killed McNamara. We don't think that's what happened. It didn't happen like that, did it, Mark?"

"No."

"You were just, like all good soldiers, following orders, weren't you?"

Simeone nodded.

"He gave the order and you carried it out. Right or wrong?"

"Right."

"You killed McNamara?"

"Right."

"But you didn't order the killing. You were following orders. Right?"

"Right."

"Who ordered McNamara to be killed?"

Simeone was now breathing hard.

"Who was it, Mark? Are you going to take the fall alone?"

"Fuck that."

"So who ordered it?"

Simeone began rocking back and forth.

"Who was it?"

"Laurence Cray."

Reznick let the name sink in. "Can you repeat that so there is no misunderstanding?"

"Laurence Cray gave the order."

"He asked you to kill Father McNamara?"

"Yes, he did."

"What did he tell you? Did he pay you?"

"He paid me two thousand dollars up front."

"What about after?"

"He said he'd give me another ten thousand in cash when the job was done."

"And has he paid that to you?"

"Yes, he has."

"Twelve thousand dollars in total. That's a lot of cash."

Simeone nodded. "I'm broke, man."

"Sure, I understand."

"And he told me to rent a car with that money."

"He told you that?"

"Said it would be safer to just rent a car. Not to use the Institute's vehicles or mine."

"That's interesting. Pretty cute."

"Not cute enough. I want to fuck that fat bastard up bad."

"So, let me be clear, you're saying Laurence Cray gave you two thousand dollars up front, ten thousand dollars after the kill, and told you to rent a car."

"That's exactly right."

"Why did you do it?"

Simeone shrugged. "I needed the money, man. Everyone needs money, right?"

"Did Cray tell you how to kill him?"

"Told me to strangle him—he was quite frail, it wasn't difficult." Simeone began to laugh. "The interesting thing is, the priest put up a real fight. Strong fucker."

"But you were more powerful, obviously."

"Way more powerful. And Cray told me to put him in the bath, slit his wrists and neck, make it look like he'd taken his own life."

Reznick nodded.

Simeone began to laugh uproariously. "I've always hated priests, to be fair. Guess it's just the way I am, right?"

Sixty-Three

Reznick suggested an hour-long break to Simeone and ordered pizza, Coke, and fresh Starbucks coffee for him. He watched in the side room with Meyerstein as Simeone ate, occasionally talking to himself, as if chiding himself about his predicament.

"He'll be looking for an attorney soon," Reznick said.

Meyerstein was checking her notes and nodded. "I thought you would be more skilled in enhanced interrogation techniques."

"There are countless ways to get people to talk. No point in ramping it up from the get-go. Sometimes it pays to play nice. Use their own prejudices and mental fragility and narcissism to do the work for you. Doesn't always work like that. But I got lucky."

"You make your own luck, you once told me."

"Yeah, well, that's true as well."

Meyerstein smiled and glanced at her notes. "There's a gap in what he told us regarding where he was in a psychiatric hospital. We need to know more about that. Which begs the question of why he would be recruited as security at a secretive psychiatric facility. That's just plain odd."

Reznick finished a slice of pizza, washed it down with a glass of Coke, and then took a couple of gulps of coffee. He stood up. "I'm going to the bathroom to freshen up and then I'll head in and try and find out more about that."

Meyerstein nodded. "Details. The more the better."

Reznick went to the bathroom and splashed cold water on his face. He stared at the reflection in the mirror. Pale pallor, sunken blue eyes, dark shadows, and the same hollow expression he had seen in his father. He didn't give much away. He popped a couple Dexedrine and washed them down with water. He let the drugs begin to rouse his system. He felt more alert. Sharper.

He headed back into the interview room, which smelled of pizza and coffee.

"I just wanted to say that we appreciate your honesty with us, Mark. But also the fact that you're brave enough to not become the fall guy for this."

Simeone wiped his mouth with a napkin. "No fucking way, man."

"The thing is, you need to say what you told me, that you killed Father McNamara, to my colleagues, who will take a formal statement, and that will ensure that you won't take the fall for this. And Cray won't expect that to happen."

Simeone showed a sly grin. "He doesn't know who he's fucking with, man."

"So you understand what I'm saying? You have to tell my colleagues what you've told me."

"Or else?"

"Or else you will take the blame for this, and Cray will be able to walk away, laughing his nuts off. Your choice, man. I've only got another point or two I need to ask you and I'm done."

Simeone dropped the dirty napkin on the desk. "What?"

"You said you were admitted to a psychiatric hospital when you came back from Iraq."

"I'd been in and out of various facilities, man. And then I ended up in some place in Florida."

"Florida's a big place. Where in Florida?"

"Hollywood, Florida."

Reznick felt a jolt to the heart. They were getting closer to how Jerry White had ended up in Wittenden. "Can you remember what it was called?"

"It was for fucked-up veterans. The Palm Hospital."

Reznick nodded. "Can't say I've heard of it."

"Neither had I. Private charity or something ran it."

"And what happened after you spent some time there?"

"I got the job working a security detail for the Wittenden Institute."

Reznick wondered again how it was possible to get a security job after being in a psychiatric hospital. "Why would they think you were qualified for that?"

"I don't know. They had me and all the other guys sit lots of little tests."

"Psychometric?"

"Yeah, psychometric, to find out what sort of people we were, what job we would fit. And I have a lot to thank the hospital in Florida for. Didn't end up so good for me in Ithaca, but in Hollywood that place at least gave me a chance."

"You said it was a private charity. I'm going to be blunt with you, Mark. It appears to me rather reckless—and I'm putting this mildly— for a charity that purports to look after the welfare of damaged veterans in Florida to get you a responsible job way up in Ithaca. I would have thought your mental health problems would have flagged something."

"So would I. But one of the doctors put in a good word."

"One of the doctors in Florida?"

"Yeah."

"You got a name?"

"Sure. Dr. MacDonald."

The name crashed through Reznick's head.

"She recommended me, said my profile was perfect for the new job opportunity up there in Ithaca."

Reznick's antennae had been turned on. "Dr. MacDonald? What was the doctor's first name?"

"Why do you want to know that?"

"Just curious, I guess."

"Eileen. Really nice lady."

"Dr. Eileen MacDonald. And she got you a security job at the Wittenden Institute. Did she specifically recommend you?"

"Sure thing. She was the chief executive of the Palm Hospital."

Reznick excused himself for a bathroom break. He left the room and headed into the adjoining room with the one-way mirror. "Jerry White was at a hospital in Hollywood, Florida, before he was transferred to Wittenden," he said.

Meyerstein stared through the glass. "I haven't seen that in any of the files."

"Jerry told me. He didn't name the place. Also, Dr. Eileen MacDonald. Now at the Wittenden Institute. And she was the head of that hospital in Florida."

"We need to get that verified."

"Let's get on it."

Sixty-Four

Gittinger was watching as the last traces of the secret operation were burned in the huge hospital waste incinerator in Wittenden's subbasement, adjacent to the mechanical room. He felt sick to his stomach. The work that had been part of his life for so long was being turned to ash.

Files, papers, videos of the patients, laptops—everything was being loaded in. An operator wearing a mask shut the lid and fired up the incinerator to the maximum. Sixteen loads had already been destroyed.

He headed back to his office, beat. He wanted to go home. He wanted to go home and sleep. And rest. But there was still much work to do.

The more he contemplated the series of events since Jerry White's escape and Reznick appearing on the scene, the more concerned he became. He needed to make sure there was nothing incriminating left behind. He had to ensure that all evidence of the Wittenden Institute's methods was erased from computers, from cloud memory, and from thousands of hours of interviews and tests on the damaged veterans.

He sat back in his seat and called his wife. She wondered if he was ever coming home. Gittinger explained that events had conspired to keep him at work for at least another few hours. She hung up, leaving Gittinger to contemplate his next move.

He knew it was only a matter of time before the FBI entered the facility. He knew Cray and his security guys had been apprehended up near Skaneateles. And it was highly possible the fallout would continue from there. No one really knew where the investigation would end up.

He wondered if the true purpose of the Wittenden Institute would ever be unearthed. His job from the beginning had been to operate in secret throughout the lifetime of the project.

Gittinger's cell phone rang, and he expected to hear the voice of his wife again. "Gittinger speaking," he sighed.

"Bob?" The voice of the CIA handler, who seemed to have left the site, echoed over the line. "Is this encrypted?"

Gittinger's stomach knotted with tension. "Fully encrypted. Where the hell are you?"

"Not far. I'll be back in an hour or so. Listen, how is the incineration proceeding?"

"We're getting there."

"I want it done within the hour."

"Will do."

"Bob, we've now had confirmation that both Cray and Simeone are in the Feds' custody."

"I know that."

"They're holding them separately."

Gittinger groaned. "What do we know so far?"

"It ain't good."

"Can you be more specific?"

"I've heard that the Feds have footage of Simeone leaving the priest's house."

"That's not possible."

"That fucking priest had cameras all over the interior and exterior of his house, he was so paranoid about getting burgled."

"That is dumb fucking luck."

239

"But it doesn't stop there. That fucker Reznick is not just satisfied with springing Jerry White. He's determined to destroy what we've built. And he's taking a lead role in all this. He has maneuvered Simeone to say Cray instructed him to do it."

"No, how the hell? Simeone is not the type to blab."

"Reznick, according to a person in the FBI office in New York, is playing this game like an old friend—they were both in Iraq—and getting him to stick it to Cray."

"There's no way I could have foreseen that there'd be video footage and that Simeone would point the finger."

"To be fair, I didn't foresee Jon Reznick breaking into the facility and breaking out with a patient. Look, Bob, what about the three remaining patients?"

"I've had them moved out, back down to Florida, for reintegration."

Gittinger closed his eyes for a few moments as the impending fallout from the events threatened to engulf not only Wittenden but those who had worked for the hospital. It had taken the best part of ten years to resurrect the methods of the MK-Ultra tests.

But Gittinger's responsibility was to take the work of the original research and explore other possibilities. And he thought he had achieved that. Not just interrogation techniques, torture, mind control, sensory deprivation, thought insertion, and memory wiping but something even more radical.

With an end result that depended entirely upon Jerry White's activation. The early release could jeopardize everything.

"Tell me, Bob, we had envisaged keeping Jerry White until the right moment. But this is earlier than we planned. Could we still activate him?"

Gittinger had his answer ready. He had no other choice. To give up now was to lose too much. "I believe we can. But we need to expose him to the trigger words."

"That can be arranged, can't it?"

"If we know where he is."

"Leave that with me."

Gittinger went quiet for a few moments.

"Are you still there, Bob?" the CIA handler asked.

"I was just thinking over the scenario we're facing, not only with the fallout and what we have to do to wind this place down, but also in light of what you've told me about Cray and Simeone." Gittinger smiled. "Our plan is very elegant. We not only activate him but we neutralize him at the same time."

There was a pause, then: "It's quite brilliant."

"First, we absolutely need to find out where he is."

"We'll find him. There is another outstanding issue, though," the CIA handler said. "Dr. MacDonald. She is privy to the innermost secrets of the Institute and our sister hospital in Florida."

"Can she be moved back down to Florida? She's been a great asset for the agency."

"She is . . . When is she due to collect her things?"

"The next hour or so."

"How is she taking it?"

"She seems to be taking it in her stride, which concerns me too."

"Bob, let's tie up any loose ends. And let's talk when I get in."

Sixty-Five

A few hours after the interrogation of Simeone, it was decided by Meyerstein that Reznick would fly down to DC to speak to Jerry White at the FBI medical facility there. The facility was situated in a faceless office building six blocks from Capitol Hill. It was late when Reznick was shown to the third floor and escorted into a locked ward, where Jerry White was the only patient. He was drinking coffee and watching Fox News.

White turned around and gave a blank stare as two male nurses watched from behind a large desk. "Hey, Jon, am I good to go?"

Reznick hugged his old friend and pulled up a seat beside him. "I don't know, Jerry. I'll find out for you. Anyway, I'm assuming this is a bit more to your liking."

"Man, this is fucking great. But my thoughts are all . . . I don't know, kind of, out of sync."

"It'll probably take you time—a few weeks, maybe months—to get over this."

"How did you get me out?"

"Long story, man."

White began to cry. "Jon, what the hell happened to me?"

Reznick got up and gave him a bear hug. "I love you, man. And you're going to be fine."

White wiped his eyes with the back of his hand. "I can't even count to ten, you believe that?"

"What?"

"I've forgotten how to count. I don't know what happened."

"Do the nurses here know?"

"Sure, they're real nice. This place is so nice. Quiet. And I've got TV, which is great."

"Can you remember the trip back to Ithaca on the plane?"

"No."

"What about your stay with Tom McNulty?"

"Vaguely. I remember him taking my temperature, said I was burning up. He gave me something to help me. I keep seeing things."

"What kind of things?"

"I see images. In front of my eyes. Like a face. A smiling face. And sometimes it's a face with a frown."

"And the nurses and doctors here know about this?"

"Yeah, they know. And they've got me on some medication to calm me down and try and stop me freaking out."

Reznick glanced up at the TV. It was showing a discussion on Iraq. The lingering mess. Hundreds of thousands dead. Maybe millions when all was said and done. Then it began showing footage of suicide bombings. "Is this sort of stuff to cheer me up?"

White stared at the TV. "That's me."

Reznick looked at Jerry and then the images. "Yeah, Iraq, man. Not good."

"Suicide vest. That's me. Boom!"

Reznick had seen dozens of suicide bombers blow themselves to pieces in Iraq. He tried to change the subject. "Is there maybe some football on now?"

White stared at the TV. "Boom!"

"Jerry, you want to change the channel? This isn't good, man. Maybe some football."

White stared at the images.

Reznick reached over and picked up the remote control. He switched channels to watch a rerun of a Green Bay Packers game. "That OK?"

White nodded but said nothing.

"Last thing I want are memories of goddamn Iraq."

"Boom . . . That's all I can hear. You remember, Jon?"

Reznick pointed at the running back. "He's a tough little guy, right?"

White nodded. "Don't like Iraq."

"No one liked Iraq."

"I see it every day. I hear it every day. The bodies. I see them. They're always there for me, Jon. Always there. Can't get them out of my head. And I've got these images in my brain. Remember the guys we saw crucified?"

Reznick didn't want to think about that.

"I keep on seeing their faces. I can't remember anything apart from Iraq. I remember every fucking detail. How crazy is that?"

Reznick cleared his throat, keen to change the subject. "You're looking better. You eating?"

"Had some nice soup. And some chicken. That was nice."

"Chicken is good." Reznick leaned closer, voice low. "Jerry, I've got a few questions for you, if you don't mind."

White shrugged. "What about?"

"About your time down in Florida."

"That was some time ago, Jon. I don't remember too good."

"I'm just trying to understand exactly what had happened to you. So just to get this straight, you came back from Iraq, panhandling down in South Beach, out of it, and you got taken to a hospital in Florida—wasn't that what you said?"

"That's right. I think."

"You think . . . OK, what was the name of the hospital?"

White closed his eyes for a few moments. "I think . . . I'm sure it was called . . . Hollywood."

"Hollywood?"

"Yeah, that's where it was. Hollywood. It's a city."

Reznick wanted Jerry to verify things and not give him leading questions. "Where's that?"

"In between Miami and Fort Lauderdale. You never heard of it?"

Reznick said nothing.

"I can't remember much else."

"The name of the hospital?"

"The Palm Hospital. That was it. I remembered."

Reznick leaned over and patted Jerry on the back. "See, your memory isn't so bad."

"The Palm . . . yeah."

"What was that like?"

"It wasn't so bad. We had our own rooms. And it was nice. And quiet."

"And then you got moved, right?"

"Right." Jerry's eyes were filling up. "I got moved. Right. That's when they moved me. Right. Right. I got moved, Jon."

Reznick thought the sequence of words he used was strange. Like a stuck song on a scratched vinyl record. He wondered if this was an aftereffect of Jerry's spell in Wittenden. Almost certainly. What had those fucks done to him? But more to the point, why?

"Really. Yes, really. Did I really?"

Reznick nodded. Jerry seemed to be talking gibberish, as if in some soporific fugue state. "Jerry, does the name Dr. Eileen MacDonald mean anything to you?"

"She was nice."

"How was she nice?"

"She treated me nice. And she thought I deserved my own room. But she thought I needed a bigger room."

"Did Wittenden have bigger rooms?"

"No, it did not."

"So who was Dr. MacDonald?"

"She was nice."

"OK, I get that, Jerry. She was nice. What was her job?"

"She picked people. She picked me."

"Why?"

"She thought I needed a bigger room."

"OK, Jerry, just relax, man." Reznick glanced up at the TV. "Packers are a helluva team."

"Big guys, Jon. Big bastards, Jon."

Reznick got up and kneeled down beside Jerry and hugged him tight. "I love you. We're gonna get you better."

"That's not going to happen, Jon."

"Sure it is. You'll get better. And you'll be fixed. We've put all that bad stuff behind us."

Reznick extricated himself from Jerry's viselike hug.

"Bad stuff is not gone. Bad stuff in my head, Jon. Can't make it stop. Can see things. Bad things will happen. Boom! I know it, Jon."

Reznick felt an icy chill wash over him. He wondered how long it would take Jerry to be rehabilitated. If he ever would be. "See you, Jerry. Take care."

Jerry's eyes were on the football game. "Boom! Boom! What?"

Reznick walked away, a part of his heart broken at the sight and condition of one of the toughest guys he'd ever known. He approached two nurses and asked about Jerry's condition. They pointed to a small side room, where the ward psychiatrist was located.

Dr. Raj Patel showed him into his office. "Take a seat, Mr. Reznick. I believe you've been working with Assistant Director Meyerstein."

Reznick sat down. "That's correct. I hope you don't mind me dropping in like this. We were just hoping to see if Jerry could remember anything about his time in Florida."

Patel smiled. "He's got multiple problems, partly dissociative, partly PTSD, partly as a result of the outrageous experiments at Wittenden, but also more complex underlying behavioral problems which we believe might be triggered in the future."

"He talked about seeing things. Faces."

"Hallucinations. Out-of-body experiences. A whole pattern of signs of acute mental health disorders."

Reznick sighed. "Do you think he's going to get better?"

Patel took a few moments to answer. "Very difficult to say. 'I don't know' would be the honest answer. But what I can say is that Jerry's condition is very worrying."

"Why so?"

"He's like a firecracker. I expect him to go off at any minute."

Sixty-Six

Reznick called Meyerstein to confirm that Palm Hospital in Hollywood, Florida—where Mark Simeone, Iraq veteran and latterly security for the Wittenden Institute had stayed—was the same hospital where Jerry had been treated.

The confirmation stunned her as much as it had stunned Reznick. She said there was a court order being drafted and that an FBI taskforce would hopefully be taking over the Wittenden facility within the next forty-eight hours.

"Jon, did you know Cray is still on the loose?" she said.

"What? I thought he had been apprehended?"

"They picked up the wrong person, someone with the same name who lived locally."

"Bullshit. That's ridiculous."

"A lot of egg on some faces, but we're looking for him."

"What about Gittinger and the rest of the gang?"

"He will be among those arrested."

"What's taking so long?"

"The attorney general is locked in talks with his counterpart at the CIA. It's very sensitive."

"Was this black ops?"

"Very much looks like it. But that's only hearsay. I haven't been able to get access to that or anything more substantial about Wittenden. The best guess from our analysis is that this started as a briefing paper by some CIA officer just after 9/11."

Reznick's mind flashed back to that day. The day his wife had died in the Twin Towers. The day his world had turned to dust.

Meyerstein's voice was kind. "I'm sorry, I forgot."

"Forget it."

"The climate afterward was fevered. And this decision to resurrect the MK-Ultra program in a different format started it all."

"So when are the Feds going to go in to shut this bullshit program down?"

"Very soon."

"When?"

"That's an operational matter, and I can't divulge that."

"But it is going to happen, right?"

"Count on it. Tell me, Jon, how is Jerry after all this?"

"Honestly, I'm worried about him."

"He's in a good place. Dr. Patel is a fantastic psychiatrist. He's doing everything he can for Jerry. And if anyone can get him better, it'll be Patel."

"I don't doubt that. But the way Jerry was talking before we left, there was something unsettling about it."

"What was unsettling?"

"His use of language. Repetition. Like a needle stuck on a scratched record."

"Isn't that just part and parcel of his condition? His symptoms?"

"Maybe. But . . ."

"But what?"

"I know Jerry. I know him well. Well enough that when he managed to get out of that hellhole, he came and saw me. So I feel like I know when something isn't right. Know what he said?"

"What?"

"'Bad stuff will happen, Jon. Bad things will happen.'"

"I don't know, probably just the jumbled-up thinking he's got right now. Can't be easy."

"Martha, I'm telling you, something is seriously wrong with Jerry. Something I missed before. He was transfixed by a program about Iraq on TV. Some suicide bombings. He kept saying, 'That's me.' It was like he was so jumbled up he couldn't think straight. Like he was getting mixed up between what al-Qaeda were doing as opposed to what we were doing. Then again, maybe it's something that's just been lying there dormant."

"What are you getting at, Jon?"

Reznick sighed. "Honestly, I don't know what I'm getting at. I'm so dead tired I'm not thinking straight myself."

"Jerry's in the best possible place. But to calm your fears, I'll pass on your thoughts to Dr. Patel."

"Thanks."

"And you're probably right. You just need some rest. You can't have slept much in the last few days."

"A few hours at most."

Reznick fell silent for a moment, thinking, until Meyerstein cleared her throat. "I sense that you're not telling me the whole story, Jon."

"I'm trying to understand what I'm even thinking. This whole thing has been truly horrifying. And I don't think it will end well."

"How do you mean?"

"I keep thinking about Wittenden and the recordings repeating those phrases over and over and over again. It's like they were priming Jerry."

"Priming him for what?"

"'Boom,' he said. I believe they were priming him to kill on command. He knows it but can't express it."

Meyerstein took a few moments to let the information sink in. "How can you be so sure?"

"I can't. It's just my gut feeling. Martha, he needs to be under 24/7 guard."

"That's already in place. But I'll also pass that on to Dr. Patel's team. Can I pass on your cell phone number in case they want to talk to you?"

"Yeah, do that. I'm going to crash. Need some sleep. Take care."

Sixty-Seven

It was nearly midnight, and Gittinger decided it was time to do what he had been putting off for days. The sealed white envelope was sitting on his desk. He picked it up and went through to the conference room, where the CIA handler was deep in conversation on his cell phone, a bottle of Scotch and two half-full glass tumblers sitting on the highly polished table.

"Can I have a minute?" Gittinger asked.

"I'll call you back," the CIA handler said to whoever was on the line. He ended the call and put down his cell phone. "What's on your mind?"

Gittinger handed him the envelope.

"What's this?"

"Resignation letter. I'm sorry, but I feel like this whole thing has been very unsettling for me. My health isn't great. And I'm not sleeping."

The CIA handler nodded. He handed Gittinger a drink and picked up one for himself. "Bob, tell you what I'm going to do. I'm going to toast your good health and wish you a long and happy retirement, finally. And since you've done such sterling work for us, despite the mishaps recently, we'll write off any of your outstanding debts and give you a one-million-dollar thank-you bonus. You've brought us so far. How does that sound?"

Gittinger felt his throat tighten. He took a sip of the whisky. It was bittersweet—leaving the project he felt so invested in. But he was old. And tired. He didn't need the sadistic and sexual thrills anymore.

The CIA handler took a drink. "Tell me, the staff—where are we with that?"

"They've been told we're winding down our research. And they've all been paid a year's salary, and they seem quite content with that."

"It's amazing what money can do."

Gittinger nodded. "Once we find Jerry and pass on the trigger words, he'll know how to proceed."

"Then your work here will soon be complete." The CIA handler knocked back the rest of the whisky and poured them both another. "So everyone is off-site?"

"Yes, apart from Eileen."

"Where is she?"

"I don't know. I've tried calling her. But there's no reply."

"I'll catch up with her later," the CIA handler said.

"The escape means that our activities, which have gone unnoticed for years, will, I fear, be coming under the microscope." Gittinger stared into his glass.

"It's unfortunate. In fact, it's terrible for us. But I'm putting a plan in place."

Gittinger said, "I'm also concerned about what happens if the Feds begin to investigate what's been going on. What do I say?"

"Don't worry. We're nearly finished shutting the whole operation down. Besides, the buck stops with me." The CIA handler took a large gulp of the amber liquor.

"I'm worried they'll want to interview me," Gittinger said. "My blood pressure is too high. And everything that's happened is not helping."

The CIA handler pulled out a shoebox-sized cardboard box. He handed it over to Gittinger.

"What's this?"

"Open the lid."

Gittinger did what he was told. Inside were dozens of lurid black-and-white photos of him sexually abusing women and children.

"From our covert cameras in Vietnam, Laos, and Bahrain. But they're yours now. I'd strongly advise you to get rid of them."

"Are these the only copies?"

The CIA handler nodded. "I burned all the negatives myself."

"Thank you."

"So back to business. I've put a contingency plan in place so that there is no fallout, Bob. It's going to be fine. And we've got your back. Head down to Florida. And put your feet up."

"You told me the day you hired me that you'd always have my back."

"I did. And I meant it. We have conducted controversial tests and experiments which some might view as psychological torture. Inhumane. But can you imagine, as a species, if we had just stayed where we were, without reaching out, trying new things, experimenting, being prepared to fail, being prepared to take risks? We would've died out long ago."

Gittinger felt his eyes getting heavy. "I agree with that . . . We had to do this."

"That's right. We had to do it. Do you think America stays number one without taking monumental risks, without pushing the boundaries of what is acceptable? This is science. And sometimes, just sometimes, the boundaries are blurred."

Gittinger's vision was also becoming blurred.

"Bob, are you OK? You seem like you're miles away?"

Gittinger put down the glass. "Guess I'm just very tired."

"We're all exhausted. Sit down."

The spook helped Gittinger into a leather easy chair. He wondered if the alcohol was mixing with his high-blood-pressure medication. He felt like closing his eyes. Heavier and heavier. He looked around the room. No one was there. The CIA handler was gone. Where was he? The room was moving.

He tried to move. Inexplicably, he found he couldn't. He urged himself to move. But nothing. He was immobile. Paralyzed.

The swirling colors of the room were making him feel nauseous.

Gittinger felt his head fall back. Staring down at him was Cray. Where had he come from?

"Don't worry, Bob, I'll get you home OK."

Gittinger tried to open his mouth but he couldn't. He sensed he was being carried. His eyes were closing. But he fought to keep them open. Willed himself to see.

He felt himself headed down a corridor. He recognized an elevator door. He tilted his head to the side and saw Cray smiling as if through a fish-eye lens.

Gittinger tried to speak. His words didn't come. He tried again. He tried to open his lips and make a sound. But he couldn't. Nothing came.

Cray stared down at him. His eyes seemed colder. Not smiling anymore.

The top half of Gittinger's vision was turning black. Like a black curtain descending slowly. Blocking out the world.

It was then he realized where he was. The putrid smell of smoke. Decay. Rotting flesh. His senses hadn't died.

Gittinger tried to turn his head. He fought to stay conscious. He was in the mechanical room. The sound of boilers. Steam. And he seemed to float through to the incineration room.

Towering over him again was Cray.

He felt himself being strapped to something. He was being hoisted up to a metal platform over the incinerator.

Waves of panic washed over him. But he couldn't move a muscle or utter a sound. The terror of what awaited him was slowly dawning.

The huge steel lid opened. Fires raged through piles of clothes, laptops, phones, papers, files, and a charred body.

He tried to scream. He saw the face up close. It was blackened, but the lips were still red. As he was lowered into the chamber beside the torched remains of Dr. Eileen MacDonald, his mind was in free fall. He tried to scream as the flames consumed him. Then all the black-and-white photos covered her face before they too caught fire, flames erasing the last traces of his crimes.

His last thoughts were of home. He thought of his wife. He thought of his obituary. He thought of himself as a boy. The happy smile, carefree. The boy was smiling at him in his mind's eye. The young man in the lab in Canada. He tried to reach out to him as he said a silent prayer.

Sixty-Eight

It was nearly dawn, and Dr. Amy Nasheem was exhausted after a long shift in the burn unit at MedStar Washington Hospital Center, following two extensive reconstructive operations on burn victims. She changed out of her scrubs, showered, and put on her jeans and T-shirt. She headed across to her mother's house in Georgetown for breakfast. She kissed her mother and hugged her tight.

"You look tired, my darling girl," she said. "You work too hard. I tell you that all the time."

"Mother, you worry too much. Long hours are part of the job. This is America, after all, isn't it?"

Her mother nodded, still unconvinced about their adopted country.

"We're very lucky to be here, Mother."

Her mother averted her gaze.

"I know you miss home."

"I miss home. I miss your father. Each and every day I miss him more. I still cry myself to sleep. After all these years, I mourn him forever."

Nasheem wanted to confide in her mother about what she was going to do. She knew it would almost certainly result in her own death. But she didn't care. She had a mission. A mission that would avenge the death of her father. Her mother would be devastated at her death. But she would over time come to see it as a beautiful chance for immortality.

She looked at her mother. Pain was still etched in her face. Eyes heavy, turned slightly downward.

Her mother took out the old photo album, which she often did when she felt down. She began to look over the grainy photos of their old life in Manama, Bahrain. They were of her mother and late father getting married in an Orthodox church. They were part of the tiny Christian Bahraini community. Her father handsome, her mother looking demure and petite. Her father had been westernized and become a prominent human rights lawyer. But three years after Amy was born, her father had been taken in the middle of the night by Saudi secret police. He had been dumped outside the family's home dead, showing extensive signs of torture.

Her mother plunged into a terrible depression. And Amy received counseling sessions from an evangelical charity working in Manama. She thought back to the couch where the man had promised to protect her and her family. But she had to do everything he said.

She was drugged. She lost her inhibitions. Months of therapy, delving into her past as she lay on the couch in the air-conditioned office while the man stroked her hair. And kissed her.

He was going to be her protector. Her father figure.

And he told her the sacred words, uttered over and over again: *No today. No tomorrow. No now.*

Ingrained in the darkest recesses of her mind, those words were lying dormant.

The man was as good as his word. He enabled Amy and her family to leave Bahrain and settled them in a beautiful new home in Georgetown, in Washington, DC. It was a new start. A boundless opportunity.

"Mother, if I could grant you one wish, what would it be?" Nasheem asked.

"I would wish to be with my husband again. Forever."

Nasheem's cell phone rang, snapping her out of her reverie.

Her mother said, "Always work with you. I don't understand why there is always work."

Nasheem checked the caller ID. The man, a Christian friend and intermediary, hadn't called in months. "Mother, I need to take this upstairs."

Her mother shrugged. "If you must."

Nasheem headed up to her old bedroom, still the way she remembered it from when she was a teenager. Pink Barbie wallpaper. Tiny single bed.

"Dr. Nasheem," she said.

"Is it OK to talk?" the man said.

Nasheem cleared her throat. "Sure, what's on your mind?"

"You're going to be receiving a new patient very shortly."

Nasheem felt her heart rate hike up. She had been dreaming that this day would come. She had been preparing for it. "An important patient?"

"Very much so. But I can't say too much more. It's a surprise."

"When will this patient be arriving?"

"Real soon."

Nasheem's stomach knotted tight. "So the *operation has been green-lighted*?" She had given the code words.

"The operation is tricky, and there are obstacles, but *we believe your skills are a perfect fit for us*." He had given his code words.

Nasheem took a deep breath. "Do I have anything to worry about? Do I need to know anything else?"

"I think you're going to be pleasantly surprised at this opportunity."

"Sounds important."

"This is a once-in-a-lifetime opportunity. You always wanted to make a name for yourself, right?"

"That I did."

"Then you've got something really exciting to look forward to. Take care. I'll be in touch."

Sixty-Nine

Reznick was free-floating in darkness, struggling to breathe. Gasping for breath in the pitch-black air. A piercing sound and he awoke bolt upright. His cell phone was ringing. He took a few moments to get his bearings. He was in a small hotel room in downtown DC. He reached over for his phone. He recognized Meyerstein's caller ID. "Yeah?"

"Jon, we got a problem."

Reznick switched on the bedside lamp. "What time is it?"

"It's just past eleven in the morning."

Reznick got out of bed and pulled on his pants. "So what's the problem?"

"Jerry has disappeared."

"You're kidding me. How is that possible?"

"You tell me. I'd imagine he has a skill set that might be useful."

"Jerry was acting very strange when I saw him last night."

"Well, he's out now."

"How?"

"Apparently, he knocked out the old guy who was cleaning his room in the middle of the night when they thought he was asleep, tied him up with wires. Used the man's swipe card to exit the ward, get down the stairwell, and disappear into the night."

"You've got to be kidding me."

"We've got police and FBI units working on this. Dog teams. We're bringing the whole intelligence-gathering operation into play."

Reznick sighed. "Have we had the timeline of what happened within this unit?"

"I've been looking over that. Just over an hour before he escaped, there was a call."

"What sort of call?"

"A man called the unit, said he was Jerry's brother and wanted to wish him well."

Reznick sat up in his bed, rubbing the sleep out of his eyes. "Jerry doesn't have a brother."

"I know that. But the nurse didn't. And she was going to ask the psychologist for permission, but he was seeing another patient. So she handed Jerry the phone."

"Shit. OK, tell me what we know."

"The call was made at 4:26 a.m. and the call, we believe, came from or around the vicinity of the Wittenden Institute."

"Fuck!"

"What?"

"You know what that'll be?"

"Orders?"

"Trigger words. Orders. Instructions. Code words. Fuck."

"NSA have managed to decrypt the call. The voice they determined to be a man's."

"Well, that narrows it down. When you say *determined*, what do you mean?"

"I mean the voice had been electronically distorted."

"What else?"

"There was a phrase used. A trigger phrase, perhaps."

"What was it?"

"No past, no future, no now."

"Shit."

"What?"

"Those were the exact words booming in Jerry's room at Wittenden."

"So some sort of brainwashing?"

"I think those words have wormed their way in. Over days, weeks, months. Conditioning him so that when they are uttered in an alien environment, he acts in a certain manner."

"What manner exactly, though?"

Reznick sighed. "I think he's been primed. Primed to kill. Programmed to kill."

"Christ. So where's he going to get a gun or rifle from?"

"Probably someone has planted the weapon or weapons at a safe location for him to pick up. Then again, he might just raid a gun shop."

"Jon, we need to find him."

"I want in."

"I thought you would. I'm outside in an SUV. You've got two minutes. Don't keep me waiting."

Seventy

Ninety seconds later, Reznick slid into the back of the waiting SUV beside Meyerstein.

"You took your time."

"Gimme a break."

Meyerstein sighed. "Let's hit it," she said, tapping the driver on the shoulder. "Straight to the Hoover Building."

The driver nodded. "Very good, ma'am."

Reznick said, "What was the last known sighting?"

"He caught a bus to Arlington."

"You think he might be headed there? Military cemetery and all that."

"We've got people there. Our analysis shows that an attack is more likely to be in DC. So we don't think Arlington is his final destination."

FBI guards stopped the SUV and scanned their credentials before they were waved through to the parking garage. Reznick followed Meyerstein and her team to a newly allocated room on the fifth floor.

Meyerstein sat on the edge of a desk. "You know Jerry better than anyone alive. What do we need to know?"

Reznick slumped in a chair. "Gimme a fucking break. Do you know that Jerry was really fucking good, better than me, better than just about everybody on my Delta crew?"

Meyerstein shook her head.

"Long-range rifle shot. He was a sniper."

"I'm wondering if in his mental state he would be physically, as well as mentally, capable of doing such a thing."

"I can't believe he escaped from the FBI ward. He told me, he begged me not to let them take him back. And then I got the fucker out."

"That was before the trigger words. I'm wondering if he had an inkling that something bad was going to happen but he couldn't tell you what it was. Maybe he couldn't remember."

"Maybe. So after this sighting of him getting on a bus, he drops off our radar?"

Meyerstein closed her eyes and sighed. "Precisely. Jon, you know this guy. Better than anyone. You know what we know. What's the playbook for this?"

"From Jerry's point of view?"

Meyerstein nodded.

"He gets into position unnoticed, unseen."

"What position?"

"If it's a sniper situation, ordinarily a tall building. But Washington is not known for its tall buildings."

Meyerstein reflected on that. "That's interesting."

"So if that's the case, we might be talking about getting in closer and lower than would normally be ideal."

"You think he's capable?"

"I think he's capable of just about anything."

"Do you think we could be overreacting?"

"Maybe. He's potentially dangerous. We have proof that trigger words or something similar have been passed on to him. And he reacted by escaping."

"That doesn't mean it will necessarily translate into a terrorist incident."

"So why the hell would these trigger words be issued? The same trigger words that have been drummed into him virtually nonstop."

"You're certain something is going to go down?"

"Yeah, something is going to go down."

Seventy-One

"Sir, you wanted to see me," Meyerstein said as she entered the office of FBI Director Bill O'Donoghue.

O'Donoghue indicated she should take a seat.

Meyerstein sat down as the woman on the sofa ended her call. She turned and smiled. "Assistant Director Martha Meyerstein, I don't believe we've met."

The woman nodded. "Nice to meet you, Martha. Holly Courtney. National security adviser. I believe we may have a developing situation."

Meyerstein nodded. "My team is working on this as we speak."

O'Donoghue leaned back in his seat. "What's the current position, Martha?"

"We have reason to believe there is an above-average probability that Jerry White has been activated."

"You make him sound like a robot," Courtney said.

"In a way, from what I've learned, he has been turned into a sort of robot. Memories have been erased and new thoughts inserted. And we are convinced that these phrases he has been given are designed to trigger him."

"My sources in the CIA say they were aware of Wittenden but that this has nothing formally to do with them. It was a private facility."

"They can say what they like. This is a special access program—we know that—and it was developed by the CIA. A retired CIA psychiatrist is leading up Wittenden—Robert Gittinger."

Courtney nodded. "Let's leave aside the purpose of the Wittenden Institute. My concern is the President and the security of this country."

"First, we've got a major league problem. We have a guy who has been activated. Is the target the White House? The Pentagon? That is what's concerning me."

O'Donoghue said, "Can we discount bioterrorism and kidnapping as the method of attack?"

"I think we can," Meyerstein said. "We have no evidence of bio-materials in his possession or any inkling that he is planning to kidnap someone."

O'Donoghue piped up: "Is there a possibility of a bombing?"

"Reznick mentioned when he saw Jerry last night that he was watching some news program about Iraq, about suicide bombings. Said something along the lines of 'That's me.' We don't know if he was in a highly confused state, but that's what Reznick reported."

Courtney closed her eyes and shook her head. "Jesus Christ."

Meyerstein said, "We can't rule anything out. White, having served in Iraq and having been part of Special Forces, would be well acquainted with all methods of killing."

O'Donoghue nodded. "I don't like the sound of any of this. Shit."

A silence filled the room as the full extent of what they were facing began to sink in.

Seventy-Two

Reznick paced the room, coffee in hand, trying to figure out where Jerry would strike. He looked across at Meyerstein, who was deep in thought, flicking through the latest analysis.

"He's out there," Reznick said. "And he'll be coming soon. I can feel it."

Meyerstein looked up. "Are you directing these comments at me, Jon?"

"Yes, I am."

Meyerstein sighed. "I'm well aware, Jon, that Jerry is out there and that he will almost certainly be used to carry out a terrorist attack."

"What's the name of your senior behavioral analyst? The guy you trust to get this right."

"Special Agent Cortez. He's a behavioral expert. A leading psychologist who specializes in the motivations of violent offenders."

"Do you mind if I talk with him?"

Meyerstein shrugged. "He's very busy."

"I get that."

"He's just down the hall. What is it?"

"It's nothing."

"Don't say it's nothing. You clearly have thoughts about what's happening. Why do you want to speak to Cortez?"

"I don't know. I just want to touch base with him. Run something past him. The suicide bomber is a terrifying tool used by Islamists in Iraq, Syria, etcetera. But is that something Wittenden was trying to replicate?"

Meyerstein went quiet for a few moments. "Using severely damaged, brainwashed, suicidal veterans?"

Reznick nodded. "Perhaps. Consider this: What sort of guy would you task with carrying out an assassination plot? A psychotic who has been brainwashed for months, his thoughts disordered, or a level-headed, cold-blooded assassin waiting in the wings?"

Meyerstein buzzed in Cortez. A few moments later there was a knock at the door, and Special Agent Cortez entered the room.

Meyerstein fixed her gaze on senior analyst Special Agent Robert Cortez. "Before I get to the point, I'm going to play devil's advocate, if I may. We don't know for sure there's going to be an attack."

Cortez glanced at figures on his laptop for a moment. "Here's the thing. No one can predict with any degree of certainty what might or might not happen as regards Jerry White. Maybe these so-called trigger words are simply a coded message for him to escape from wherever he is. We've heard from the CIA that they knew the Wittenden Institute was an advanced facility that was testing the faculties of mentally ill soldiers under unbearable stress. Which, incidentally, is breaking the law, as we all know. But let's assume this secret program, which is linked to the CIA, has a purpose. Common sense and experience would suggest that the CIA is not going to be too bothered about enabling a Special Forces soldier to escape from captivity. It is my opinion, looking at the scraps of data we've got on this, that we're looking at a seventy-three percent possibility of a nefarious action, perhaps terroristic in nature."

"Let me clarify so I'm up to speed," Meyerstein said. "There is an above-average chance that this is going to happen."

"Precisely. Now, we've read about this psychosis, breakdown, and prolonged episode of perhaps bipolar disorder with PTSD symptoms for years, almost certainly heightened by the incarceration at this Wittenden facility. But we're already working through some scenarios."

"Sniper attack?" Meyerstein asked.

"That was the number one scenario on our list," Cortez said. "All the way through to a car bomb, suicide bombing, and killing someone on live TV."

"And you're as sure as you can possibly be that this will happen?"

"If I were a betting man, which I'm not, I'd put money on some kind of lone wolf attack."

"Where?"

"This is where it gets tricky. Where will depend on the method of delivery. If it's a sniper attack, who will be the target?"

Meyerstein went quiet for a few moments as she contemplated what Cortez had said. "I'd like you to consider a different scenario."

Cortez shrugged. "Sure."

"I'm looking for a quick answer. Jon raised the possibility of Jerry White as a suicide bomber. Can we rule that out?"

"Not at all. The mistake a lot of people make when it comes to suicide bombers is that it's all about ideology or religion or some such motivating factor. But the reality is—and research of would-be or failed suicide bombers has backed this up—that many of them have had suicidal feelings before."

Reznick nodded, listening intently.

"There was research carried out in Israel, I believe, that asked terrorists if they had ever considered a suicide mission. Eleven out of twelve said they had not. None had suicidal tendencies. But for the would-be suicide bombers, eight had depressive tendencies, six had been suicidal, and two had even attempted suicide in the past. So to answer your question, perhaps this is what Wittenden has been working on. Breeding a generation of American suicide bombers to be used as and when they decide. And yes, Jerry White must be considered to be in that category."

Seventy-Three

Dr. Amy Nasheem was checking the medical file in front of her when her cell phone rang. She headed out into the hallway for more privacy. "Yes?"

"It will be today."

"Who?"

A silence opened up between them. "I don't think you're going to believe it."

"Who?"

"Who do you most wish to kill?"

"I think you know who."

"It is him."

"You cannot be serious?"

"I'm deadly serious. It is him!"

Nasheem's mind flashed on her memories of her father's tortured body.

"Please do not toy with my emotions."

"I will tell you one final time. It is him. And you have been chosen. You have the opportunity to avenge. To slay the man who signed your father's arrest warrant."

Nasheem felt her heart rate quicken.

"He was the man in charge of the Saudi General Intelligence Presidency when your father died. He was the man who signed the orders. And he is here in Washington, DC, with his entourage as we speak. He is the oil minister now. A crown prince."

Nasheem felt giddy with excitement.

"My next call will be the last. The operation has begun. So do not leave the hospital. This is a Code One. I repeat, this is a Code One."

The line went dead.

Seventy-Four

Sandwiches, water, and coffee were brought as the discussions on the fifth floor of the Hoover Building continued apace.

Cortez tore into a roast beef sandwich. "Tell you what, how about I bring Ben Goldman in here? He's the only guy who's talking about your scenario."

Reznick looked at Meyerstein, and she was nodding. "Yeah, absolutely," he said.

Goldman was called in and introduced to everyone. He was a frail middle-aged special agent with an intense gaze.

Cortez said, "Ben, tell me again what you think might develop. We're all intrigued."

Goldman flushed. "I don't know, it's just my take on it." He pressed his hands together as if part of some OCD ritual before he spoke. "I believe this private company that owns the Wittenden Institute, staffed by former CIA types and associated with the CIA, might be developing a new strategy based on what we faced in Iraq."

Meyerstein said, "Iraq? What strategy?"

"Maybe I didn't make myself clear," Goldman said. "What I'm talking about is suicide bombers and suicide car bombings. The Baathists, al-Qaeda, and ISIS have used these to devastating effect."

Meyerstein said, "So why would the CIA, even if the Agency is involved in the most tenuous way, come up with this?"

Goldman said, "It is a weapon of war to be used at home or abroad. Is this a trial run? I don't know. What about the plans the CIA drew up for Operation Northwoods in 1962? A false flag operation to blame the Cubans. Part of the plan was to carry out bombings on US soil."

Meyerstein nodded but didn't comment.

"I'm with you," Reznick said. "Jerry seemed fixated on suicide bombings when I spoke with him last night."

Goldman looked at Reznick. "He was?"

Reznick nodded.

"Now that is interesting."

"Like he was in a trance. Repeating phrases. Even used the word *boom* as he watched a Fox News report showing footage from Iraq."

"Then, if that's the case, I would say my analysis would now predict, after what Mr. Reznick has told me, a brainwashed veteran either shooting or bombing some innocent people. The fact that the phone call to his ward earlier today came with the code words he had been absorbing indicates a high probability that whatever he's going to do, he's going to do it today."

Seventy-Five

Cray escorted the CIA handler in charge of shutting down Wittenden's operation through the tunnels underneath the Institute. Up ahead he saw the arch-shaped opening, which Cray had carved out a few hours earlier with concrete drills and rotary hammers. They walked for nearly a mile until they reached an exit door.

Cray keyed in the code and pushed the door open. It revealed a near-deserted underground parking garage. A white BMW SUV sat at the far end. He turned and shut the door, the heavy clunk of the electronic lock making it impregnable again.

The CIA spook slid into the back seat and Cray pulled away. "There's no one left on the premises, is that right?"

"That's correct."

"The databases have been wiped, laptops, phones, cell phones, and servers all incinerated?"

"Everything is gone or destroyed."

"What about the video material?"

"Wiped. Deleted. And overwritten a hundred times."

The spook gazed out the window at the passing green fields. "How about the exterior gates and fences? All activated?"

"Still in place, sir. If anyone wants in, they'll have to drill their way in, but it's been set up to take time in case we had to evacuate."

"Not how I'd imagined the facility closing."

"Me neither. But you do what you gotta do, right? The operation is king."

"What about you, Laurence?"

"What about me?"

"Where will you go?"

"Guatemala. Got a few friends down there. And you, sir?"

"The company that owns the Wittenden Institute is offshore, so I believe the Caymans will be my first stop. I will get an update to the shareholders and backers. Then our plane can take you directly to Guatemala afterward. Unless you want to stop over in the Caymans."

"No, if it's alright with you, I'll head straight there."

"As you wish. The money, three million dollars, was transferred just over an hour ago."

Cray grinned. "I know. I checked."

"Then you're good to go."

"Damn straight."

It was a fifteen-minute drive to a tiny airfield in the middle of nowhere. The Gulfstream was waiting on the runway. They parked the SUV and walked the short distance to the plane, climbed the stairs, and slumped into their seats. The CIA spook began to think about what was going to unfold in DC as the plane taxied and took off into the gray afternoon skies.

Seventy-Six

During a short break, Cortez's cell phone rang. He answered and immediately handed it to Reznick. "It's Assistant Director Meyerstein. Urgent."

Reznick pressed the phone tight to his ear. "Yeah, Reznick. What've we got?"

"I'm in the Director's office. Face recognition has picked out Jerry White at the underground parking garage at CityCenterDC."

"How far?"

"Not far. Cortez will take you."

Reznick and Cortez were already on the move. "Martha, do we know if this is going to be a shooter situation? Or maybe worse?"

"Jon, we have no idea. All you need to know is that you have to take him down."

Reznick ended the call and returned the phone to Cortez. An SUV with two other agents whisked them to the site in under three minutes. He had an earpiece to hear what operational SWAT command were saying. Cops were trying to clear the upscale shops. His earpiece crackled into life. "He's on the move on foot, walking very close to a larger group of people. He's holding something in his right hand."

"Shit," one of the SWAT team said. "I think that's a trigger in his hand."

Reznick's heart sank. "Not good. Get this mall cleared! Now!"

Meyerstein was in his ear. "Jon, he's tagging along close to this group. A very well-dressed group of women surrounded by a phalanx of what look like male bodyguards."

"And Jerry is a few yards behind them?"

"Fifteen yards or so. Appears to be browsing, but it looks like he's following this group."

"And he's got a handheld thumb switch?"

"That's what they're saying."

Reznick didn't need to know any more. "We're talking a bomb."

Reznick bounded down some stairs and was in the mall, being guided to the scene via the earpiece. Suddenly, up ahead he saw the crowd of affluent female shoppers about a hundred yards away. He was staring at them as they approached. They were Middle Eastern in appearance. Superwealthy Saudis, maybe. They stopped to look in the window of an upscale jeweler, pointing at the gold rings and watches.

The voice in his earpiece. "Jon . . . not too close. You're too close."

All of a sudden, Jerry emerged. He seemed dazed as he stared at Reznick, maybe sixty yards away.

"Jerry," Reznick said, "you don't need to do this, whatever it is. This doesn't have to happen."

"You can take me down, Jon," he said, holding up the trigger, his thumb pressed down on the mechanism. "We all know how this ends."

"This doesn't have to happen."

The Middle Eastern women were looking alarmed as the bodyguards ringed them, speaking into cell phones.

Reznick took out his gun. "Leave them alone, Jerry."

Jerry unzipped his jacket, exposing explosives strapped to his body. "They told me to come here, Jon. They told me to do this. They told me last night, Jon, what I had to do and when. It has to be now. That's what they said."

"Jerry, this doesn't have to happen."

"No today. No tomorrow. No now." Jerry recited the line two more times.

"Please, Jerry, don't do this!"

"You know all about trigger mechanisms, Jon. It'll blow the place sky-high."

The Middle Eastern women began to scream, and a few ran away from Jerry.

Reznick had his gun trained on Jerry. He knew a bomb was going to go off. "Ladies, get the hell away from him! He has a bomb! Bodyguards, do not shoot him or the bomb will go off!"

The women sobbed and screamed as they fled the scene.

One of the Saudi bodyguards took aim.

"Do not shoot, I said!"

The man shot Jerry, and his grip released, dropping the switch mechanism. In a split second the Semtex strapped to his body exploded, blowing apart Reznick's old friend in a terrible blast. Then everything went black.

Seventy-Seven

The ringing in his ears and screaming echoed around Reznick's head as he lay sprawled amid glass, bloody body parts, and pieces of shrapnel. He wondered if his eardrums had burst or if he was just in shock. He crawled for a few yards and then managed to get to his feet. He headed over to where the Middle Eastern women were bloodied, moaning, and crying on the ground. He watched over them until medical help arrived. A short while later the Feds and the mall's security guards began to set up a cordon and field hospital.

Reznick saw carnage wherever he looked. He saw that the blast had killed all the bodyguards and perhaps three of the women, whose bodies were all missing arms and legs. Four were still alive.

"Jon!"

A few minutes later, Reznick turned, dazed, and saw Meyerstein. She waved him toward her. He staggered to her as a paramedic dabbed his wounds, shining a penlight in his eyes. "I'm fine, goddammit."

The paramedic ignored him and continued to swab the wounds. The smell of antiseptic alcohol was filling the air, stinging his face.

"Fuck!"

Sirens were going off.

The paramedic escorted Reznick to an ambulance. "Forget it."

"Not an option, Jon," Meyerstein said, "you're injured."

"Clean it up. We can stitch it all up later."

The paramedic shook his head. "Not an option, my friend. You're going to the hospital."

The minutes that followed felt like a lifetime. Slowly, Reznick was wheeled into a hospital room on a gurney. Cortez and Meyerstein came into the room.

His mind was racing as he tried to process what he had just witnessed. "There's something else," he said, looking toward the ceiling. "This is just one part of it. I'm sure of it."

Meyerstein leaned over him. "You're in shock, Jon. Just relax. It's over."

"Maybe not."

"What do you mean?"

"I'm just trying to think of how a military operation could be at its most devastating. I know about this stuff. You think it's over. But it isn't. It's just the start."

Cortez frowned. "What are you getting at, Jon?"

"Bear with me for a few moments. Jerry was used as a suicide bomber. But what if we are wrong to fixate on only one man, Jerry White?"

Cortez shrugged.

"What if Jerry was just part of the threat?"

Cortez took a few moments to reflect on that. "Sure, it's a possibility."

Meyerstein said, "What the hell are you talking about, Jon?"

"Wasn't it Sun Tzu who said all war is based on deception?"

Cortez and Meyerstein exchanged glances.

"There are countless diversionary tactics, decoys, and the like. What if we're making the assumption, a false assumption, that this guy, this hugely damaged veteran, Jerry White, was the lone assassin? The lone wolf. What if there are others?"

Meyerstein glanced at Cortez, whose face was like stone. "What if there was more than one? Part of a coordinated attack?"

Cortez reflected on what they had just said. "I think something like that, a strategy like that, would have to be high-level, government-level thinking."

Reznick shrugged. "What, like the CIA? Wasn't this program devised by the Agency? Wasn't it being led by Gittinger, former CIA?" He looked at Cortez. "I'm just putting this out there."

Cortez nodded as the lines bunched up on his forehead. "Do you know what Machiavelli said about deception?"

Meyerstein rolled her eyes.

"He said, 'Although to use deception in any action is detestable, nevertheless in waging war it is praiseworthy.'"

Reznick nodded. "We believe that one man was responsible for this terrorism act. But as we've learned, this project at Wittenden wanted to erase memories and put new ones in place. Destabilizing and unhinging already seriously damaged veterans. What better way to apportion blame than to have a psychotic veteran on hand who's primed to go off. Except we believe he poses the real threat. But meanwhile another genuine threat might very possibly be waiting in the shadows for their moment."

Meyerstein's cell phone rang. "Goddamn." She pressed the green button to answer. "Quantico? Put them through." She paced the room. "Are we sure? Positive? Triple checked? And it's her? We're not far."

Reznick's head was pounding and his ears still ringing as he got off the gurney. "What is it?"

"That was Quantico. Cray's keys that you took—there was a flash drive on the key ring."

"And?"

"NSA have been looking over this after Quantico checked. The FBI saw extensive footage inside the facility. But the NSA have uncovered an encrypted contact too."

"What about it?"

"The cell phone belongs to Dr. Amy Nasheem. She works at MedStar Washington Hospital Center here in DC. She's a burn specialist. That's where they've taken all the most seriously injured, including several prominent Saudis."

"Bullshit."

Meyerstein shook her head. "There's more. Her father was tortured to death in Bahrain by Saudi intelligence. The man who signed the order to detain and torture him, resulting in that death, was none other than the current Saudi oil minister."

Cortez said, "So where is he now?"

Meyerstein said, "That's the thing. He's in Washington."

"Right now?"

Meyerstein nodded. "And one of the Saudi women who was hit by the blast was his wife. She's seriously injured, suffering terrible burns, and is now fighting for her life."

Reznick's mind was racing to keep up. "And she's been taken to the same hospital?"

"She's there as we speak. And her husband, who signed the order to detain the doctor's father, is en route."

Seventy-Eight

Dr. Amy Nasheem was overseeing the treatment of the Saudi oil minister's wife. The woman's ripped and burned clothing, blackened and shredded by the blast, had been cut off and the burns cooled with cold water. Then her body had to be dried to prevent hypothermia.

Her team had applied Burnshield to cool and dress the injury. High-flow oxygen was being given through a mask. An IV line was supplying the patient with fluids and morphine to kill the pain.

She checked her vital signs.

"She's dropping in and out of consciousness," a nurse said.

"Let's keep the fluids going, morphine steady flow."

Within a few minutes, she was aware of huge men in suits outside the room.

"What is this?" she asked.

A doctor popped his head around the door. "Bodyguards of the crown prince of Saudi Arabia. He will be arriving in less than five minutes."

Nasheem nodded. "Keep them out there." She pulled down the blinds for privacy. *No today. No tomorrow. No now.*

It was nearly time.

Seventy-Nine

Reznick was traveling in the back of an SUV with Meyerstein and some heavily armed SWAT guys. He had been given painkillers and popped a couple of Dexedrine. The amphetamines were now coursing through his veins. He turned to Meyerstein, who was still on the phone. "How is it that nobody can get through to the crown prince?"

"We're trying multiple numbers, but no one is answering."

"Fuck."

The vehicle was traveling fast, taking corners at breakneck speed. But it wasn't going quick enough for Reznick. Time was running out.

Reznick turned to Meyerstein. "So we believe we know this doctor's motivation to kill the crown prince?"

"Precisely."

"Question is, what's in it for the CIA?"

Meyerstein said nothing as she glanced out at the people of DC going about their business.

"You know more than you're letting on."

Meyerstein sighed.

"Do you know what's in it for the CIA?"

She lowered her voice to a whisper. "I just spoke to one of our most senior geopolitical analysts. He said the crown prince has been infuriating the Pentagon, apparently, with private talks in Moscow and Tehran. He was talking about a rapprochement of sorts."

"And the CIA hawks don't want that, right?"

Meyerstein sighed and nodded.

"Fuck."

"This is a very complex plan they've put in place."

"It's a slow-burn operation. They've got this doctor, who's going to be the patsy. Plausible deniability straightaway. The fingerprints of the American military are not on this. And once it's revealed that she has motivations . . . You can see how it would look and how the media will portray it."

Meyerstein sat in silence.

"The Agency doesn't care about who gets killed or blamed or taken down. They don't want Saudi Arabia aligned in any way with Russia or Iran. That's a red line that can't be crossed. And that's why the crown prince is going to be next to be neutralized."

"I don't know," Meyerstein said. "It all sounds crazy."

"It is crazy. And you know what? I'll guarantee that this doctor, this Bahraini doctor, will be framed as an Iranian spy with links to Shias in Bahrain. I know the playbook."

"You really believe this is a covert CIA operation?"

"CIA, Pentagon, Joint Chiefs of Staff, whatever name you hang this on . . . it's all the same. They put plans in place. They put people in place. Then if they don't do what they're told, they take those same people out."

Meyerstein dialed another number on her cell phone. Still no answer. "Are you kidding me?"

Three long minutes later, the SUV pulled up at the hospital. Reznick had a fresh earpiece in and a 9mm Beretta in his hand. The elevator took too long. So they took the stairs to the third level and headed toward the burn ward.

J. B. Turner

The voice of Meyerstein crackled to life in his earpiece. "Jon, you guys, be aware the crown prince can't be contacted. We don't know where he is. You're going in blind."

The lead SWAT guy said, "Copy that, ma'am."

"Is she definitely on this floor?" Reznick asked.

A long silence filled the void.

Meyerstein said in his earpiece. "Jon, this isn't right. We have the crown prince's wife on the third floor, according to the hospital. Now we're being told she was moved to the seventh floor."

"Which floor?"

"Head to seven," Meyerstein said. "Damn!"

Eighty

The red second hand on the clock in the large ICT room was ticking remorselessly.

Dr. Amy Nasheem knew she had to act. "OK," she said to the nurse by the side of the crown prince's wife's bed, "this woman's husband will be visiting very shortly and I'm sure he'd like to have some privacy with his wife. I'll take over from here. Why don't you check on the others?"

The nurse nodded and quietly left the room.

Nasheem looked at the woman, eyes shut, attached to the morphine and fluid drip, swathed in Burnshield. She was still alive. And the next twenty-four hours would be crucial to her recovery. But as it stood, Amy had another matter to attend to.

A matter of honor for her family. An eye for an eye. But there was something else.

She sensed a trigger had been switched inside her. As if she was now primed and almost incapable of pulling out of the action. There was an inevitability about what she was going to do. And she liked that feeling.

A bodyguard opened the door. "You need to leave while the crown prince is in attendance," he said.

"No. That's not possible. I'm in charge of this woman's treatment."

"This is not a request. It is unacceptable in our culture for him to be alone with a woman who is not his wife."

Nasheem took a step closer. She had been wanting to say this for a lifetime. "Well, this is America. I'm staying. If he doesn't like it, he needs to speak to the medical director. In the meantime, I will be saving this woman's life."

The bodyguard stared at her long and hard.

"I need to explain intimate medical details to the crown prince in confidence, do you understand? Very intimate details."

The man's contempt for her was palpable in his cold brown eyes.

"After that, he can be alone with her," Nasheem said. "Am I clear?"

The bodyguard sighed. "Very well," he said as she shut the door.

Nasheem checked that the woman's vital signs were stable. She was enjoying dragging it out. Each and every second a delicious pleasure. Stalling the rush she was about to experience.

A minute later, a sharp knock at the door. Nasheem opened the door, and the bodyguard was standing there.

"The crown prince has agreed to speak with you. But you can only be with him for two minutes."

"I've already discussed this with you. I will speak with him for as long as necessary to discuss his wife's condition and treatment."

The bodyguard turned and bowed low as the crown prince came into view.

"My wife," he said. "Where is she?"

Nasheem ushered him inside. "Sir, I must speak to you urgently."

"With regards to?"

"Your wife's condition. She's been very badly injured and we should discuss her treatment immediately."

The crown prince nodded and strode into the room. He wore an impeccably cut single-breasted navy suit, white shirt, navy tie, and black shiny oxford shoes. Gold cuff links. Light-blue pocket square.

Nasheem shut the door behind him and quietly locked it from the inside. "Sir, your wife's condition is giving us cause for concern, but she has stabilized in the last fifteen minutes since she arrived. We are delivering the highest quality of care."

The crown prince stared down at his wife, tears in his eyes. "Thank you."

"Sir," Nasheem said, pointing to a seat, "please sit. Your wife is in critical condition. She was very badly burned in the explosion."

The crown prince sat down and sighed. "Will she live?"

"At this stage, sir, I don't know."

"Whatever she needs, she gets," he said.

"Of course."

Nasheem picked up the clipboard with a medical form attached to it. "You need to sign this to ensure she receives all the treatment we have at our disposal. It's just routine."

The crown prince reached into an inside pocket and pulled out an expensive-looking pen.

While he was distracted, reading over the form she had handed him, Nasheem carefully reached into an inside pocket of her white coat. She held her breath as she felt the syringe. She pulled it slowly out of her pocket. Then she stabbed it hard into the carotid artery of the crown prince's neck. Blood dribbled out of the pinprick wound.

He gasped and gaped, as the huge dose of cyanide took hold. The crown prince began to convulse, eyes wide as he slipped into unconsciousness. His skin turned a bluish gray.

Nasheem checked his pulse. He was close to death.

She turned the chair, with the crown prince still in it, around so he would appear to be facing the window.

She felt elated. She looked around the room. And smiled.

Then she quietly opened the door, making sure to automatically lock it from the outside.

The bodyguard towered over her.

"The crown prince would like to be alone with his wife," Nasheem said. "He must not be disturbed. Are we clear?"

"Thank you. Yes, of course. His personal physician is on the way."

"Very good. I will be back in five minutes, and I can speak to him then."

Nasheem headed down the corridor and to the stairwell, thinking only of the last thing she had to do.

Eighty-One

The FBI SWAT team with Reznick at the front moved stealthily down the seventh-floor corridor, brushing past the bodyguards.

Reznick tried the door. "Locked!"

The voice in his earpiece: "Break it down!"

Reznick took a step back and kicked it in. Inside, the crown prince had slumped to the ground, blood spilling from his neck. Reznick checked for a pulse. Nothing.

"He's dead." It was pandemonium as the SWAT team kept the bodyguards at bay. He turned and stared at a colossal bodyguard. "Where is she? The doctor who was in here . . . Where the hell is she?"

The guy fell to his knees and began to cry and pray. "She has killed him!"

"Where the hell is she?"

The bodyguard indicated a long corridor. "She went down there to the exit sign not more than three minutes ago, I swear!"

The voice of Meyerstein sounded in Reznick's ear as nurses and doctors rushed past him into the room. "Jon, we got a visual. She's on the roof. Ready to jump. Shit."

Reznick signaled to the SWAT team leader, and his men followed him to the stairwell and bounded up the stairs and out through an emergency door to the roof. At the far end, looking out over DC, stood a woman wearing a white coat. She spun around. Reznick pointed the Beretta at her.

"Freeze!"

She stared at him. "Leave me alone. This is my time."

"You need to step toward me, ma'am," he said.

"Stay away from me!"

"No can do. You need to take off your coat."

"No."

"We need you to take it off to prove to us you are not carrying any weapons or explosives, ma'am."

"I want to die." The woman began to sob hard. "I want to die, do you hear me?"

The SWAT team fanned out across the roof as Reznick took a step toward her, gun trained on her. "You need to move away from the ledge."

The doctor took half a step back. "I want to die, don't you get it? You don't get to define what I shall or shall not do."

"Why did you kill the crown prince? Who is your handler?"

The doctor bowed her head. "Please leave me to die alone."

Reznick said, "Ma'am . . ."

"My name is Dr. Amy Nasheem."

"Dr. Nasheem . . . Amy, don't do this. Your death will devastate your family."

"I'm avenging my father!"

Reznick nodded. "You've avenged him."

"I want to join him in heaven. I want to walk with him. I want to be with him. Do you understand? I need to do this!"

"I want to walk with my father too. But I know it's not the time. The time will come. But that time is not now. Amy, listen to me. You want to walk with your father again?"

The doctor nodded, shaking profusely.

"Now is not that time. He will still be waiting for you, won't he? He won't desert you, will he?"

The doctor took a step back, now on the edge of the roof, inches from death.

"One more step back, Amy, and all the dreams your father had for you will be gone. And your mother. Find the courage to go on. To live. You need to live."

The doctor began to shake uncontrollably. "I want to go."

"No. Here's what you're going to do, Amy. Take a step forward. And then another. And come to us. I will not harm you. I swear you will not be harmed!"

"I want to die!"

"If you die, they win. Simple. If you live, you have won."

The doctor said nothing.

"Tell us what you know. Tell us how this happened. Help us understand. And the FBI can do a deal. But you have to help us know how this transpired. So take a step forward. Can you do that, Amy?"

The doctor stood and stared at him.

"So one step forward . . . Let's do this."

Tears streamed down the doctor's face. She stepped forward and dropped to her knees, arms outstretched, facing Reznick, sobbing hard.

Reznick was handed handcuffs by one of the SWAT guys. "You need to show me you have no devices attached."

"I give you my word. On my father's life, there are no devices. I am unarmed."

A SWAT guy spoke into his earpiece. "She's lying, Jon. Do not trust her. Repeat, do not trust her."

Reznick turned and ushered the SWAT guys off the roof. "I got this."

They reluctantly complied.

"It's just me and you, Amy. Can you see that? If you're lying, you'll be leaving my daughter without a father. Do you understand?"

The doctor sobbed hard.

"I don't want to leave my daughter, Lauren, just now. She needs me. So I'm going to ask you again to show me you have no devices."

Slowly, the doctor unbuttoned her coat and dropped it on the ground. She was wearing a white T-shirt.

"I swear . . . it's done."

Reznick stepped forward and cuffed her. He frisked her. "I'm sorry but I've got to check."

The doctor was wailing as he pushed her facedown on the ground.

"He had to die! He had to die! Father, forgive me!"

Reznick hustled her off the roof to the SWAT team waiting in the wings.

The lead SWAT guy spoke in his earpiece. "You done it, man. Fuck. You really done it!"

Eighty-Two

In the minutes that followed, Reznick was whisked away from the hospital with the SWAT team. He felt deflated as he sat opposite the sobbing, handcuffed doctor. He tried to put himself in Amy Nasheem's shoes. Would he have done the same to avenge his father? The answer was almost certainly yes.

The more he thought about it, the more he realized what a mess the whole thing was.

A mess which had begun with Jerry White tailing him and ended with the slaying of a Saudi crown prince by a Bahrain-born doctor.

You done it, man.

The words echoed in his head. The truth was he hadn't done it. Reznick realized that tiny delays getting to the room had cost the Saudi crown prince his life. He did get there in time for Jerry. But not before Jerry had blown himself and half-a-dozen innocent people to smithereens.

Reznick felt a deep sense of sorrow about Jerry more than anything else. A guy he had fought with. A guy that had read his daughter stories as a child. A guy she had called Uncle Jerry when she was just a little girl. And to see him end his life in that way hurt him deep down in his soul.

The look in Jerry's eyes for that split second was a memory Reznick would not be able to erase.

The more he thought about it all, the more he recognized he had been behind the curve and unable to see the big picture until it was too late. This was a parallel operation. While Jerry White had been brainwashed into being the suicide bomber, hidden like an iceberg under the water, another killer was in waiting.

A doctor. Not on anyone's radar. This was a complicated, slow-burn, false-flag operation to point the finger at a fucked-up veteran and a crazy Bahraini-born doctor. This was high-level CIA stuff. Complex. Perhaps years in the making.

When everyone, including the doctor, was back inside the Hoover Building, the FBI began a major debrief. Then Reznick's wounds were cleaned and dressed before he was shown into Meyerstein's seventh-floor office.

"We have to stop meeting like this," she said.

Reznick pulled up a seat and slumped down. "What a mess."

"I'm sorry about your friend. That can't have been easy for you to witness."

Reznick sighed. "It's too much to contemplate . . . a guy like that. Terrible end."

"I suppose, as a crumb of comfort, there will be no more Jerrys. At least, not coming from Wittenden. You stopped that."

Reznick felt uncomfortable to have the focus on him. "The whole thing is fucked up. I don't take any crumbs of comfort from any of it."

"Believe me, it could've been a lot, lot worse."

"How?"

"Well . . . indications are that the doctor is going to spill the beans on how and why she got involved in this conspiracy."

Reznick leaned back in his seat and whistled. "In return for . . ."

"A severely lighter sentence."

Reznick said nothing.

"It's important we understand what happened. What transpired. Bottom line? No one must ever know that elements of a government intelligence agency are rogue."

Reznick closed his eyes for a moment and sighed. "It's an old story. Same old same old."

Meyerstein nodded.

"And we got there too late. Too late for Jerry, too late for his dad, the priest. Too late for the Saudi women and their bodyguards."

"Out of all that bullshit, you saved a life. You saved the doctor."

"The killer."

Meyerstein said nothing.

"So what exactly is she saying?"

"She's been explaining how her family were one of only a few hundred Christians in Bahrain. Her father was a human rights lawyer whose arrest and torture were authorized by the man she just killed."

"It's starting to make more sense. Biblical justice."

"She mentioned an evangelical charity in Bahrain. Run by? Dr. Robert Gittinger."

"Bullshit. Who recruited her?"

"She wasn't so much recruited as she fell under his spell. She's talking about flashbacks with Gittinger, who she knew as Uncle Bob."

"Fuck."

"Possibly a CIA operation in Manama, which was running parallel to the Wittenden project."

"Wow."

"It's early yet, but we believe Laurence Cray, director of security at Wittenden, is also former CIA. Former posting? Riyadh."

Reznick nodded. "So this operation to kill the Saudi crown prince . . . Do we know if this was green-lighted in Riyadh? Were they aware of it?"

"Jon, let's not go there."

"This has all the hallmarks of a deep-state operation."

"I don't subscribe to conspiracy theories. But I am aware that many national security experts believed that a new oil minister would be much more amenable to American thinking on oil supply, prices, and OPEC generally. This guy was a maverick."

"And paid for it with his life. It sounds like business as usual for the CIA."

Meyerstein said nothing.

"How was that Institute able to operate without anyone asking some serious questions?"

"That in itself is a good question."

"Cray made an encrypted call to the doctor's number, and this was the thing, along with the call to Jerry, that brought it all together, right? So they were inextricably linked."

"Pretty much. You managed to get the keys, and we're assuming the videos of the patients and footage inside the facility he took on his cell phone were for his own voyeuristic purposes. Former staff have said he was a sadist. An evil bully who lorded it over everyone in Wittenden. They said he was untouchable. So maybe he got his kicks watching that stuff in the evening."

Reznick looked across at Meyerstein. "Not exactly *Monday Night Football*."

"Indeed."

"So where's Cray?"

"No one knows."

"Left the country no doubt."

"I wouldn't bet against it. What about you, Jon?"

"What about me?"

"You seem to attract malevolent forces wherever you go."

"Yeah, tell me about it."

Meyerstein smiled. "There's one thing you still haven't answered yet, Jon."

"And what's that?"

"You've signed the forms to join the FBI for the next year. But we're still waiting on an answer from you on your longer-term plans."

Reznick smiled and got to his feet. "You got to be kidding me."

Meyerstein shook her head.

"I need a vacation."

"An answer, Jon. One way or the other. Otherwise, the Director is going to freak."

"Tell him to take up meditation. The last time I saw him on TV, he looked really strung out."

"Why won't you commit, Jon, to the longer term?"

"I will. I promise. One day."

"When?"

"When I get back from vacation."

Meyerstein looked at him and smiled. "I want you on my team, Jon. Can you deal with that?"

"I can deal with that. The question is, can you deal with me on your team?"

Meyerstein smiled. "I guess we'll just have to wait and see."

Epilogue

Three days later, Reznick was back home in Rockland, wrapped up against the cold as he sat down in the sandy cove beside his daughter, Lauren, home from college for a couple days. He'd taken her out for a pizza earlier and wandered around the town. Walked onto the breakwater and then to the lighthouse, talking, father and daughter. She talked of one day moving back to Rockland. He smiled. He knew the opportunities were far greater in cities like New York. But it was nice to know she hadn't forgotten where she was from.

The town he called home. The same streets his father walked.

Past the deserted sardine-packing plant. He bought her an ice cream as he got himself a coffee to go. They walked, his hands thrust into his jacket pockets, her arm intertwined with his.

"You're all cut up, Dad," she said, pointing to the marks on his face, neck, and hands.

"Don't worry about it." He sighed. "Lauren, there's something I've been meaning to tell you. About Jerry. Uncle Jerry."

"Sure, what is it?"

"I don't usually talk about what I do."

"I'm fine with that."

"It's usually government work, you know?"

"I guess. Is Jerry alright?"

"Jerry's dead."

"Oh my God."

Reznick closed his eyes for a few moments as he gathered his thoughts. "I just wanted you to know. He sat on this very spot with you all those years ago. Right here."

"What happened to him, Dad?"

Reznick felt awkward as he tried the best he could to explain the circumstances surrounding the death of Jerry White. He found his voice breaking a couple of times as he thought back to the warrior he once knew.

"So you were there when he died?"

"I saw him blow himself to pieces."

Lauren looked sad. He wrapped an arm around her. "Why?"

"Why? I guess that place made him like that. But then again, maybe they just accelerated the process. Pushed him over the edge that little bit quicker. He had been suicidal for years. But he's at peace now."

"I saw something on Twitter about an explosion in a mall. That it was an Islamist. But there was nothing on TV."

"It wasn't an Islamist. I guess it was hushed up. Best not to share that with any of your friends, though."

"I understand."

"I was thinking about Jerry earlier today, before you came back. And I went into the attic and pulled out all the photographs. So many memories of your mom. Everything came flooding back all these years later."

"What was she like, Dad?"

"What was she like? She was like you. Real smart. Beautiful. Bit of a pain in the ass, if you must know."

Lauren's eyes filled with tears as she smiled.

"Know what else I found?" Reznick wiped the tears from her eyes. "I found a photograph I hadn't seen before. Never seen it in my life."

"A photograph of who?"

"Of Jerry. And you." Reznick took the faded color photograph from his pocket and handed it to his daughter.

Lauren held it carefully at the corner. She stared at the image for nearly a minute. "He's holding me, smiling."

Reznick nodded and turned to stare out at the waters of Penobscot Bay.

"When was that taken?"

"Not long after Mom died."

"Right on this spot?"

"Right where we're sitting."

Lauren shook her head. "I miss not having a mom."

"I know you do, honey. Just remember she loved you so, so much. And you know what she would've wanted more than anything? Simply for you to be happy."

Lauren looked thoughtful for a few moments.

"God I miss her. Each and every day. I always pictured us sitting down here as a family."

"Did Mom ever meet Jerry?"

"Yeah, she did once. A few months before she died, we met up for drinks. And Jerry was tagging along with a girl too."

"Why didn't you tell me about him before, Dad?"

"There's a lot I didn't tell you. I guess it's just the way I am."

Lauren looked again at the photograph. "He read me stories?"

Reznick nodded. "Yeah. A lot of stories."

"He's got kind eyes."

"It's probably the last time I saw him happy. A few years after that, he became a different person. We drifted apart. And I hadn't seen him for nearly a decade since I left Delta. In and out of institutions. I should've made more of an effort to keep in touch."

Lauren held his hand as they both stared out at the ocean, waves crashing onto the shoreline. "I'm going to make more of an effort to keep in touch with you."

Reznick held her close as he felt his throat tighten.

"I'd like to come home for weekends maybe, if that's OK."

Reznick nodded. "I'd like that. I'd like that a lot."

"Maybe you could visit me too."

"At Bennington?"

"Yeah, why not?"

"Do they allow people like me into places like that?"

Lauren frowned. "They damn well better. I'll make sure of it."

Reznick smiled.

"What?"

"You sound like your mom. Just the way you said that."

Lauren bowed her head. "I love you, Dad. I couldn't have asked for a better father."

Reznick stared out at the sea as the tears spilled down his face.

Acknowledgments

I would like to thank Jane Snelgrove and my editor, Jack Butler, and everyone at Thomas & Mercer for their enthusiasm, hard work, and belief in the Jon Reznick series. I would also like to thank my loyal readers, who have made the Reznick books such a success. I'd also like to thank Faith Black Ross for her terrific work on this book. Also Caitlin Alexander, who looked over an early draft. Special thanks to my agent, Mark Gottlieb, of Trident Media Group in New York.

Last but by no means least, my family and friends for their encouragement and support. None more so than my wife, Susan.

About the Author

J. B. Turner is the author of the Jon Reznick series of action thrillers (*Hard Road, Hard Kill, Hard Wired, Hard Way,* and *Hard Fall*), as well as the Deborah Jones political thrillers (*Miami Requiem* and *Dark Waters*). He loves music, from Beethoven to the Beatles, and watching good films, from *Manhattan* to *The Deer Hunter*. He has a keen interest in geopolitics. He lives in Scotland with his wife and two children.